Into the NETHERLANDS

By: V. J. Koning-Keelan

Into the Netherlands

Copyright © 2018 by Valerie Koning-Keelan

All Rights Reserved

Published by Septimal Publishing

Septimalpublishing.ca

ISBN-13: 978-0-9811795-7-5

This is a work of fiction. Although general events may have similarities to actual events, all characters and detailed events are products of the author's imagination, and any similarities to actual persons is coincidental.

Cover design © Septimal Publishing. Images used with permission

First edition: November 2018

Chapter	Page
Acknowledgements	v
Prologue	1
Chapter 1:	9
Chapter 2:	15
Chapter 3:	25
Chapter 4:	32
Chapter 5:	37
Chapter 6:	43
Chapter 7:	52
Chapter 8:	59
Chapter 9:	65
Chapter 10:	73
Chapter 11:	79
Chapter 12:	83
Chapter 13:	87
Chapter 14:	91
Chapter 15:	96
Chapter 16:	102
Chapter 17:	109
Chapter 18:	115
Chapter 19:	120
Chapter 20:	128
Chapter 21:	135
Chapter 22:	143
Chapter 23:	151
Chapter 24:	154

Chapter 25:	163
Chapter 26:	170
Chapter 27:	179
Chapter 28:	184
Chapter 29:	188
Chapter 30:	193
Chapter 31:	197
Chapter 32:	203
Chapter 33:	208
Chapter 34:	215
Chapter 35:	220
Chapter 36:	225
Chapter 37:	230
Chapter 38:	236
Chapter 39:	240
Chapter 40:	246
Chapter 41:	251
Chapter 42:	256
Chapter 43:	261
Chapter 44:	271
Chapter 45:	274
Chapter 46:	279
Chapter 47:	281
Chapter 48:	285
Chapter 49:	291
Chapter 50:	297
Chapter 51:	304

Chapter 52: 308
Chapter 53: 315
Chapter 54: 320

Acknowledgements

Thank you to:

My parents – Their lives provided me with the inspiration for this story. My father died before I started writing, but he was a Dutch soldier who came to Canada in 1941. He met and married my mother in Stratford ON in 1942 and she joined him in Holland for a year at the end of WWII.

Sadie – for getting me started and making a story out of all the words!

Jean, Atty, Harry, Carrie, Marianne, Margaret, Mary, Henry – for their remembrances of life in Holland at that time.

Truus de Bruyn, Jaap Salentijn – for letting me use their names.

Liesel, Bill – for their assistance with the German section of the book.

Geoff – for his expertise in the historical aspects of the book,

Richard, Rosemary – for their editorial assistance.

Meghan, Barb, Blake, Dawn, John, Sheila – who read the book and offered suggestions.

My husband Bryan – for his ongoing love and support and for the title, Into the Netherlands.

Any errors or omissions are my fault.

Prologue

May 1940

They were surrendering? Already? Willem Spelt could not believe it. They'd barely even started fighting! He looked around at his fellow soldiers gauging their reactions. After a moment of complete silence some soldiers started jeering and others soon joined the protest. As the noise level grew, Willem glanced at his brother Harrie who stood silently at his side, a similar look of disbelief on his face.

The General's words were being broadcast nation-wide and Willem wondered what his mother's reaction would be. She usually listened to the radio as she was preparing the evening meal. He had not been in touch with his parents for several months and after this declaration he had no idea when or if he'd ever see his mother or father again. The General made quieting motions with his arms and gradually order was restored. After a few more remarks he dismissed the men.

The soldiers had gathered at the General Headquarters in Den Hague to hear their leader make his proclamation. As they left the barracks Willem and Harrie discussed the news. They both would have preferred that Holland stay neutral as it had in The Great War.

They joined their brigade, Jagers, in a separate building and Willem wondered how *Luitenant-Generaal* Pietersen was going to sell it to the troops. From the comments he'd heard around him no one was pleased with the announcement. He doubted even Pietersen was happy and he wondered if Pietersen had known what was coming.

Willem liked *Luitenant-Generaal* Pietersen. He was not a big man but he demanded obedience by his very presence. In this case the discord was so great that not even Pietersen's stature quelled it. The noise continued as he started talking.

"Let's hear what he has to say," Willem called out in Dutch. A few men near him nodded and began to glare at their noisy neighbours. The *Luitenant-Generaal* had to convince the men this was the correct course of action, but from the grumbling Willem had heard so far it would not be an easy job.

"You've come from every region of Holland to defend our country," *Luitenant-Generaal* Pietersen said in a formal Dutch that was understood by all. "And I thank you." He paused to acknowledge a few shouts before continuing.

"Now we must stop fighting," he said. "If we persist Hitler will continue to drop bombs and destroy our cities. We have no choice; we must lay down our arms."

A chant began, "*Nee! Nee!*" and it became louder as it spread throughout the building. Pietersen stopped speaking. In the mounting noise he began speaking in a softer voice and as the noise subsided he repeated his words.

"We decided to defend our country to the very limit," he said, "and to-day we have reached that limit. We must stop fighting. We must lay down our arms."

Some men shouted into the sudden silence; others turned to their neighbours and voiced their objections. The noise level grew again. Willem pushed his way through the crowd until he was standing near the front.

"We must lay down our arms," *Luitenant-Generaal* Pietersen repeated. When he didn't continue Willem looked at his superior. Pietersen's face was grim, his back straight.

"We will lay down our arms," Pietersen said in a stronger voice, "but we will not lay down our love for our country and our queen." He hesitated before echoing the general's words, "Long live Her Majesty the Queen! Long live The Fatherland!"

§ § §

Two days after Hitler invaded Poland in September 1939 France and the United Kingdom declared war on Germany. Over the next week the Dominions of Australia, Canada, New Zealand, and South Africa made their own declarations of war. In Holland speculation increased dramatically: would they stay neutral as they had in the Great War or would they join the fight against Hitler? Willem and Harrie Spelt listened to the speculation while trying to decide when to sign up for their one-year compulsory service. Willem wanted to wait to see what would happen but Harrie was in favour of signing up immediately voicing the opinion that "it might be fun" if they had to go to war. The decision was taken out of their hands when their father told them to sign up immediately.

As the German army marched across Poland the brothers, with the rest of the Dutch army, practised basic maneuvers and learned how to handle their weapons. Throughout it all Willem still believed that Holland would remain neutral. He had no intention of remaining in the army for any length of time; after his year of conscription he would get out.

In the spring of 1940 and already at war with France and England plus its dominions Germany turned its sights on its immediate neighbours. German soldiers pushed into Belgium, the Netherlands, and Luxembourg. Belgium held out for several weeks but the Netherlands crumbled in days. Four to be exact. Suddenly Holland was at war.

§ § §

As the cheers faded *Luitenant-Generaal* Pietersen continued his speech clarifying why the General had ordered them to surrender. The German army had already landed spies in Dutch territory to infiltrate cities and prepare the way for enemy soldiers to take control of the small country. The city of Rotterdam had been bombed destroying almost the entire historic city centre, killing 900 civilians, and making 85,000 homeless. The German *Oberkommando der Luftwaffe* had threatened to also destroy the city of Utrecht unless the Dutch government surrendered.

The Dutch militia consisted of a standing army of 280,000 men who were poorly equipped and for the most part badly trained. Fortress Holland, as the army brass was known, had alarmingly low ammunition caches. With no tanks and few aircraft, they were in no condition to repel the German war machine. By invading Holland Hitler had removed the general's option of remaining neutral.

Willem detested the idea of going to war but he would do as his superior commanded. He looked at his brother. Harrie grinned and shrugged his shoulders as if he had known all along that this would happen. Pietersen dismissed the soldiers telling them "get to England any way you can." They had two weeks to get to the coast and find a boat that could take them to England. Two weeks – if they were lucky. And if a Dutch soldier didn't make it to England? What then? Willem didn't want to consider that possibility.

When the new day dawned Willem awoke to a new reality: the army had been disbanded and the *Luitenant-Generaal* had left. That intensified his resentment. He hadn't wanted to be in the army at all and now he was in a war. Life looked bleak.

§ § §

The more senior soldiers suggested splitting the brigade into groups of three or four that could travel quickly and escape detection. Willem, Harrie, Hans de Wolfe, and Kees Posthumous formed one group. They set out travelling west: going from Eindhoven through Tilburg and Breda to Middelburg.

As they passed through one community after another Harrie wondered aloud if the Krauts' invasion might be disrupted by beer and young women. Hans joined in with his own rowdy comments laughing and slapping Harrie on the shoulder. Kees regarded them with contempt and rebuked them both.

"This is no time for joking," he said. "We're running for our lives."

Hans stopped laughing and looked around perhaps expecting to see enemy soldiers chasing them. It might have been amusing in other circumstances.

§ § §

They were walking through a small Dutch village when a friendly shopkeeper gave them half a loaf of bread to share. It wasn't much, but Willem was so hungry he'd found himself looking longingly at the vegetation contemplating how tasty a tulip would be. He was happy to have a few bites of bread. What he wouldn't give for a glass or two of beer to go with it!

"Do you think these villagers resent the fact that the Queen has escaped to England?" Willem mused to distract his mind from food. As they trudged through towns, women came out to wave at them. "And do these women resent the fact that we're leaving too?"

"They must know that the only way of saving Holland is for the Queen to remain safe," Harrie replied. "She can't govern if she and her Ministers are captured." Kees shook his head.

"I disagree," he said firmly. "The people will feel the Queen has abandoned them. And now we are abandoning them too. What will happen to the women who can't flee? They will have to stay and face the Germans." Willem heard the pain in the other man's voice.

He slowed until he and Kees were walking together so they could talk more easily. Kees was from a different part of Holland and even though he was speaking Dutch Willem had to listen carefully to catch what he was saying.

"Most people will understand why the Queen had to leave," Willem said. "Our job now is to get to England as well. We'll meet with the rest of the troops and we'll all return no matter how long it takes. We'll drive the Nazis out and Holland will be a free country again. Our Queen will return in triumph!"

Once at the coast they searched for boats with room to take extra passengers but there were none. They kept walking. Civilians were also trying to leave the country. Willem thought of his months of training, of preparation, of performing drills. All that effort and what was he doing? Running away! It felt wrong. Getting out of the country and off the continent ran counter to his instinctive desire to remain and defend all he held dear. But he had no choice.

§ § §

Harrie was walking backward in front of Kees and Willem so he could watch a girl who was standing outside a shop smoking a cigarette. He stumbled and nearly fell.

"Hey watch where you're going," Willem cautioned. Harrie righted himself and waved cheerily at the young woman.

"She's pretty. I may not see girls like her for quite a while," he said. Willem looked at him and raised an eyebrow.

"You think there will be no pretty girls in England?" he asked.

Harrie waggled his eyebrows and smirked.

"No girls are as pretty as Dutch girls," he said. But his smile faded as he looked to a windmill that wasn't turning.

As one week passed into the next even Harrie's humour waned. The four of them had met several other groups of soldiers and they were all hungry, tired, and dirty. In Belgium they were forced onto roads further from the coast. Towns and villages were deserted. No one came out to watch or to cheer.

Conversation among the men dwindled. As they pushed through France Willem caught sight of a dark-haired girl whom he mistook for his neighbour Anneke Biel at first. As he drew closer he realized it wasn't her but it reminded him of a conversation he'd had with his mother. His mother and her friend, *Mevrouw* Biel, wanted him to marry Anneke. He and Anneke had decided they were good friends but they did not love each other enough to get married. If he lived through this however he would do what his mother wanted and ask Anneke to marry him hoping that her feelings might have changed by then as well. He would like to be married and perhaps even have children. That thought cheered him and lightened his step for several hours.

§ § §

A crowd of civilians had congregated at the pier in Brest France. Willem surveyed the boat tied to the dock. They all wanted to leave the continent and get to England but would a boat of that size have enough room for all of them? He supposed this one looked sturdy but it wasn't that big. Could it outrun the Germans until it reached British waters?

Willem made his way onto the dock. He was so tired and afraid not only for himself but also for his fellow soldiers and his country. Would Holland ever be free again? Would they be successful in driving the Germans out of their country? Would he ever be able to return to the life he remembered? His mind snapped to the present. Where was Harrie?

He searched frantically swivelling his head but was unable to spot his brother in the mass of humanity. People crowded in trying to reach the gangplank.

Harrie, where are you? he cried silently. He spotted him among the mob of people but just as he yelled, "Harrie!" his brother disappeared from sight.

The crowd shoved from behind and Willem almost lost his balance. Sailors came to untie the vessel as he jumped. He landed on the crowded deck and felt the boat jerk as it left the dock. A woman fell against him. As he fought to get to his knees he prayed.

"Jump Harrie, please jump."

Chapter 1:

November 1945

Standing at the railing towards the stern of the ship Gloria had hoped for one last glimpse of Canada but she was out of luck. The mist obscured the land. She was turning away from the railing in disappointment when the storm hit. Rain lashed down hiding the view even more.

"Oh no," she cried bending forward and trying to cover her hair with her hands. She slipped but caught herself before she fell.

A voice called out and she looked up to see a sailor gesturing to her. Just then the ship pitched and, losing her balance, she staggered and this time she did fall. She got her hands out in time to soften the impact of hitting the deck but she lay still for a moment to catch her breath. The man muttered to himself as he moved closer and reached towards her. She stretched out and grabbed his hand. Somehow, he managed to pull her to her feet. Keeping a protective arm about her he guided her towards the door.

Safety was still ten or twenty feet away when the ship rolled and Gloria grabbed wildly for the sailor's other arm. His crewmate appeared mouthing words that were lost in the wind. Her saviour said something in return but to Gloria it sounded like gibberish. The wind stopped blowing momentarily and Gloria realized they were speaking Dutch. The sailors conversed as they all struggled to stay on their feet. Slowly, slowly they made their way to the main part of the ship and safety.

Once inside the door the man let go of her arm and both men hurried away. She'd been expecting her vision to clear once she was out of the rain but the corridor was a shadowy maze of shifting shapes. It was disorienting. In the gloom she heard a voice over the loudspeaker.

"There has been a problem in the engine room," the voice said, "but there is no cause for concern; things are under control. If there is a doctor or nurse on board can they report to the engine room? Thank you."

Gloria sighed in relief. There was something she could do! She tugged the sleeve of a sailor as he passed. He stopped.

"I'm a nurse," she said pointing to the loudspeaker.

"Follow me," he said curtly. His accent reminded her of Willem and thoughts of her husband helped to calm her. The sailor led her around a corner into a total suffocating darkness and she stopped, paralyzed with dread. Panic returned threatening to swamp her.

"This way miss," the sailor said giving a soft tug on her arm.

Concentrating on that tug she was able to move her feet and follow him. The ship was wallowing and the up and down motion made it hard to stay on her feet. She was blind and disoriented. Her companion's breathing was reassuring. He was panting slightly as he struggled to keep them both upright. His body odour was strong but it was comforting to know he was there.

They proceeded along the corridor and down a flight of metal steps. As they went further into the ship the darkness became blacker. The stench of oil and other foul-smelling odours became almost unbearable forcing her to breathe through her mouth. Finally, they arrived at a doorway to a small room. A faint light glowed inside.

Her guide pushed her into the room and introduced her to the Second Mate before leaving. This close to the engine Gloria realized what was missing – there was no engine noise. They were no longer moving forward; they were floating in the Atlantic Ocean.

"I'm a nurse," she said to the Second Mate.

"These men were scalded by a steam leak," he replied. "Can you help?"

"Certainly," she said assuming a familiar role. "Do you have a first aid kit?"

While a sailor went to get it, she observed the three injured men. Two were sitting on chairs and one was lying on a blanket on the floor. One sailor on a chair was barely more than a boy. He was biting his lip and holding a dirty towel wrapped around his arm. Gloria carefully removed the towel frowning as she glanced at the Second Mate. He shrugged his shoulders.

"It was all we had," he said ruefully. The sailor returned and handed the kit to Gloria.

Gloria cleaned the wound with antiseptic ointment and applied burn cream before wrapping a clean bandage around it. She turned to the man on the other chair. He was bent at the waist his head almost in his lap his good arm cradling his injured arm. She went through the same procedure treating his arm. Then she turned her attention to the man on the floor. It looked like he might have been closer to the engine and had thus received the brunt of the steam. His face was white, his lips were drawn tight, and he was moaning softly. Kneeling beside him she encouraged him to turn over and she lifted his clothing to get a better look at the wound.

She thought it was closer to a second-degree burn rather than the first-degree burns the other two chaps had on their arms. She'd had experience treating burns when she worked in the hospital in Stratford. There'd been an accident when two young children had been playing with matches and had set their clothes on fire. In that case they'd received third-degree burns and the little girl had almost died. This sailor wasn't as badly injured as the girl had been but Gloria was without the medicine, equipment, and supplies she'd had in the hospital.

Gloria examined the red blistering mass of skin. The affected area, covering a good part of his abdomen, looked wet and shiny. She wished she had something stronger than aspirin to give him for the pain but she knew the real problem was the danger of infection.

"How are you doing?" she asked gently gauging his response. He shook his head but didn't say anything and Gloria could see fear in his eyes. Taking his wrist in her hand she ascertained that his pulse was good. Signalling for water she encouraged him to drink knowing that he would need fluids to prevent dehydration. She cleaned the wound, applied burn cream, and covered it with gauze.

"This needs to be watched for signs of infection," she said as she stood. "When can he be seen by a doctor?"

"We will not reach Holland for ten days at least," said the Second Mate speaking with that familiar clipped accent. He put his hand on the wall to steady himself.

"Is something wrong with the engine?" asked Gloria.

"We had to turn the engines off because of the leak. That cut the power," he said. Just then the lights flickered on.

"Power is back," he said unnecessarily. Gloria closed her eyes briefly against the glare of the light.

"This man," she said indicating the man on the floor "will need aspirin if you have it."

The Second Mate looked to his assistant who nodded and left. Gloria looked briefly at the other two men both of whom seemed to be resting comfortably. Before leaving she touched her patient's forehead. He was warm to the touch but not dangerously so.

"I'll check on him every day or for as long as is necessary," she said. Fortunately, there was plenty of antiseptic cream.

Back in her cabin Gloria was glad to see her roommate Maartje. The young Dutch woman had introduced herself as Maartje Smit, pronouncing it "Martya", when they'd met. After four days together, Gloria felt Maartje was a friend. As well as the six women who shared Gloria's and Maartje's room there were twenty-five male passengers plus the crew. The men all slept in a different part of the ship.

The ship was a tramp steamer – before the war it had sailed wherever it was needed delivering cargo. Gloria could tell that it was old; it looked like it needed a good cleaning, a bit of elbow grease, as her mother would say. It had been slated to be sold for scrap before the war but was pressed into service because the Dutch Army needed all the ships it could get after the German invasions.

The ship had space to carry passengers as well as cargo. In the sleeping area each woman had a single bed with a table beside it and room under it to store her trunk. Three beds were against one wall and three were against the opposite wall. A small room with a toilet and a sink was down the hall.

"What happened to the lights?" asked Maartje as Gloria sat on her bed. Gloria recounted her adventure.

"Turning the engine off knocked out the power," she added, "but they must have emergency power. I hope it lasts until the engine is running again." Maartje shrugged.

"I do not understand how it works. I just hope the ship gets going again," she said. "I want to get to Holland as soon as possible."

Gloria understood Maartje's concern. The two women had shared stories as they'd walked around the deck while the ship sailed up the St. Lawrence River. Maartje had gone to Canada with her aunt in the spring of 1939 after her aunt's visit to Holland. She'd planned to return immediately but her aunt had taken ill and Maartje had ended up staying longer than she'd intended. By the time her aunt was willing to let her leave Maartje was unable to get passage on a ship. It was deemed unsafe for passenger ships to cross the Atlantic Ocean. Maartje had spent the war years in Canada.

Gloria had her own reasons for wanting to be in Holland. She wanted to discover what had happened to her husband.

Chapter 2:

Gloria had met Willem in 1942 but it seemed like a decade ago. The Dutch army had sent a contingent, the Royal Netherland Army Recruiting Unit, to Canada in January 1941 to set up headquarters in an empty furniture factory in Stratford Ontario after the Perth Regiment moved out. The centre put out word that Dutchmen from anywhere in the world could go there to enlist since Holland was in enemy hands by then. Within weeks men stranded in countries around the world were making their way to Canada to become soldiers. Soon men in uniforms, slightly different than Canadian ones, became a familiar sight in the Southern Ontario town.

In the fall of 1942 Gloria's friend Mary was going to the Stratford Fall Fair with her boyfriend, Jan, a Dutch soldier. Mary invited her to accompany them and Jan asked his friend Willem to go too. Gloria had never been on a blind date before and she was thrilled.

When she first met Willem, she was impressed with his courtly manners; he treated her like royalty. He was 28 – five years older than she – but he seemed much more mature. She loved his accent and his way of speaking. At times she felt she was living in an earlier century since Willem and his soldier friends spoke formal English without using contractions. Gloria found herself occasionally speaking more formally as well.

The four of them – Gloria, Willem, Jan, and Mary – walked around the fair looking at exhibits, the livestock, and the baking exhibits. They even went for a ride on the Ferris wheel. By the end of the afternoon Gloria was smitten. She was in love.

Willem invited her out again the next time he had leave. They went for a walk and laughed at puns and word plays. Willem had quite a sense of humour. She invited him to her house to meet her parents and they liked him too. Soon Gloria and Willem were spending all of his time off together.

They went for walks and they went to the show – although there were not many new shows in the theatre. They played card games. When it was cold enough Willem used a pair of Mr. Macdonald's skates and they skated together on the river. Mrs. Macdonald even let Willem take a shower, a rare treat for him. It was while he was under the running water, singing Figaro, that Gloria discovered he was not musical. His singing was so off-key – he had the rhythm correct but he failed to hit many of the notes. Hearing it she loved him even more. Those times came to an end later that fall when the Dutch army moved to Guelph.

For Gloria it had been love at first sight and after Willem kissed her she knew he must love her too. She'd been kissed before but never with such passion. This was the man she wanted to spend her life with – the one she would love till death did them part. After dating for a year, she was more convinced than ever that she and Willem were meant to be together, that they were destined for a happily-ever-after. Perhaps that accounted for their behaviour one evening.

Willem had just said he was leaving. The Dutch army was being sent to England to prepare for the invasion of Europe and Gloria was heartbroken. They started kissing and soon they were doing more than just kissing. She knew with one part of her brain that she should say no and they should stop before things got out of control, but she didn't listen to her brain. Willem was leaving and she might never see him again. She loved him and she was sure he loved her. It was dark, they were alone, and – she stopped thinking.

Two days later her period should've started but didn't and her concern began. She was never late. There was only one reason for that to happen. If only, if only…but it was pointless to think that. What was done was done. Her biggest fear was telling her mother. What would she say? Gloria spent an agonizing day and night wondering what she should do. There was only one way to resolve this predicament.

She would ask Willem to marry her and the marriage would have to happen before he returned to England. Without a "Mrs." in front of her name Gloria could not announce that her mother was going to be a grandmother. Once it was settled in her mind Gloria put action to words and wrote to Willem.

§ § §

"Willem has asked me to marry him and I've accepted," Gloria called to her mother as she ran down the stairs waving a sheet of paper in her hand. She'd taken the letter to her room to read in solitude after seeing the return address.

"He asked you by letter?" her mother asked raising her eyebrows.

"No. He asked me when he was here on the weekend," Gloria lied willing herself not to blush, "but we didn't want to tell anyone until he'd found out whether he could get leave. We want to be married at the church in Stratford." That part at least was true.

Her mother held out her arms and Gloria stepped into her mother's embrace hugging her in return. Her mother seemed unaware of any artifice in Gloria's declaration.

"You've only known him for a year," Mrs. Macdonald said. "Are you sure this is what you want?" Her mother released her and peered at her intently. Gloria raised her eyes to meet her mother's.

"We know each other well enough to know we want to spend our lives together," Gloria said defiantly. She softened her voice before adding, "And we want to get married before Willem leaves Canada. He's returning to England with the rest of the Dutch army in a month."

"What…!" her mother shouted in alarm pushing her daughter to arm's length. "You want to be married in a month?" Gloria hesitated.

"Three weeks actually," she said. "I know it's not much time. But you're so good at these things. We can work together. Mary will stand up with me and Jan will stand up with Willem. It will be a very small wedding. I don't need a fancy white wedding gown." She stopped talking as tears threatened. She didn't want her mother to think there might be another reason she couldn't wear white.

"Oh my dear," said her mother hugging her again and smoothing her hair like she used to when Gloria was little. "You'll have to give up working at the hospital, but if you and Willem want to get married quickly before he leaves Canada that's what we'll do.

"Come to the dining room and we'll organize what needs to be done," her mother said releasing her. Gloria obediently followed her mother into the dining room and sat at the table trying not to think about having to give up working as a nurse.

"The first thing," said her mother pulling a piece of paper towards her and reaching for a pencil, "will be to make sure we have enough food. Beef hasn't been rationed yet – I'll cook a roast of beef. It won't be fancy – just a regular Sunday meal except it'll be a Saturday!" She smiled at her joke and Gloria breathed a sigh of relief. Perhaps getting involved in the planning would keep her mother from wondering why she and Willem wanted to get married on such short notice.

"It may be a good thing you don't want to wear white," her mother added. "I'm not sure I could buy the material to make you a proper wedding gown. We'll have to go to Northey's Dress Shop tomorrow to see what they have in stock. It's too rushed to order a dress to be made." She bent her head and made some notes.

"I'm sure they'll have something suitable," said Gloria trying to appear excited. "You bought some extra material last month. Could you use it to make a bridesmaid dress for Mary? I don't think she'll be able to afford a new dress."

"That's a good idea," said her mother making another note. "Since she's almost your size I could use the pattern I used to make you that yellow patterned dress. I'll make hers a different colour."

Gloria assured her mother that Mary wouldn't mind having a dress similar to one of hers. She felt some of her tension dissipating now that her mother was taking charge. Maybe, just maybe, she could get through these next few weeks without her mother noticing anything was amiss.

Willem came to visit for the weekend as usual. They spent Friday evening and Saturday talking with her mother and getting caught up on the plans. On Sunday Willem and Gloria went for a walk. Willem seemed preoccupied as they sauntered along the sidewalk.

"It is strange," he said after a few minutes. "Jan is a good friend. We have been through a lot together and I know he is happy I asked him to be my best man but I always thought my brother would stand up with me."

Gloria turned quickly to look at him, her eyes searching his face. He hadn't talked about his brother since mentioning that he had one when they'd first met. In fact, she'd forgotten about it. He was staring straight ahead his face somber.

"I'm so sorry," said Gloria stopping to put her arms around his waist and leaning her head against his shoulder. "I'm rushing you into this," she said in a muffled voice.

"I wish we could wait," she said stepping back, "but I'm so worried. I've only missed one period but I was sick this morning. Luckily Mom didn't notice. If we get married in two weeks and have a week together before you leave for England, I hope my mother will think that I became pregnant after we got married." She looked at him again.

He was handsome with regular features: dark brown eyes and darker brown, almost black, hair which he wore long in the front. It constantly fell forward and he had a habit of running his hand through it trying to keep it out of his eyes.

"I really do not understand why you are so afraid," said Willem pushing his hair back before pulling her close and encircling her with his arms. He looked into her face. "Would she care so much if you have a baby before we are married?"

"She would," said Gloria not meeting his eyes. "It's hard to explain but that's just the way she is. I grew up believing that you had to be married to have a baby." She tried to laugh but it ended in a sob and Willem held her tighter.

"Never mind; it is okay. I want to marry you and if we have to do it quickly before I go to England that is what we will do." He pulled his handkerchief from his pocket and gave it to her.

They strolled along the river. The town of Stratford and the Avon River were named after Stratford–Upon–Avon in England. She watched the white and black swans swimming sedately. They seemed blissfully unconcerned about her predicament. Was she making too much of this? She remembered how horrified her mother had been upon hearing the news that her cousin in Detroit had had a baby six months after getting married. She could not have a baby without being married; her mother would be mortified.

"We will have a small but happy wedding. I do not mind." Willem smiled as he said this but Gloria could see sadness in his eyes. Was it the issue of the best man? Why would he prefer having his brother there instead of Jan? She and Isabel weren't close and it had never occurred to her to ask her sister to be her maid of honour. Of course, she was six years older than Isabel. Was Willem older than his brother? She turned to ask him and spotted Isabel running towards them. As her sister got closer Gloria heard what she was saying and her question remained unasked.

"Come home quickly!" Isabel yelled. "Dinner is ready!"

They returned post-haste and during the meal they all discussed wedding plans. Isabel was delighted that her mother was making her a new dress too even though she wasn't in the wedding party. Willem seemed pleased with the arrangements Mrs. Macdonald had made.

After dinner he talked to Mr. Macdonald about Montgomery's victory over Rommel in Africa. Gloria could not detect even a hint of unhappiness or discontent in her fiancé. The worry about his brother receded and was forgotten.

It wasn't easy saying goodbye to Willem before he caught the train to Guelph to return to his regiment but in a couple of weeks they would be husband and wife. She tried to keep that thought in mind as she waved until the train was out of sight. The joy she should have felt at her impending nuptials was missing and she blamed it on the war. Then she chided herself because without the war she wouldn't have met Willem.

§ § §

Two weeks passed in a blur and suddenly it was her wedding day. She woke early but lay in bed not thinking of anything. When she heard a knock on the door downstairs she jumped out of bed. She would have to hurry to be ready for the 11:00 a.m. ceremony.

Mary dressed herself before helping Gloria into her wedding gown, a lovely blue crepe creation. It had been bought off the rack, but it fit Gloria like a glove, hanging to just past her knees. Mary's dress was a lighter blue and not as fancy but they looked good together Gloria thought as she surveyed their images in the mirror.

Mary wore a headband covered in the same material as her dress while Gloria wore a white pillbox hat with a short veil made by her mother's friend who had a hat-making business in Toronto. Fortunately, they had each bought shoes prior to the beginning of the war. Gloria's black patents had high heels. Mary's were black patent as well but with a lower heel.

Gloria's father drove them to the church in his 1935 Dodge. He was proud of it – he'd bought it used the year before from the widow of an acquaintance. There was little traffic as they drove through town. When they arrived at the church Mary made sure that Gloria looked perfect before they entered the building. After parking the car Gloria's father joined them just inside the door.

Gloria watched as Willem and Jan followed the minister out of the sacristy. When she saw Jan, she remembered that she'd never talked to Willem about his brother. But then the music started and all her thoughts focused on it. This was her wedding day!

Mary started walking slowly down the aisle. Gloria and her father followed arm in arm. The procession was just the three of them. Gloria concentrated on Willem as she walked closer returning his smile. When they reached the groom and best man her father squeezed her hand gently before she let go of his arm. She smiled at him fondly before turning her attention to the minister.

Thinking back on the marriage ceremony she could only remember scenes – Willem waiting for her as she walked down the aisle; his eyes as he spoke his vows; the ring slipping onto her finger. After it was over she and Willem walked together towards the back of the church arm in arm. The actual words she and Willem had spoken were already a jumbled memory. But his steadying presence beside her throughout the ceremony had comforted her. Surely, they were meant to be together!

The wedding party and guests went to her parents' house for the wedding meal – a Sunday dinner on Saturday – as her mother had observed. Only one picture was taken of the bride and groom with their attendants. When she looked at it later Gloria thought she looked a happy bride. Her nose was a bit big she'd always thought but she had an attractive mouth. Her brown eyes were large and wide-spaced and her short brunette hair curled naturally framing her face.

Standing outside the church after the ceremony Willem had seemed happy and free of misgivings. He clapped Jan on the back and shook her father's hand. He even bent to kiss her mother on the cheek which had made her blush.

§ § §

Gloria lay in bed that night waiting for Willem to join her. She shivered in anticipation. They were married! Willem was now her husband. He closed the door behind him beaming at her as he walked to the bed. He was dressed in only his robe and it fell open as he sat beside Gloria.

"My dear sweet Gloria," he said raising her hand to his lips. "We are husband and wife now. If it turns out you are pregnant your mother will have no reason to complain."

Smiling warmly at her he stood and let his robe fall to the floor. As he lifted the covers and slid in beside her she snuggled against his warm body. They were joined for life.

Chapter 3:

"Please come," the sailor said after poking his head in the doorway and gesturing with his hand. Gloria reached behind Maartje as she grabbed her sweater and put it on. She said a quick goodbye to her friend before she left.

Gloria followed the sailor into the hallway. He moved quickly and she had a hard time keeping up. The only reason for this summons that Gloria could think of was the fact that she'd treated the three sailors the day before but she didn't question the sailor. He might not have told her and he probably didn't speak much English. She concentrated on keeping her balance. The sailor stopped outside a small room, the infirmary, where her patients had been moved. The Second Mate and another sailor stood just inside the door.

"Please can you help?" asked the Second Mate. His face was creased in concern as he pointed to the man lying on the bed in a corner.

The patient with the bandage on his abdomen was lying still. His face was deathly pale and he was moaning softly. Gloria felt her stomach drop. She knew what she'd find before she checked. Loosening the bandage, she could see the blisters had broken and his abdomen was covered in pus.

"It's starting to get infected," she said. "I'll have to clean it again." When she was finished she turned to look at the Second Mate.

"I don't suppose you have any penicillin?" she asked. He shrugged.

"What is it?" he asked.

"It's a new drug that is useful in treating infections," said Gloria. She put the bandages and cream away. "He needs to been seen by a doctor but I'll do what I can until we reach Amsterdam." She asked for another basin of cool water and a clean cloth which she used to bathe the sailor's face. She offered him a glass of water to drink.

"He needs to drink as much water as he'll take," she explained to the waiting sailor. He nodded.

"Do you have any more aspirin?" she asked. The Second Mate handed her a small package which she opened to reveal six small white pills.

"He should be given two every four hours," she said handing the package to the uniformed sailor. "I'll come back this evening to see if the aspirin is helping."

As Gloria returned to the sleeping cabin, she reflected on the differences between treating these sailors and treating the children who been burned. The children had been in a hospital where every effort was made to have conditions as sterile as possible. The ship burned coal which meant there was soot everywhere. Even surfaces in the infirmary were covered in gray dust.

Back in the sleeping area she explained to Maartje what had happened. Maartje grimaced slightly when Gloria recounted changing the bandage. She'd barely finished talking when a gong sounded calling them to the mess deck.

They joined the rest of the passengers heading in the same direction. Gloria lost sight of Maartje and caught up to her as they reached their assigned table where they sat beside each other. Only two of the other seats were occupied but no one spoke.

The First Mate stood at the front of the room and explained what had happened concluding with the changes that would be in place until the engine was fixed.

"We will only be serving two meals a day," he said swaying a bit as he rolled with the ship. "A light meal served mid-morning and sandwiches at 1600 hours. The leak should be fixed in a day or two. I am sorry for the inconvenience but please do not be alarmed. We have enough food and water to last until the ship is repaired."

He looked around perhaps to see if there were any questions. Gloria checked as well but no hands were raised. The First Mate left the room.

§ § §

The crew was kept busy the rest of the day holding the ship on course as much as they were able and working to repair the damage. Most of the passengers stayed out of their way. Gloria was glad of a chance to rest on her bed and study the other women sharing her sleeping quarters. She knew and liked Maartje best; partly because they were nearly the same age.

Mevrouw Dekker was five to ten years older than Gloria. She was friendly but spoke English with a very thick accent which Gloria had trouble understanding. She wore her hair in a long braid like Maartje did but Maartje's hair was blonde and Mevrouw Dekker's was brown. From their brief conversation Gloria gathered that Mr. Dekker had been a businessman in the Dutch West Indies. He'd died sometime during the war – Gloria wasn't clear on the details – and Mrs. Dekker wanted to return to Holland to be with her family.

Greta and Hilda Rutgers were sisters. Greta walked with a limp which made it very difficult for her to get around now that the ship was floating in the ocean. They'd been in the Dutch West Indies where their brother owned some businesses but now they were looking forward to returning to their native country. They mostly kept to themselves. Gloria wasn't able to converse with them since they only spoke Dutch. The other woman was travelling with her husband but Gloria hadn't met her yet.

When Gloria returned to the infirmary she found all three men resting comfortably and another sailor there to watch them. She examined each injured man in turn and before leaving she asked the able-bodied sailor to call her if any of the patients got worse.

The next day was the same. The crew was kept busy and the passengers were left to fend for themselves. Gloria made her way to the infirmary and treated her patient. His wound seemed to be getting better but it still looked red and inflamed. Gloria tried to remain positive when she spoke to the Second Mate about the sailor's chances for survival, but privately she was less optimistic.

The remainder of the day was spent resting in the sleeping area. She talked briefly with Maartje but most of the time she was alone with her thoughts.

§ § §

Willem had left for England in September 1943 a week after their wedding. Gloria had moved back to Stratford to live with her parents. She and Mary who was still living in Stratford helped with the war effort knitting socks and scarves to be sent overseas. Knitting was not one of Gloria's better talents and she was embarrassed at the results of her efforts. The socks were too big and the scarves were misshapen.

After a while her mother interpreted Gloria's morning sickness and mood swings as proof that Gloria was pregnant. She accompanied her mother to the doctor and was not surprised when the pregnancy test revealed that she was going to have a baby.

"Have you written to tell Willem he's going to be a father?" Mrs. Macdonald asked.

Gloria didn't answer but that evening she forced herself to write the letter. Three weeks later she received a reply. She was pleased that Willem seemed happy to hear her news.

"I hope you have a son," he'd written. "We will name him George, after your king."

When Gloria read that to her mother, her mother laughed.

"Willem will be a good father, I'm sure," she said.

Gloria wanted to believe that Willem really was happy at the news but she couldn't be sure. She wanted to believe that Willem loved her and he was glad they'd gotten married, but was it true? Did he love her? She'd been the one to pop the question. With him so far away her doubts grew.

Then the spotting started. Being a nurse, she knew what it meant but she didn't say anything to her mother. A couple of days went by with no spotting and Gloria felt her hopes lifting. When the spotting returned and she was too ill out of bed in the morning her mother called the doctor. He came to examine Gloria and admitted her to the hospital. A week later she lost the baby. She was heart-broken. She felt in her heart it had been a boy although she didn't think anyone could tell for sure.

At home again, she stayed in bed and refused all visitors. Her mother came into the bedroom and sat on the bed but Gloria lay with her face to the wall. She did not want to talk to anyone. Finally, her mother left the room but she left several pieces of paper, a pen, and an envelope on the bedside table. Gloria got the hint – she had to at least tell Willem even if she didn't want to talk to anyone else.

Gloria sent the letter to the only address she had for Willem – the one in England. It was early 1944 but she hadn't been following the news of the war closely and she didn't know if the Dutch army was still in England. Months went by with no answering letter although Gloria checked the mail every day. She wasn't sure the postal service was still working but her father said that letters would get to England as long as the ship carrying the mail was not attacked. When more weeks passed with no letter she even roused herself to go to the Red Cross office to check for word of where Willem's unit was. Nothing!

Each day Gloria grew more bewildered. She found it harder to smile, to pretend nothing was wrong. What did his silence mean? Perhaps he hadn't received the letter. Or it could be that he was glad there was no baby. How was she to know?

Her mother, suspecting that Gloria's depression stemmed from the baby's death, asked Mary to visit. Gloria and Mary had trained as nurses together. Since Mary now worked in labour and delivery at the Stratford General Hospital she understood the emotions surrounding the birth of a baby. And perhaps she had an inkling of what Gloria might be feeling since her miscarriage. Seeing her friend's kind face creased in concern struck a chord in Gloria. When her mother left the two of them alone Gloria started crying. She told Mary the whole story.

"I don't know what to think," Gloria cried when the tale was told. "Did Willem marry me because he loved me or not? I don't know anymore."

"Gloria," said Mary in her characteristically straightforward way, "I know you. This is not how the Gloria I know would react. You and Willem love each other. I could see it as soon as you met. Go to Holland when the war is over. It won't last much longer now. Find out why Willem didn't reply. Talk to him directly. It's the only thing that will put your mind at rest."

Gloria stopped crying. After a few minutes she took a deep breath. "You're right," she said in a steadier voice. "I will do something. I will go to Holland." She hugged her friend.

Gloria had to wait a few months until the war in Japan was over before going to check with the Red Cross but when she did she discovered she could get passage on a ship to Holland because she was married to a Dutch soldier. No one questioned her assertion that she and Willem were married. She had the form the minister had signed and that was proof enough.

During one visit to the Red Cross she was told a ship would be leaving from Montreal in a week and a spot would be held for her on it. It was a mad scramble but Gloria was packed and ready to go in time. As the train pulled out of the station in her hometown she waved good-bye to her parents. When she could no longer see them, the realization hit her – she was going to a foreign country where she didn't know anyone and she couldn't speak the language. After a few hours the panic subsided. By the time the train arrived in Montreal Gloria was feeling stronger having remembered what a music teacher had told her prior to a singing contest many years before.

"Don't think of your jitters as nervousness," the teacher had said, "think of them as excitement for your performance."

As the train sped through the country-side Gloria told herself she wasn't afraid; she was excited. By the time the train pulled into Montreal she almost believed it.

Chapter 4:

Gloria sat up quickly placing her feet on the floor. The ship was moving again! The rumble of the motors was a soothing sound and together with the faint vibrations under her feet it felt like the ship was waking from a long sleep.

"Repairs have been completed successfully," a voice announced over the loudspeakers. "We will arrive in Amsterdam in ten days."

Gloria ran to the deck and peered over the railing. She saw the wake — another indication that they were underway. Soon she would have answers; soon she could continue with her life. Holding the rail, she danced a little jig.

"It looks like someone is happy," called one of the sailors.

She waved at him and laughed as she made her way back to the sleeping area. Maartje was up and ready to go to breakfast. At the mess deck Gloria and Maartje headed over to their table. Three men were seated at the table talking. Enough English was spoken that she was able to ascertain that it had been touch and go for a while as to whether they could fix the engine without waiting for assistance from another ship.

Their table had a full contingent at dinner that evening for the first time since the ship had left Montreal. As Gloria and Maartje approached the table the five men sitting at the table stood immediately. A woman stayed seated and took no notice of Gloria and Maartje.

As soon as Gloria and Maartje were seated the men each nodded in turn, said his name, and sat. Ruben Alders and Daan Ebberts sat to one side of the couple. Martin Hinrichs and Piet Boswel sat to the other. The younger men looked similar with short dark hair and mustaches although one of them also had a beard. Piet and the husband, who introduced himself as Gregor Korman, were older than the other three. Gregor presented his wife Beatrix who didn't acknowledge Gloria or Maartje at all although she had perked up as the men introduced themselves. In the silence she turned to her husband.

"I thought this ship was for Netherlanders returning home," she said unkindly glaring at Gloria. Her husband didn't say anything but the woman's reaction reawakened Gloria's fears.

Would her mother-in-law also reject her – especially if Willem hadn't told his parents he was married? Gloria was counting on being able to stay with Willem's parents. What if they didn't believe her story? She didn't know what she would do. Gloria lowered her eyes and bit her bottom lip. Piet Boswel glanced at Gloria before speaking.

"How do you know Gloria is not Dutch?" he asked Beatrix. He turned to Gloria and put the question to her. Gloria stared at Beatrix briefly before answering.

"No," she admitted, "I'm not Dutch but I am married to a Dutch soldier. I'm meeting him in Amsterdam."

"My mistake," Beatrix said leaning forward and smiling sweetly at Piet. She looked to both sides including the other men at the table in her comments. "We are returning home to visit with our son. He married a good Dutch girl."

She surveyed the table triumphantly once again before turning her attention to the young man sitting beside her – smiling at him like a fox inspecting a chicken. Resting her hand on his arm she said something meant for his ears only. Gloria glanced briefly at Gregor. She was embarrassed by the woman's actions but Gregor was oblivious to his wife's behaviour. Piet turned towards Gloria.

"You are married," he said sounding disappointed. "I am heartbroken," he added putting his hand over his heart.

As others at the table laughed Gloria welcomed Piet's deflection of the other woman's spite. Conversation resumed in Dutch which Gloria couldn't understand but she didn't mind. She hadn't learned the language when she was dating Willem because he and the other soldiers had wanted to improve their English.

Servers arrived setting a plate of food in front of each person. Gloria waited until the others had plates in front of them before picking up her knife and fork. Nobody spoke for several minutes while food was consumed.

"Do you play ping pong?" Piet asked suddenly catching Gloria's attention. When she nodded, he continued.

"There is a table set up in the games room. If you and Maartje want to play Martin and I will take you on in doubles." He looked from Gloria to Maartje and back again. Martin Hendricks on Piet's other side leaned forward to hear her reply.

"I do play," said Gloria. She turned to Maartje. "What about you?"

"I play," she said smiling shyly, "but not very well."

Piet assured her that didn't matter and said he would make arrangements for them to play a game. It was the first of many games the four of them were to play during the trip. The two couples were evenly matched for playing doubles but they rarely kept score. Playing ping pong was a welcome change of activity from walking never-ending circuits of the deck.

After a week Gloria wondered if Maartje's flush was as much from exertion as it was from the attention Martin paid her but Gloria told herself it was none of her business. And if Piet seemed more interested in Gloria than was warranted she ignored it. To her Piet was the older brother she'd never had. She would remain faithful to Willem until after she'd heard from him. She owed him that much at least.

§ § §

"Tell me about your life in Holland before the war," Gloria said. She and Maartje had arrived at the common area on the ship after their third circuit of the deck. As the chairs were vacant they both sat.

"My father owns an *apotheek* much like your drugstore in Canada," Maartje said. Her voice became animated as she talked about her life before the war. "My mother stayed home to look after me and my brother Theo who is four years younger than I am. I started dating a boy Mathias de Vries just before the war started but I had known him for many years. It was not very serious yet." She hesitated staring into the distance as she relived what was clearly a pleasant memory.

"We liked to skate on the canals," she said glancing at Gloria.

"Willem and I liked to skate too on the Avon River," said Gloria. "He told me what it was like to skate on a canal. I used to think how romantic it would be to glide arm in arm along the frozen water, blue skies overhead, and windmills with large arms turning gently swooshing the air." She closed her eyes briefly and sighed dreamily.

"It was like that although we did not skate arm in arm so much as Mathias used to chase me. Of course, we were quite young then," Maartje said with a touch of melancholy. "Later we did not have so much time for skating because he had chores to do. And I helped in the shop once I was old enough."

Gloria leaned back in her chair glad to be wearing slacks. The sun was deceptive – it was not warm; it was actually quite cool. In Canada before the war it was just starting to be fashionable to wear slacks. Gloria's mother liked to be in the forefront of fashion and she also liked to sew. She'd made two pairs of pants: one for Gloria and one for herself. Called "beach pyjamas," they were made of a floral-patterned material. The wide pant legs kept Gloria and her mother looking decent.

Gloria had been barely into her teens but even at that age she'd felt very daring wearing the pants. As soon as the war in Europe ended she'd ordered a pair of tailored slacks from a dressmaker. Made of a Margaret Rose tartan they were very swish, very stylish but they kept her warm and that was more important on the ship.

She tried to imagine what it would be like when she reached Holland. What would she do and how would she manage? Her goal was to find Willem – but how would she accomplish that? She now knew one person who lived in Amsterdam, Maartje, but she needed to be in touch with the army. She missed her father who had helped her deal with the army when she was still at home. Being on her own and responsible for her own actions was a new experience. But it was also exciting and having made it this far she was confident she could manage in Holland. Feeling better about her situation she stood and turned to Maartje in the other chair.

"It's almost time for dinner," she said as Maartje got to her feet. "Let's do one more circuit before we eat."

Chapter 5:

Gloria struggled to wake up. Someone was talking. She opened her eyes to see *Mevrouw* Dekker and a sailor standing together on the other side of the room.

"Tell Mrs. Spelt to come to the infirmary immediately," the sailor said. He turned and left.

"I'm awake." Gloria spoke in a quiet voice before Mevrouw Dekker could say anything. The others were still sleeping. Gloria got out of bed and dressed quickly. Her patient must have taken a turn for the worse.

She spent the morning in the infirmary bathing her patient's forehead and upper body. He was barely conscious as she tried to get him to drink. She knew by touching his skin that he was becoming dehydrated.

She spent the better part of the next two days with her patient trying to keep him comfortable and to keep the wound clean. She mentally reviewed the treatment for burns but there wasn't much else she could have done. Without medicine or machines, such as an IV unit, she felt useless.

Each time she went to the infirmary the other sailor left to have a break. She'd discovered her patient's name was Willem although on the ship he was called Vim. While she was alone with him her imagination ran wild. Was the fact that he had the same name as her husband an omen? She hoped not. What would it mean if the patient died – that her Willem was dead too?

After two days the other two sailors were fit to go back to work although they were given a reduced workload for another week. Gloria spent another day with her patient trying to get him to drink and bathing his face to keep his temperature down. As the evening descended she asked if the Second Mate could meet her in the infirmary. When he arrived, she stood to face him.

"I'm sorry," she said. "The infection has set in too solidly and there is nothing more I can do. Without medication and a way to get fluids into him there is little hope he will recover."

"You mean he is going to die?" the Second Mate asked softly.

"I'm afraid so," said Gloria. "It will be another few days until we reach Holland, right?" At his nod she continued. "He needs to be in a hospital so he can be given fluids by IV and he needs to be seen by a doctor."

A burial at sea was held five days before they reached Amsterdam. A wind had sprung up whipping up waves and making it hard to stand on the deck. The body had been sewn into canvas with weights attached to it. Looking around at the men's faces Gloria could see everyone felt the injustice. This soldier had survived the war but was not going to return to his family and his homeland. She felt tears on her face as she watched the body plunge into the icy depths.

§ § §

That afternoon after the wind had calmed she walked around the deck by herself thinking about life and death. She tried not to think that because the sailor had died and because his name was Willem it necessarily meant her husband was dead too. She had to believe that her Willem was still alive. It was the only thing that kept her going.

She stood at the railing gazing at the sea. With no wind the sea stretched endlessly with no hint of danger or risk. But other times the sea was treacherous and unforgiving. Fighting in the war must have been like that — enemy fire coming suddenly and unexpectedly.

Her friend Betty's brother George had been fighting in the south of Holland at the end of the war. He was sleeping in a barn with some other chaps when they heard someone coming but before they'd had time to gather their weapons they were attacked. George was hit all up his left side including his stomach. He'd been taken to a hospital in the south of England where he'd been given penicillin to prevent him getting peritonitis. Luckily for him the nurses there also knew how to help him get his collapsed lung working again. By the time he returned to Canada he was partially recovered.

Gloria didn't know if anything like that had happened to Willem. She would have to wait to ask him in person — if she ever saw him again. With that thought her eyes filled with tears.

"Are you really meeting your husband in Amsterdam?" a voice asked. Gloria looked up quickly blinking back her tears. She'd almost walked directly into Piet.

"I'm not sure," she said. "I hope he will be."

"I can give you my address," said Piet, "before we leave the ship." Gloria was unsure how to respond.

"Thank you," she said hesitantly. "I'm not sure…"

"If you need help finding your husband I mean," Piet interrupted his face softening as he smiled at Gloria.

"Th-Thank you," she stammered wondering what sort of help he was offering.

"My father worked for the Dutch government before the war," he said. "He may still have a few connections that might be useful." Piet smiled cheerily as he raised his hand in farewell.

"Thank you," Gloria repeated before ducking into her cabin.

Gloria had just gotten out of bed the following morning when Maartje returned from breakfast. Kippers had been on the menu but since Gloria couldn't face eating fish in the morning she'd slept in. Maartje brought with her the news that they were having a captain's dinner that evening.

"How are they managing to have a captain's dinner?" Gloria asked in surprise. "This is not a cruise ship! It's not even a real passenger ship for heaven's sake."

"Two of the men returning to Holland worked in the embassy in New York," said Maartje. "They mentioned it to the captain and he thought it was a good idea. Also," she said pausing to take a breath, "the cook travelling with us is a pastry chef returning to his home in Belgium and he wants to prepare some fancy dishes."

"That sounds like fun," said Gloria, "but what are we supposed to wear? It's customary to wear formal clothes to a captain's dinner. Do you think anyone has fancy clothing?"

"The chaps from New York have tuxedos that they'll wear," said Maartje, "but the rest of us can wear our regular clothes. Although I do have a skirt and sweater I could wear." Gloria brightened suddenly.

"I brought a dress with me," she said, "Let's you and me dress up even if it's just us and the guys from the Embassy who do so." Maartje agreed.

Talking to *Mevrouw* Dekker later Gloria discovered she also had a dress to wear. Gloria felt something – not excitement exactly – but certainly a change from the usual anxiety and apprehension welling up inside her as she got into her dress that evening.

"I only have one pair of silk stockings," said Gloria, "I hope I don't get a run in them. During the war silk stockings were unavailable; we only had cotton stockings because all silk was used to make parachutes. When I saw this pair for sale last month I bought them."

The two women entered the mess deck and waved to their friends seated at the makeshift bar. The chaps in tuxedos were easy to spot. Most of the other men wore their usual attire of dark pants and a dark shirt but Gregor was wearing a suit. Beatrix was in a red dress with a flared skirt which showed off her legs as she walked. *Mevrouw* Dekker wore a plain dress with a high neckline and a hem that fell past her knees. She smiled brightly and waved to Gloria and Maartje in passing.

Gloria hesitated momentarily when she saw Piet but he merely nodded and smiled. Gloria relaxed as she and Maartje made their way to the table which was being used as a bar. Gloria ordered a whiskey sour but Maartje had a soda pop. Both Dutch and English were heard in the conversations around them but Gloria didn't try to follow the foreign language. From the many outbursts of laughter, she knew the men were in a good mood. Gloria approached Gregor who was sitting by himself further along the table. He took a handful of nuts from the bowl and turned to Gloria.

"You will be meeting your husband in Holland soon," he said popping a few nuts into his mouth.

"Yes," said Gloria, stalling to recall what he was referring to — ah yes — her boast to Beatrix, "although he might not be at the dock to greet me. He's um…he's in the hospital," she said. It was the first thing that came to her mind and she groaned inwardly. Now she'd have to remember to keep up that pretense.

Oh, what tangled webs we weave when first we practise to deceive, she thought dryly.

"I hope he'll be better soon," Gregor said absentmindedly. He looked to where his wife was talking to the captain. She was smoking a cigarette with one hand and holding a glass of amber-coloured liquid in the other.

"I had better go to Beatrix," he said. "She does like to play that is for sure," he added in a soft voice almost to himself. Gloria didn't think he was referring to ping pong.

§ § §

Before dessert was served there were speeches and toasts spoken in Dutch. Gloria didn't understand the words but she grasped the sentiment. The men were happy the war was over and they were glad to be returning to their native country.

After dessert they were given coffee with a choice of cigars or cigarettes. Gloria and Maartje each smoked a cigarette while joining the others for a walk on the deck. Many times in the months to come Gloria would think back fondly on this meal.

Chapter 6:

"You killed him!"

It was the only thing she remembered from her dream but the thought was enough to fill her with dread. In her half-awake state she tried to make sense of the terror she felt. Had she done enough to try to save the sailor? Panic threatened to overwhelm her and she had trouble catching her breath. Was it her fault that he'd died? She tried to review what she'd done to help the sailor but memories of the dream intruded. She knew with one part of her mind that things would make sense once she was fully awake but it was small comfort.

A horrible thought took shape in her mind – what if there was an inquest? She didn't know what happened when someone died at sea. They were in International waters – which country's rules would be in effect? That would govern whether she was charged with murder when she reached Amsterdam. She didn't even know the Dutch word for lawyer, let alone someone who could represent her in court. She tried to clear her mind to grab a few more hours of sleep.

§ § §

When Gloria awoke Maartje was already up and dressed. She was brushing her hair getting ready to plait it into two braids. It took Gloria a minute to collect herself. She sat and blinked trying to banish all traces of her dream. Perhaps no one would mention anything about the sailor dying.

"We'll dock tomorrow," Maartje said. "Do you want to do one last circuit of the ship after we eat breakfast?" Gloria nodded.

"I'll be ready in a minute," she said.

After breakfast the two women completed their circuit and stood at the rail gazing into the gray mist. Gloria stared in silence but Maartje sighed contentedly. She turned to Gloria.

"I am so glad to be back," she said. "Even if the news is very bad at least I am home again." Gloria envied Maartje her feeling of home-coming. Her own arrival was fraught with worry.

"I'm also happy to be here at last," said Gloria trying to sound as if she meant it.

"Where will you stay in Amsterdam?" asked Maartje. "I would invite you to stay with us but our apartment is small."

"Don't worry about me," said Gloria. "I have the Spelts' address and if I can't stay with them I'll contact the Red Cross and find someone to live with that way." She tried to smile but she felt it was more of a grimace. Maartje didn't seem to notice.

"If Willem's parents are not there to meet you," said Maartje, "my brother will drive you to their place."

"That would be swell," Gloria said. "Do you think he'll mind? Are you sure your brother will be there to meet you?"

"He was the one who sent the telegram telling me to come home," said Maartje turning to look at Gloria. "When I was at my aunt's we knew the war was over of course but like your parents she did not want me to come until I knew what had happened to my family. My aunt contacted the embassy and asked if they knew anything about my parents. They did not. There was no way to get any information and we did not know what to do. My aunt is too frail to make the trip. The next day a telegram from my brother arrived."

As Gloria listened to Maartje she realized that their situations were similar – they were each travelling to Holland without knowing what awaited them.

"Perhaps we can get together when we're in Amsterdam," she said.

"I would like that," said Maartje softly. "I will give you my address."

The rest of the day passed without incident. Gloria fretted inwardly about what would happen with regard to the sailor's death when they docked but outwardly she maintained a sunny face. The First Mate and the Second Mate were both busy with their duties and no one else seemed the least bit interested in what she was doing.

Going to sleep that night was difficult. Gloria tried to summon her excited feelings about Willem but her mind was filled with fear. Had she done enough to save the sailor? Was it her fault that he'd died? She shook herself mentally. This was senseless. She'd make herself crazy if she continued thinking like this. She had to believe she'd done everything she could. It wasn't her fault if it hadn't been enough. If she'd been a doctor or if she'd had more supplies perhaps she could've saved his life. But under the circumstances she'd done her best.

She fell into a restless sleep with that thought.

Gloria joined Maartje and the other passengers on the deck as the ship slowly made its way to the dock. Maartje greeted Martin and Piet but Gloria moved away. After all the months of worry and dread – hoping for the best, but fearing the worst — she was finally in Amsterdam and would soon be able to discover the truth about what had happened to her husband. Perhaps.

Fishing boats emerging through the mist indicated that people were working already. She took that as a good omen. Life in the beleaguered country was starting to return to normal. After a few minutes Piet joined her at the railing.

"Here is my address," he said handing her a piece of paper. "You can send someone to my house if you want my father's help."

Gloria was startled at first trying to recall what he meant. Ah yes! Piet's father had worked for the government. She took the paper and put it in her pocket smiling her thanks.

"That was a German submarine base," Piet said pointing to a partially ruined structure behind a fence a few hundred yards from the edge of the river. "It was bombed by the British Air Force. It's ruined now but those walls were fifteen feet of solid concrete when it was standing."

Gloria thought it looked like an igloo with one side smashed to smithereens. She surveyed the other buildings along the water's edge but none had been damaged as much as the base had been. Piet was still looking at the shoreline.

"And see those pieces of wood sticking out of the water?" he continued, "The Germans stuck them in at the entrance to the harbour early in the war to keep the Allies from being able to land supplies. Five years later they are still here." Gloria followed his gaze.

"All this," he said sweeping his arm in an arc to indicate the debris in the water as well as the buildings along the shore, "will have to be cleared out before Amsterdam can be a workable port again."

As they sailed closer to the dock the first people Gloria saw were the German prisoners of war in camps on either side of the waterway. The men stood with heads bent and shoulders rounded – the image of the defeat their country had suffered.

Turning away from the sight of the detainees Piet said, "I hope to find my father has survived the war. He was too old to join the army and since my mother died several years before the war he is all the family I have."

"My father was also too old to join the army," said Gloria. "But he still wanted to help. Since he is a garage mechanic by trade he was involved in setting up a school to train the Canadian Women's Army Corps to drive and service jeeps." She stopped talking as a sudden sound drowned out her words.

Looking to see where the racket was coming from she saw crowds of people on the dock. They were stamping their feet shouting and waving at the ship. Everybody seemed happy. Looking more closely Gloria noticed many were wearing ill-fitting clothes in browns and grays; there were no bright colours. Many women wore faded kerchiefs, also in dark colours, on their heads. The ship slowed and gradually came to a complete stop but rather than everyone lining up to leave, people rushed onto the ship. Gloria was confused. Leaning in to be heard Piet explained.

"Family members are allowed onto the ship while immigration procedures are carried out," he said. "Is someone meeting you?"

She started to answer but he suddenly let out a whoop and headed off towards the ramp. Gloria watched him making his way towards a young woman who was waving her arms. They came together in a hug. Piet's body acted as a bulwark against tides of people pushing in both directions. He had a girlfriend! Gloria suddenly felt quite a bit better. Just before she looked away Piet raised his head and caught her eye. He smiled sheepishly and waved. Gloria waved back. Looking around she spotted Martin his head partially visible above the crowd. Next to him she thought she spied Maartje and she took off in their direction. It was tough going but gradually a channel opened for her.

"Gloria, my brother is here! Theo is here!" exclaimed Maartje almost jumping up and down in her excitement. "I saw him on the dock. He has to get clearance to come on board. Oh, look there he is. Theo! Theo!" She started off in that direction. Gloria watched her until she reached her brother.

""Let's wait over here," she said touching Martin on the arm and signalling to the side of the deck. "Are you watching for someone?"

"I do not expect Karin to be here but I am looking for her anyway," he said. He moved towards the railing and Gloria followed in his wake.

"Where did you spend the war years?" asked Gloria when they were standing at the barrier watching people on the dock. It was only marginally quieter and they had to speak loudly to be heard.

"In the Dutch West Indies," he replied. "I worked there when we were not able to get home before the war began." He had been scanning the people on the dock while he was speaking. He gasped unexpectedly and yelled, "Karin! Karin!"

He repeated the name plus a sentence in Dutch several times before a young woman holding a child by the hand finally spotted him. She waved and began a more determined effort to reach the ship. She grasped the little boy by the wrist and pulled him behind her stopping only to speak briefly to an official. He waved her to the gangplank. Gloria stepped back as Martin pushed past her. She saw them come together; they stood and stared at each other before he grabbed her in a hug. He didn't even look at the little boy.

Gloria watched the scene as it unfolded although she couldn't hear anything. Karin and Martin clung to each other for several minutes and when they stepped apart Karin spoke, her hand resting on the boy's head. She picked him up and held him as she talked to Martin. The child glanced at Martin before burying his head in his mother's neck.

A man stepped in front of Gloria blocking her sight but she thought she realized what had happened. Somehow the Dutch woman had heard about the ship arriving and she had met it hoping her fiancé would be on it. She must have given birth to his son while he was away. Gloria put her hand to her mouth. This could have been her and Willem. She with a young son and Willem returning from service — she had to swallow the lump in her throat. She turned around to survey the crowd and began pushing her way to where Maartje was talking to a young man.

"Hi Maartje," Gloria said. "Is this your brother?"

"Yes," she replied stepping back as Gloria joined them. "This is Theo. And Theo this is my friend Gloria Spelt."

Gloria extended her hand to the boy who looked so much like Maartje they could've been twins. Gloria was fast learning that the proper Dutch greeting was to shake hands.

"I'm pleased to meet you," she said.

"I am pleased to meet you," he responded in faintly accented English bowing slightly but with a grin tugging at the corner of his mouth. She thought he was gently mocking her formality but she didn't mind. She turned as an official-looking gentleman approached.

He and Maartje had a short conversation in Dutch. When Maartje and Theo began following him Gloria tagged along. As they walked Maartje explained that the gentleman wanted to talk to them since they were new arrivals in Holland.

As they made their way off the ship and to a small room Gloria could see other rooms occupied by groups of people. She looked for the other people she'd met on the ship but didn't see anyone she knew. She regretted not being able to say goodbye to *Mevrouw* Dekker at least.

The gentleman led Gloria and Maartje into a room with a desk and two chairs. He spoke English inviting them to sit. Theo leaned against the doorjamb.

"I am a Dutch citizen," said Maartje, producing her papers. The officer looked at them closely before stamping one paper and handing it back. He turned his gaze to Gloria.

"My passport is in my maiden name," she said placing it on the table. She began rummaging through her purse as she talked.

"I haven't had a chance to get it changed. But I have my marriage license with me. I can prove I'm married to Willem Spelt." She extracted a paper from her purse and tried to flatten it on the table before handing it to him.

"Why is he not here to meet you?" asked the man, in a confused but not unfriendly tone as he took the paper.

"He is missing," she said.

The man didn't respond. He scrutinized the paper carefully, glanced at Gloria again before stamping it, and handed it back. Gloria thanked him in Dutch, gathered her papers, and followed Maartje out the door.

While looking for Willem's parents, Gloria imagined a couple her parents' age who might be looking for her. She stopped and scanned the remaining throng of people on the dock but saw no one matching that description.

Catching up to Maartje and Theo she gratefully accepted a ride. After Theo helped them put their luggage in the truck Maartje asked him about it. Theo admitted he'd borrowed it from a friend.

"He had gas to put in it too or we would all be walking," he added with a grin as they settled themselves in the front seat. There was barely enough room for the three of them.

Gloria showed Maartje the address - Griftstraat 2-III - which Maartje explained was number 2 on Grift Street the third floor.

After a few minutes' drive they arrived at the address: a narrow street with buildings so close they looked to be one big building. Maartje followed Gloria out of the truck and began to help with the luggage. Gloria waved off the help.

"It's all right," she said. "I'll be fine." She shooed her friend back towards the truck.

"What if there is no one home?" Maartje asked anxiously.

"Oh, someone will be," Gloria said cheerfully. "Don't worry about me. Go and find out how your family is. I'll see you in a couple days." She held the door while Maartje climbed in.

The two women waved at each other as the truck drove away. Missing her new friend already Gloria faced 2 Grift Street feeling very alone.

Chapter 7:

Gloria took a deep breath and squared her shoulders. This was it. After many years of worry and uncertainty she was finally in Amsterdam. She picked up her suitcase but after several glances at the building she set it down again and studied the building. She headed towards the only door that was visible but as she got closer she saw that it was the entrance to a single apartment.

She took a few steps back and looked around. The building was white concrete with the one wooden door. To her left she could see three steps leading to a landing. The steps turned ninety degrees and disappeared into the building.

As she stood in the middle of the sidewalk puzzling over what to do she noticed a young woman rounding the corner of the building and coming towards her. She walked with a slight limp and her head was down. In her left hand was a bag presumably of groceries. Gloria could see a loaf of bread sticking out the top. The woman turned towards the single door. She transferred the bag to her other hand and reached into her pocket. Gloria knew it was bad manners to stare but she hoped the woman would feel her gaze and look her way. It didn't happen — the woman pulled keys from her pocket and entered the building.

Holding her jacket tighter against the slight breeze Gloria started to turn towards the steps thinking that she'd have to see where they went. The woman reappeared at the doorway and walked towards Gloria speaking a sentence in Dutch. Gloria halted. Assuming it was an offer to help she stammered to say, in Dutch, that she was there to visit Mr. and Mrs. Spelt.

"Are you English?" the woman asked. Gloria smiled on hearing her native tongue.

"I'm from Canada," she said. When the other woman didn't respond Gloria added, "I'm married to Willem Spelt." The woman continued to stare at Gloria still without smiling.

"Willem is married?" she asked in surprise pronouncing the name "Villem".

Gloria nodded but didn't say anything. The woman had said his name with ease as if she knew him. What was their relationship? She and the woman stood facing each other for a minute before the other woman finally spoke again this time in precise English.

"My name is Anneke Biel. Come in," she said extending her hand. Gloria shook the proffered hand hesitantly, aware of the other woman's aloofness. She followed the Dutch woman through the doorway into Anneke's kitchen, dragging her suitcase.

"*Mevrouw* Spelt and my mother were best friends," Anneke said as she closed the door behind Gloria. "My mother died last winter." Anneke had still not smiled.

Gloria murmured words of sympathy as she stood just inside the door unsure what to do. The bag of groceries rested on a table; two chairs were pushed in on either side. The counter was bare but two plates, two mugs, and two knives were piled in the sink. The floor appeared to have been swept recently. Anneke started taking groceries out of the bag.

"Willem and I have been married for a couple of years," Gloria said willing her voice to remain calm and steady. "I guess Mr. and Mrs. Spelt don't know that and they must not know I'm arriving today." Anneke didn't respond.

Gloria stood silently watching the other woman put the food away. The few vegetables were fresh not canned. There was no meat and only the one loaf of bread which Anneke put in the bread keeper.

"Put your suitcase there," Anneke said sharply indicating a spot beside the door. "You can sit here." Gloria did as she was told. Anneke sat on the other side of the table.

"*Mevrouw* Spelt did not mention that Willem was married," Anneke said.

Her tone was accusatory as if it was Gloria's fault. Gloria began rummaging in her purse. She pulled out her marriage license and offered it to Anneke who looked from the paper to Gloria's face several times before finally taking hold of the document. She stared at it for several minutes before handing it back to Gloria.

"*Mevrouw* and *Meneer* Spelt did not say that you were arriving today," Anneke said. "They would have told me if they had known."

In the silence Gloria looked at Anneke, sizing her up in the same way that Anneke seemed to be observing her. Anneke appeared to be in her twenties. She was very thin and her long brown hair was pulled back in a ponytail.

"I'm a nurse." Gloria blurted into the silence that was quickly becoming awkward.

She didn't know why she'd said that but when Anneke glanced at her Gloria saw a flash of interest in Anneke's eyes.

"Are you a nurse too?" Gloria asked taking a stab in the dark. Anneke nodded once.

"I am," she said.

"Where do you work?" Gloria asked.

"The Queen Wilhelmina Hospital," Anneke replied. She took a breath as if to say more but then stopped and fell silent. Gloria tried a new topic.

"Have you known Willem a long time?"

"Willem and I have lived in this apartment building for nearly our whole lives."

Hearing that, Gloria had a sinking feeling. With the two mothers being friends had Anneke and Willem played together as children? And might Anneke have hoped the friendship would continue into adulthood? Gloria thought it was prudent to change the subject. She told Anneke about her hometown of Stratford, her sister, and her parents. Anneke listened but didn't speak; her facial expression remained neutral. As Gloria ran out of steam Anneke stood.

"Come," she said. "I will take you to meet Willem's parents. We leave your suitcase here." It sounded like an order.

Gloria followed Anneke out of the apartment trying to calm the butterflies in her stomach. She recognized the feeling — she'd felt a similar apprehension prior to writing an exam at school but this was unlike any test she'd ever faced before. Gloria followed Anneke up the stairs to the Spelts' third floor apartment and hung back as Anneke knocked on the door.

An old man, stooped and gaunt, opened it and Anneke launched into a speech in Dutch. Gloria smiled uncertainly tucking her hair behind her ear. When Anneke stopped talking the man looked at Gloria before stepping back to gesture them in. Gloria hesitated but Anneke strode in calling, "*Mevrouw* Spelt?" as she walked through the kitchen.

When they were all seated in the living room Anneke began talking in Dutch. She gestured to Gloria several times as she spoke but kept her attention centred on the older couple. Not able to understand what was being said Gloria observed her parents-in-law, looking for similarities to her husband. She thought he looked more like his mother; her colouring indicated that her gray hair may have been darker in her youth. His father projected the same sense of calm confidence she'd seen in her husband.

When Mrs. Spelt glanced at her momentarily, Gloria smiled but the older woman ducked her head and looked away. Gloria was baffled. Was the woman shy or had she taken a dislike to Gloria? Perhaps Mrs. Spelt had wanted Willem to marry Anneke and now she felt that Gloria had somehow "stolen" him. Mr. Spelt looked slightly bemused all the while Anneke was talking but as she finished speaking he beamed at Gloria with what she felt was real pleasure.

He spoke to Anneke in Dutch while Mrs. Spelt removed her glasses and wiped her eyes. Gloria wondered if she'd passed the test but Anneke gave no hint of that as she turned to her.

"They have not received any letters from Willem," Anneke said. "They did not know he went to Canada or that he was married." She sat back in her chair relaxed and at ease.

Anneke's attitude had changed when she entered the older couple's apartment as if she had adopted her nursing persona. Her concern for the couple was obvious as the three of them talked easily for several minutes but Gloria was unable to understand any of it.

At a prolonged break in the conversation she asked Anneke, "Do they know where Willem is? Why is he not home yet?"

"The Red Cross has told them Willem is missing," said Anneke. "They do not know what to do. And I cannot help them because I am not family."

Gloria gathered from her tone of voice that she had tried to help but failed. It suddenly occurred to Gloria that the army was still treating Willem's parents as his next-of-kin. Her marriage to him must not have been recorded by the army. Mr. Spelt leaned forward talking to Gloria in heavily accented English.

"Willem's brother, Harrie, no come home. You see him with Willem in Canada?" He too pronounced Willem's name as "Villem."

Gloria hesitated before answering. What could she say? How much should she tell them? She didn't want to upset them unduly but neither did she want to give them false hope.

"I didn't see Harrie in Canada," she began tentatively consciously slowing her speech. "Willem said Harrie was not on the same boat to England as he was. When Willem signed up to go to Canada he was out of touch with the soldiers in England."

Anneke translated what Gloria had said and the couple reached out to grab each other's hand. Tears slid silently down the older woman's cheek. Mr. Spelt spoke softly to his wife in Dutch patting her hand.

"Because they have heard nothing they fear he must be dead," Anneke said softly.

Gloria nodded silently. She knew what they were feeling. When she didn't hear from Willem at the end of the war she'd been frantic with worry.

Gradually though the feelings of panic had become less intense and she'd begun to believe her husband was alive. That belief had sustained her while she found passage to Holland going against her parent's wishes at first. It had given her the courage to get on the ship in Montreal and it had remained with her throughout the two-week journey across the ocean. She couldn't explain that to Mr. and Mrs. Spelt though.

"He might not be dead," Gloria said gently. "There could be any number of reasons why they haven't heard from him. The man at the Red Cross office in Canada explained that many soldiers were in POW camps in Germany and not all of them were freed at the same time. It could take quite a while for some of them to make their way home."

Listening to Anneke speaking Dutch Gloria reflected on the conditions the Dutch people had lived with for the past five years. An occupying army had taken over their land making it difficult to retain a sense of hope. She recalled what Piet and Gregor had said about food being scarce in Amsterdam. Had Mr. & Mrs. Spelt had enough food to eat? They both looked very thin so perhaps not. If the Spelts had barely enough to feed themselves how would they feel about having to feed her as well? Maybe she had been rash to come on this trip without hearing from Willem first. There was nothing to be done about it now. She was here and she would have to make the best of it. She smiled at the older couple offering silent encouragement but only Mr. Spelt returned the smile.

"Willem didn't talk much about his family," Gloria said during a lengthy pause, "other than to say he regretted not having his brother there to be his best man at our wedding. Were they close as children?"

"Close?" exclaimed Anneke taking Gloria and the Spelts by surprise. "They are twins!"

Chapter 8:

Gloria stared at the three of them as Anneke repeated the exchange in Dutch. It suddenly made sense. That was why Willem had said what he did about thinking his brother would be his best man! But why hadn't he told her he was a twin? Gloria realized her mouth was open and she closed it. Mrs. Spelt left the room saying something to Anneke in passing.

"*Mevrouw* Spelt is going to get a photo album," Anneke explained.

Gloria sensed that they all doubted her story especially if she didn't even know her husband well enough to know he was a twin. She was having a moment's doubt too wondering why Willem also hadn't told her about Anneke. What if he'd wanted to marry Anneke? Why would he have agreed to marry her, Gloria, if he'd wanted to marry someone else? After a minute her common sense prevailed. He was an adult and he could make his own decision about whom he would marry. One thing she did know about her husband – he was not dishonest.

"Willem was extremely protective of Harrie," Gloria said while they waited for Mrs. Spelt to return. "He felt guilty that he hadn't made sure Harrie was on the boat to England. Because of that I assumed he was the older brother but I never asked him. Was Willem born first?"

Gloria had never known any twins but she'd read in a textbook that the first-born twin often assumed the role of "older" brother or sister. When Mrs. Spelt re-entered the room carrying a large photo album Anneke spoke to her in Dutch.

"*Ja. Ja.*" Mrs. Spelt said. Anneke looked at Gloria and nodded. Willem had been born first.

The four of them spent the next quarter hour looking at small black and white photographs stuck on black sheets of paper. Gloria could see that Willem and Harrie had looked very similar when they were babies. As young children each had begun to develop his own distinct features but even into the teenage years they still looked remarkably similar.

The pictures showing two brothers playing together led Gloria to wonder again why Willem hadn't told her about his twin. But she was given no chance to ponder the question. Mrs. Spelt pointed to a picture and spoke a sentence in Dutch. Anneke peered at the picture and translated.

"Willem was more serious. Harrie always had a joke," she said.

Gloria smiled and nodded thinking that Willem was serious at times, with his old-fashioned manner but there were other times when his humour caught her off-guard. She remembered once when she'd been telling him about the kind of dress she was searching for and how difficult it had been to find the perfect one especially with the country at war. They'd been walking in downtown Stratford when he suddenly stopped and grabbed her arm.

"Wait!" he said.

"What? What?" she replied swivelling her head thinking something dreadful must have happened.

"Let me put on my interested face," he said gazing at her with his head tilted to one side and a look of intense concentration on his face. "Okay, continue."

Gloria cracked up. She doubled over with laughter not caring that they were blocking the sidewalk and people were staring at them. After that episode she didn't bore him with questions of fashion but she was glad he was still willing to discuss other plans for the wedding.

A picture in Mrs. Spelt's album suddenly caught Gloria's attention. It was of Willem, Harrie, and Anneke. The boys were about five years old, Anneke a year or two younger. Willem was in the middle holding a hand of the other two. Anneke pointed to the picture.

"Willem always treated me like a younger sister," she said. "He looked out for me as well as Harrie." She stated it in a matter-of-fact tone without looking at Gloria who didn't know what to make of it. Had Anneke liked Willem? Might she have thought their childhood friendship would continue into adulthood? Or was Anneke speaking the truth when she said she regarded Willem as a brother?

Anneke closed the album and handed it to Mrs. Spelt. She stood and said it was time to go. Gloria panicked. No one had mentioned anything about her staying with the Spelts. She put her hand on Anneke's arm.

"Could you ask Mr. and Mrs. Spelt," she asked in a low voice although they couldn't understand anyway, "if I could stay here? I have nowhere else to go." She willed herself to remain dry-eyed and to keep her face expressionless.

Anneke looked at her in astonishment and started to say something. Then she shut her mouth firmly and spoke to the Spelts in Dutch. To Gloria's surprise it was Mrs. Spelt who answered. She turned towards Gloria.

"You want stay here," she said. Gloria didn't know if it was a command or a question but she grinned in relief.

"Oh, thank you," she said taking both of Mrs. Spelt's hands in her own. "That's swell!"

Mrs. Spelt extricated her hands from Gloria's grasp and nodded without smiling. She turned and went down the hall muttering in Dutch. Anneke called a farewell to Mrs. Spelt as she led Gloria and Mr. Spelt downstairs. After retrieving her suitcase from Anneke's apartment Gloria and Mr. Spelt returned to the third-floor apartment. He put her suitcase in a small bedroom and left.

Gloria sat on one of the two single-size beds feeling anxious and cold. She took a deep breath and let it out slowly. She could almost see her breath. How was she going to sleep in a room this cold? Hearing a soft tap at the door she raised her head.

"Glorie?" said Mrs. Spelt shyly mispronouncing her name. She stood just outside the door clutching something to her chest. She spoke a sentence in Dutch and shoved what she was holding towards Gloria.

"Thank you," Gloria said. "*Dank u wel.*"

She took the sheet and blanket from Mrs. Spelt's outstretched arm. The older woman left quickly. Their shared worry about Willem was a shaky basis on which to build a friendship but that's all there was for now. Gloria spread the sheet and blanket on the bed. There was no pillow. Gloria sat in the bedroom unsure what to do. If Mrs. Spelt had hoped Willem would marry Anneke, Gloria's job was to convince her that she and Willem had married for love. And in Gloria's present state of mind she wondered if that was true. The cold drove her to move to get her blood circulating again. She stood and raised first one knee and then the other. As she marched she tried to supress her qualms and misgivings.

Mr. Spelt came to the door. Gloria stood still, feeling her face flush as he beckoned to her. Ignoring her discomfort or perhaps not aware of it he showed her around the kitchen. He offered her a glass and pointed to the faucet. She filled the glass with water and drank. It tasted good. She nodded to him before he left the room. Walking into the living room she looked for something to read but there were no magazines or books lying around. Not that she would have been able to read them anyway she thought sheepishly. There weren't even pictures on the walls to look at. It was too dark to look out the window.

She sat with her eyes closed and must have dozed because she wakened as Mr. Spelt entered the room. She sat straighter and smoothed her hair but he simply said, "*Goedenavond.*" Mrs. Spelt trailed behind him and repeated the word. Gloria mumbled, "Good night" before the couple left the room. She returned to her bedroom.

She put her pyjamas on without even bothering to brush her teeth. A sense of complete and utter desolation swept over her. She shouldn't have come to Holland. She should've waited as her parents had suggested. The feeling of certainty which had sustained her for so long was gone. What was she going to do?

After cocooning herself in the sheet and blanket she lay on the bed and gave in to her tears. She berated herself, telling herself she was a fool. The romantic notion of crossing the ocean, finding Willem, and having them fall into each other arms was simply too far-fetched to be believed. She wished she hadn't come. She wished she could go home. This was a disaster.

§ § §

Gloria was startled awake hearing someone moving about in the kitchen. Donning her dressing gown, she moved towards the sounds. Mr. Spelt was in the kitchen making coffee. He turned, saw her, and smiled.

"You like?" he asked holding a mug aloft.

"Yes thank you," she said nodding and adding as an afterthought "*Dank u wel.*" They sat at the table companionably drinking their coffees.

"You find Willem?" Mr. Spelt said finally.

"I will try," said Gloria. "I'll do my best." She smiled and nodded several times since she was unsure he had understood her words.

"Good. Good," he said standing. "Harrie. Find him too?" he said as he put his jacket on. Gloria nodded again. Mr. Spelt smiled briefly before leaving.

Gloria consulted her watch and realized it was four in the morning. She went back to bed. Mr. Spelt's belief in her triggered a reciprocal belief in herself and the certainty that Willem was alive replaced the despair she'd been feeling earlier. She fell into a dreamless sleep.

Chapter 9:

Gloria awoke feeling sore and out-of-sorts, her mouth dry, and her head aching. Slowly memories of the day before returned. It was the middle-of-the-night encounter with Mr. Spelt that had made the greatest impression however. She felt he was on her side even if Mrs. Spelt and Anneke didn't approve of her. Her empty stomach soon drove all other thoughts from her mind. She hadn't eaten since leaving the ship. Untangling herself from the sheet and blanket she dressed quickly.

She pushed the bedroom door open and heard sounds coming from the kitchen. Uncertain of the welcome she'd receive she moved towards the kitchen. As she entered the room she saw the lone person there was Mrs. Spelt. Gloria paused and coughed. Mrs. Spelt was bending over and at Gloria's cough she straightened quickly.

"*Goedemorgen,*" she said. She didn't smile but her eyes seemed softer.

"Good morning," Gloria said and smiled. Mrs. Spelt put a plate with a piece of dry toast on it on the table motioning to Gloria that it was for her. Gloria sat and began eating. Never had dry toast tasted so good! Mrs. Spelt placed a glass of water on the table and Gloria nodded her thanks. There was a knock at the door.

Mrs. Spelt opened it to reveal Anneke holding a pail of coal. Gloria looked between the two women's faces while they conversed in their native tongue. Afterwards Anneke spoke to Gloria in English.

"Coal is rationed. My father and I can spare this to help until you can apply to buy more," she said. She placed the pail on the floor.

Gloria was at a loss for words. A shortage of fuel had never occurred to her as she had planned her trip. She carried the bucket to the living room and placed it next to the small stove. When she returned to the kitchen Anneke was saying good-bye to Mrs. Spelt. Prior to leaving Anneke turned to Gloria and stared at her for half a minute before speaking.

"You really are married to Willem?" she asked the doubt apparent in her voice.

"Yes, we've been married for two years. Doesn't Mrs. Spelt believe me?" asked Gloria anxiously. "I know Willem sent them a letter informing them. I'm sorry if they didn't get it." She shrugged her shoulders.

"It is a surprise," Anneke said simply adding a sentence Dutch directed at Mrs. Spelt. It sounded like good-bye and perhaps that she'd be back later. She neither spoke to nor looked at Gloria again before walking out the door.

After Anneke left Gloria tried to ask Mrs. Spelt if she could help her with anything. When Gloria's Dutch elicited a vacant stare, she resorted to charades. "Me…help…you?"

"*Je kan me helpen*," Mrs. Spelt said in a matter-of-fact tone, which Gloria took to mean that the other woman had somehow understood Gloria's arm gestures. Mrs. Spelt went to her bedroom and returned with a bed sheet. She motioned for Gloria to hold two corners while she took clothes pegs from a container on a shelf. They hung the bedclothes out the window.

In the days to come Gloria realized this was a daily activity although she wondered what good it did since it rained almost every day and when it wasn't raining the air was still damp and clammy. She got used to seeing sheets hanging in the courtyards around which the apartment buildings were constructed. Mrs. Spelt acknowledged Gloria's help with a small sad smile. When they'd finished she put her kerchief and jacket on. Gloria thought she said she was going to the market.

Once she was alone in the apartment Gloria sorted through her clothes separating a pile that needed to be laundered. She'd have to ask Mrs. Spelt about doing laundry. Or maybe she could ask Mr. Spelt although he was probably like her dad and didn't help with the housework.

§ § §

Laundry was done in much the same way it was done in Canada she discovered later. Mrs. Spelt used a washtub, scrub board, and bar of soap. The main difference was that the laundry soap used in Holland was a big orange-coloured rectangle rather than the smaller white bars that her mother used. After receiving instructions Gloria was pleased to be able to do her own laundry. The clothes were dried by hanging them on clotheslines out the windows.

Gloria and Mrs. Spelt survived that first day with very little conversation but not much was needed. In actual fact Mrs. Spelt ran her household in much the same way as Gloria's mother ran hers. One big difference was the hot water. In Canada Gloria was used to turning on a tap and having hot water readily available. In Holland it was different. A little gadget was fitted at counter level to the water intake pipe in the kitchen. It produced heated water but Mrs. Spelt had to put coins in to make it work. Immediately after the war the hot water supply was further limited — it was only available at certain hours of the day.

Gloria was relieved when Mr. Spelt arrived home. He knew more English than his wife and his manner was friendlier. Willem had told her his father was a baker. Mr. Spelt likely had to know some English to run his business but he could understand more than he could speak. As he talked he paused to think of an English word and when Gloria guessed which word he was searching for he nodded and smiled.

His working day began at 5 a.m. and lasted until 3 p.m. Since bakers hadn't been under the same restrictions as the rest of the population during the war, its end didn't bring much change to Mr. Spelt's routine. The German army had wanted bread to eat so the bakery had produced bread all during the war. But not having to use rations cards hadn't meant much if the ingredients simply weren't available.

Gloria's second evening and night in Holland were slightly more pleasant. Although there was no meat for their evening meal there were vegetables. It was cold in the bedroom when she went to bed but she was so tired she fell asleep immediately.

When Gloria awoke she could only remember parts of the dream. It had been about Willem again or someone who looked like Willem — his twin perhaps? Whoever it was he'd been in trouble. She woke up before she discovered what the problem was. Shivering as she climbed out of bed she put her dream from her mind. She didn't believe in dreams anyway.

Mrs. Spelt, no, *Mevrouw* Spelt — now that she was in Holland she would speak as much Dutch as she could — was up and moving around. Gloria went to the kitchen and got herself a glass of water. She smiled at her mother-in-law when their eyes met but neither woman spoke. *Mevrouw* Spelt put a piece of bread spread with something resembling margarine on a plate on the table and Gloria sat to eat. It didn't taste like the margarine she was used to eating in Canada but the bread was good. She was so hungry she ate it without complaint.

When Gloria finished eating *Mevrouw* Spelt was busy with the household tasks. Not wanting to bother her Gloria retrieved the paper and pencil her mother had urged her to bring. She needed to let her parents know she'd arrived safely and was staying with Willem's parents. She sat in the living room where she could hear sounds of children playing in the park outside. Thinking that it would interest her mother and maybe even her father she explained some of the differences between the two countries.

The bathroom was called the WC. Her mother, being British, would know the term WC or water closet but In Dutch it was pronounced "Vee-say". She assured her mother that she wasn't going hungry — there were usually vegetables for dinner even if there wasn't meat. She didn't mention the meal of bread and margarine or how awful-tasting the margarine was.

She stopped writing and reminisced about the meal they'd had on the ship the day before they'd arrived in Holland. The pastry and cakes had been sweet and delicious. Even the vegetables she recalled with pleasure. She started writing again before she began drooling and finished the letter without mentioning that she was homesick or how much she missed Willem. After sealing the letter, she put it in her room intending to ask Anneke how to mail it.

Returning to the living room she took a seat by the window. Thoughts of her mother and sounds of children playing outside brought a lump to her throat. She'd grieved for her baby when she'd had the miscarriage but her sorrow had been mingled with the general grief of war. The whole town had been mourning the loss of brothers, fathers, cousins, uncles.

When Willem had first left for England she'd missed him of course, but her family had been close enough to offer support. Like her friends and neighbours, she was proud that her husband was fighting with the Canadian army to keep their country safe. She absent-mindedly watched a child chasing another in the yard below the window. The noises were muted but she could tell they were yelling. One of the children tripped and fell and a young woman ran to comfort him. Gloria couldn't see if it was a boy or girl.

Her thoughts returned to the letter that never came. Without knowing what Willem was thinking her imagination filled in the blanks with bad thoughts. Perhaps Willem was happier she hadn't had the baby because then he could ignore the fact that they were married. Perhaps he was sorry they'd been alone together when... *it* had happened. Perhaps he was sorry he'd agreed to marry her. Perhaps...perhaps...perhaps. She sighed.

She'd finally decided to make this trip and now here she was – living with the Spelts but not really accepted by *Mevrouw* Spelt and Anneke didn't like her either. She wasn't doing anything to find Willem and even if she did find him maybe he didn't want to be married to her anymore. Willem was a twin and he hadn't cared enough to tell her. Anneke had been Willem's friend and she might've wanted to marry him. It was all wrong and Gloria didn't know how to make it right. She shouldn't have come. Leaning over she put her head on her arms and started crying.

She sobbed silently but after a few minutes she felt a soft hand gently rubbing her back. After another minute Gloria sat up and reached into her pocket for her hankie. She wiped her eyes and turned to face *Mevrouw* Spelt who was sitting in a chair beside her. The older woman spoke a sentence in Dutch in a gentle voice. Gloria started crying again.

"Willem and I had to get married," she whispered between sobs. *Mevrouw* Spelt sat in silence.

"I thought we loved each other," said Gloria trying to control her breathing. "I thought we'd be happy. But now…but now…" she waved her arm helplessly as her tears flowed.

The older woman stood and pulled Gloria into a hug. She may not have understood what Gloria was saying but she knew Gloria needed comforting. They stood together hugging each other until they heard a soft knock at the door. As they stepped apart Gloria dashed the tears from her eyes. The door opened to reveal Anneke looking anxious as her eyes travelled between the two women. She spoke to *Mevrouw* Spelt and after the older woman replied Anneke's gaze shot to Gloria.

"What did you tell *Mevrouw*?" Anneke asked

Gloria collapsed into a chair and the other two sat facing her. She took a moment to compose herself rubbing her face with both hands. She reached into her pocket to check for her hankie just in case she needed it. *Mevrouw* Spelt was looking at her kindly but Anneke looked angry. Her eyebrows were creased, her mouth tight.

"Willem and I had to get married," Gloria began and paused. Turning to *Mevrouw* Spelt Anneke talked in Dutch for a few minutes.

"Willem left for England a week after we got married," Gloria continued after Anneke had stopped talking. "I lost the baby after four months. I sent Willem a letter telling him but I never heard back. I don't know why he didn't reply. Perhaps he didn't get the letter or perhaps he did but he's decided he doesn't want to be married to me anymore," Gloria sniffed as tears threatened. She moved her hand to her pocket. "And now I find out that maybe he wanted to come back and marry you. I'm sorry, so sorry." She slouched in the chair holding her hankie to her mouth. She looked at the floor.

"Well," Anneke said finally. "That is quite a story." She took a few minutes to repeat it in Dutch. Gloria sat straighter and wiped her nose but continued to look at her feet.

Anneke turned towards Gloria who raised her eyes to look at the Dutch woman. Anneke didn't look angry or upset. She'd adopted her nursing persona and was sitting with her back straight, her feet flat on the floor, and her hands clasped in her lap.

"First of all," she said briskly, "Willem and I were never going to marry. We are good friends but even though my mother and *Mevrouw* Spelt tried to get us together it could not be. I think of Willem as my older brother not someone I want to marry." She hesitated a moment but continued talking. "I am sorry your baby died but if you and Willem married because you love each other he will still want to be married to you."

When Anneke stopped talking Gloria had her emotions under control again. She put her hankie in her pocket and smoothed her hair tucking one side behind her ear. She watched as *Mevrouw* Spelt got up to put the kettle on the stove and thought that making tea must be a panacea everywhere.

Chapter 10:

Gloria's outburst did have some slight effect on *Mevrouw* Spelt's behaviour towards her but almost none on Anneke's. In the following days Mevrouw Spelt often looked at Gloria with concern and patted her arm. She listened when Gloria tried talking to Meneer Spelt although she didn't attempt to initiate a conversation.

Anneke continued to visit the older couple but for the most part she ignored Gloria. The only time she wasn't cold and unfriendly was when they talked about nursing. This troubled Gloria at first but later she came to believe neither woman was being intentionally unfriendly. The Dutch people had had five years of experiencing mainly negative emotions and it was hard to switch it off. Gloria might have felt and behaved the same way under similar circumstances.

But Gloria couldn't let negative emotions swamp her. She had to stay positive, to keep focussed on finding Willem. Only by talking to him would she know what he was thinking. Only then would they be able to continue their married life together.

Since the Red Cross office in Canada had been helpful she wondered if there was one in Amsterdam. After asking Anneke she discovered there was an office in the city but she would need to take a bus to get there. Since

Anneke didn't offer to help Gloria used the phone box on the corner to call Maartje's house. Maartje's father was a druggist and he had a phone in his store. Maartje agreed to accompany her to the Red Cross office.

On her way back to the apartment after calling Maartje Gloria stopped to watch four teenage boys who were playing in the street. She thought about the pictures *Mevrouw* Spelt had shown her and wondered if Willem might've played like this in earlier years. Two of the four youths were dressed in long sleeved shirts and pants; the other two wore pants with jackets. It was cool and Gloria felt a little embarrassed in her fur coat but she couldn't very well offer it to them.

§ § §

Gloria sat on the bus and gazed about since Maartje didn't seem inclined to talk. This vehicle was not what Gloria thought of as a bus. It was more like a trolley car although it didn't run along tracks. It made one trip into the business district in the morning and one back out to the suburbs in the afternoon. As they made their way through the rest of the city Gloria craned her neck looking around.

"You must think I'm a real country hick looking at all the tall buildings," Gloria said tentatively glancing at her friend. Maartje raised her head.

"Amsterdam is quite different from Canada," she said in a soft voice, "but it is good to be home again. I have missed my country."

After that brief conversation they sat silently for several more minutes. Gloria was unsure what was bothering Maartje but she didn't want to pry. Finally, Maartje sighed turning her head to gaze out the window.

"I am glad to see people are putting up window boxes again," she said. She took a breath and continued. "In the park near where we live our neighbours have planted flowers. Gardens were not tended during the war years and the flowers died. The country will not be the same until flowers are growing again. There is still a long way to go before Holland will be back to what it was but it is starting." She sat back.

Gloria gazed out the window and nodded in agreement although it was all new to her. The streets were very narrow and ran beside canals throughout the city. The sidewalks and even some streets were cobblestone which was confusing if you were walking. Were you on the road or the sidewalk?

There were very few cars; most people rode bicycles. Without engine noises to alert her Gloria had to be careful crossing the street. She found the silence disconcerting — so many city noises were lacking. She missed hearing factory whistles announcing lunch time and the end of the workday. There were few people on the streets. Even the bustle of a small town like Stratford was absent. Amsterdam was home to many people and before the war it must have been a thriving city. She asked Maartje about it.

"It is quite different from what I remember before the war," said Maartje. "When I was younger there were people with booths set up on the streets selling bracelets and rings and always many, many people, sometimes so crowded it was hard to walk. Boats travelled along the canals —" Her voice faded and she sniffed.

Gloria looked around again not wanting to further upset Maartje. The buildings looked two-dimensional as if they were fronts in a movie set. She remembered seeing a movie set once when her mother had taken her shopping in Detroit. Here in Amsterdam gazing at the shops and apartment buildings she almost felt claustrophobic – the buildings started at the sidewalk's edge and went up three or four stories into the air.

When the bus slowed down and stopped the two women got off. The shops were so close together they looked like one big building the length of the block. A few shop windows were completely bare. On the corner was a small garden area devoid of plants. One or two windows above the shops had flower boxes attached although they too were empty. Gloria gazed about as she followed Maartje who seemed to know where she was going.

The two women ascended the outside stairs of a building halfway down the block and entered the building. The door of an office to their right stood open. As they went into the room Gloria's gaze swept over the desk observing the telephone, a typewriter, and a nameplate: *Meneer* de Haas. A bookcase partially filled with books stood along one wall. A man who looked to be in his fifties was sitting behind the desk. He held a pen loosely in his hand. As they approached he put his pen down and took off his glasses. His shoulders sagged but his eyes were friendly.

"*Goedemorgen,*" he said as he stood. He added another sentence, his gaze travelling between the women's faces. Maartje answered in Dutch after which she turned to Gloria.

"I told him you were looking for your husband who is a Dutch soldier," she said.

"I speak English," *Meneer* de Haas said. "Please sit down." He placed another chair beside the one in front of his desk. When the two women were seated *Meneer* de Haas sat too.

"I haven't heard from my husband for more than a year," Gloria said leaning forward. "I checked casualty lists with the Red Cross in Canada looking for his name without luck. I want to find him and I was hoping you could help." *Meneer* de Haas looked confused for a minute but he shook it off as he stood.

"What is his family name?" he asked turning to the bookcase.

After Gloria told him he pulled a binder off the shelf. He opened it and flipped back and forth between pages. Resuming his seat, he announced that the name Willem Spelt was not on the most recent casualty lists.

"It appears your husband's unit was assigned to the Queen's Own Rifles a Canadian regiment," he said.

Gloria leaned forward in her chair anxious for him to continue. To her disappointment he closed the book.

"He may come home yet," he said peering at Gloria. "The war has only been over for a few months. We are still getting names of men who were in POW camps in Europe. We may get word of him soon or he may make his way home on his own. I would not give up hope."

"Do you know where he was fighting at the end of the war?" she asked. "That would give me an idea of where to start looking for him."

"I am sorry but I do not follow," he said. "You do not have to look for him." And then he repeated, "As I said before we may get word of him soon or he may make his own way home."

"I have to find my husband," said Gloria a little impatiently. "I can't just wait for him to come home. I'm a nurse and if he's wounded I can look after him."

"The Red Cross will care for him," he said picking his glasses off the desk and polishing them with his handkerchief. He puffed his chest and assumed an air of importance as he placed his glasses on his face.

"We have a long history of helping wounded soldiers. In 1859 a man from Geneva Switzerland helped wounded soldiers at the battle of Solferino. Later he came up with the idea of forming national societies to help the military medical services which took dead and wounded soldiers off the field."

As he talked Gloria felt her temper rising. Why was this man giving her a history lesson? She wanted to know where her husband's regiment had been at the end of the war. She tried to interrupt.

"I only want to know…"

"Three years later he published a book. After reading the book people organized an international conference out of which a national society was formed using a red cross on a white background as its emblem.

"This first Geneva Convention made it compulsory for armies to care for all wounded soldiers regardless of which side they were fighting on…" He barely stopped for a breath.

Gloria looked at Maartje who shrugged. It appeared she had no idea how to stop him either. The man seemed oblivious to Gloria's discomfort.

"We have had many challenges in this war since we are carrying out humanitarian work on five continents."

Gloria clenched her fists in her lap and blew her breath out through pursed lips but the man paid her no heed. She started to speak again but he steamrolled over her.

"This new United Nations is helping as well. But we are still the best hope for finding your husband. It is not safe for a young pretty girl like you to travel around the country. He may show up yet. Go home and wait for him."

This was too much! Gloria stood and glared at the man.

Chapter 11:

"I most certainly will not go home and wait for him," she exclaimed. "I came all the way from Canada to find my husband and I will. I'm not afraid." She turned and stalked out of the room hoping Maartje was following.

"The nerve of him," said Gloria after they were out of the building. "As if being too young or too pretty meant I didn't have any courage." She took a deep breath expelling it forcefully.

"I don't need the Red Cross," she said firmly. "I'll find him myself." Gloria took another deep breath and tried to calm herself. Maartje was giggling.

"It's not funny," said Gloria sternly. She was still furious but after a minute's reflection she began to relax. Perhaps she had over-reacted. She looked at her friend who was still giggling and she smiled briefly.

"Maybe it was a little funny," she amended. "He did look silly gaping like a fish. But I will not sit still and wait for Willem to return. I'll think of something else."

The women walked on in solemn silence for half a block until Gloria, remembering Maartje's demeanour on the bus and feeling a little ashamed at her thoughtlessness, asked Maartje how she'd found things at home. Maartje took a deep breath.

"Things are not good," she said slowly. "My mother is in the hospital still. She has a bad heart and last winter was very hard on her. Also, she was very worried about my brother. He spent the last two years of the war with my uncle in Friesland so the German army would not take him to work in a factory in Germany." Maartje paused and swallowed before continuing.

"That is what happened to our neighbour. One day he did not come home from work. It was a few days before his wife discovered that he had been rounded up and put in a truck driven by German soldiers. My mother was horrified when she heard that. She and my father sent my brother to my uncle's in the north of Holland at once."

Gloria listened with increasing dismay. Poor Maartje. What a shock that must have been!

"I'm so sorry to hear that, Maartje. Is there anything I can do?" Gloria said stopping to look at her friend. Maartje halted too and shifted her gaze to stare into the distance.

"There is nothing anyone can do," she said stoically. She turned and continued walking. "Netherlanders are suffering in all parts of the country." She started to say more, but stopped as her eyes filled with tears. Gloria spotted a bench that had been placed in what used to be a little park and she guided Maartje to it. Maartje took a deep breath.

"My brother did not want to tell me when we drove home but my boyfriend, Mathias, died last year," she paused. "A bomb landed on his house killing him and his parents."

"Oh Maartje, I'm so sorry to hear that," Gloria said.

"Yes. I will miss him and his parents. But so many people have died," said Maartje her voice becoming gloomy. "My girlfriend died and two neighbourhood friends died. They both starved to death last winter. They were all people I grew up with."

Gloria remained silent for a minute giving her friend a chance to regain her composure. She tried to imagine what it would be like to have a boyfriend or anyone your age die but she couldn't. It was unimaginable. Maartje sniffed and turned to Gloria.

"How did the meeting with Willem's parents go?" she asked her voice muffled by her hankie. Gloria was glad she had better news to report.

"They were still living at the address I had and they are letting me stay with them," she said. "I met a young woman Anneke who lives in their building and she came with me to make the introductions. I was glad of that; I'm not sure how I would've managed otherwise."

Maartje stood and pulled her duffel coat tighter. The time was getting on and they didn't want to miss the return bus. Gloria stood too and readjusted her coat.

"I'm glad I brought my fur coat with me," she said.

"My aunt bought me this coat in Canada," said Maartje. "*Tante* knew I would not be able to buy a coat here. I bought it in Winnipeg and it is very warm." She fastened the top toggle. Gloria wondered if her aunt had money since the coat looked expensive but she didn't want to ask.

"I did not realize while I was in Canada," Maartje continued as they started walking, "how much people in Amsterdam were suffering. My cousin Bente and her mother went on hunger trips into the countryside to gather food last winter when supplies couldn't get through the lines. Bente said fuel was so scarce that my uncle had to go out after dark to chop limbs off trees. If they were caught by the German army they were punished. My uncle took a baby carriage with him to carry the firewood home."

Noticing the bus was coming Gloria ran with Maartje to where others were waiting. After a long journey winding through the city each got off at her bus stop making vague statements about getting together again.

Walking home Gloria noticed reminders of the past five years everywhere. Sections of houses stood with one or two walls gone and the roof missing; their innards lay bare and abandoned. Blackened tree stumps stood silent and forlorn amid small patches of black or brown grass. Roadways were cracked and uneven damaged by German and Allied tanks.

There was an aura of apathy permeating the country and Gloria could feel it robbing her of her will to act. She knew it was cathartic for people to talk about what had happened during the war, but it was hard to listen to — mainly because there was nothing she could do. She had no way of helping to fix what was wrong, no way of making things better. The only thing she could do although it would only help her parents-in-law was to find Willem. She bent her mind to that task.

Chapter 12:

The trip to the Red Cross had been a disaster. What was she going to do? She'd hoped for inspiration while sleeping or while helping Mevrouw Spelt around the house but that hadn't happened. She put her coat on and gestured to her mother-in-law that she was going out. She had to do something!

She hadn't gone more than half a block when she spotted a group of Dutch soldiers. Her desperation caused her to act rashly and she approached them. Without stopping to think she spoke in English.

"Can you give me some information please?" she asked looking at each of them in turn. One of them said something in Dutch and two of the others laughed.

"I'm sorry," she said suddenly realizing that they likely couldn't understand her. She started to turn away. One soldier stepped in front of her saying something unintelligible to her prompting the other two to laugh again. As she tried to walk around him he reached out and she backed up so quickly she tripped. The one who had been ignoring her until then grabbed her arm to steady her.

"Do not scare her," he said to the others holding her until she regained her balance. "She cannot understand what you are saying." He urged his friends to keep walking and as he turned to Gloria he said in surprise, "Mrs. Spelt – is it you? I did not recognize you."

Gloria looked at him again recognition suddenly dawning. She remembered him from the ship although he looked different.

"Ruben Alders," she said. "You've shaved your beard off." He nodded and stoked his chin.

"The girlfriend prefers this," he said smiling. He offered her his arm and escorted her walking behind his friends.

"What information are you looking for?" he asked. Collecting herself she matched his pace and explained her situation.

"I talked to a man at the Red Cross," she added, "but he could only tell me my husband was fighting with a Canadian troop - the Queen's Own Rifles. I'm trying to find out where they were fighting at the end of the war."

"I have heard of that regiment," Ruben said, "but I am not sure where they were fighting." He thought for a minute and then nodded toward his friends.

"I doubt any of them know either," he said, "so I am afraid we are no help."

"It was a long shot I know," said Gloria. They'd caught up to the others but at a nod from her companion the three men turned the corner and continued walking.

"What about going to the hospital?" Ruben said after a minute. "I know several chaps who are being treated there but they are not too sick to talk. Perhaps one of them is from that regiment. Or they might know more than my friends and I do." The others were waiting for him to catch up. "I have to go now. I am sorry my friends frightened you. Good luck on finding your husband." He sprinted to rejoin his friends.

As Gloria turned to walk away she heard the others laugh again but she ignored it. Ruben's suggestion made sense. She'd enjoy working at the hospital while she searched for clues to Willem's whereabouts.

"I could also improve my Dutch," she muttered.

§ § §

"Does the hospital you work at need more nurses?" Gloria asked Anneke the next time she came to visit. *Mevrouw* Spelt was preparing dinner. They were having vegetables and kidney since kidney was the only meat available at the grocer's. *Mevrouw* Spelt used her ration card or "op de bon" to buy meat. She was only allowed to purchase meat on one day of the week and if there was no meat available on that day she was out of luck until the next week.

"We always need more nurses," said Anneke in response to Gloria's question. "Tomorrow I will ask if there's a position open."

Gloria thanked her and told her about meeting the Dutch soldiers and how the man she'd met on the ship had rescued her.

"Working at the hospital is perhaps a good idea," said Anneke. "It will give you more opportunities to talk to soldiers. And they will pay you so that will help too." She paused and as she started speaking again she blushed. "Have you heard any word of Harrie?"

"No, I haven't," said Gloria feeling badly that she'd forgotten about him. "I can ask about him at the hospital too if I'm working there," she added.

When Anneke arrived the next evening, Gloria was anxious while Anneke spoke first to *Mevrouw* Spelt. Watching the young woman's face Gloria tried to discern whether the news would be good or bad but Anneke's demeanor didn't betray anything. After a short conversation with *Mevrouw* Spelt she turned to Gloria.

"Nurse van den Berg has a temporary position that you can fill," she said. "One of the nurses has to stay home because her aunt has come to live with them."

"That's swell," Gloria said beaming at Anneke. "Thanks for asking."

"The shift starts at 07:00," Anneke added. "We can walk together; it will take us one half hour to get there."

Mevrouw Spelt asked Anneke about another neighbour and as the two of them talked about people Gloria didn't know she let her mind wander.

Becoming a nurse had been her life-long dream. As a child she'd liked taking care of her younger sister, Isabel. Her sister had never seen it that way though. She'd always maintained that Gloria was bossy. One time when Gloria thought Isabel was sick she'd told her sister to lie down. Her sister refused insisting Gloria wasn't the boss of her. Later Mrs. Macdonald had put Isabel to bed with a temperature. Gloria grinned inwardly at the memory.

Several hours later lying in bed she was too excited to sleep. Her mind was whirling. There was so much to get used to and so much she didn't understand. It wasn't just the language – it was the Dutch way of looking at life.

Or maybe it was the fact that Holland had been at war for five years. At least working in a hospital and caring for patients was familiar. And as Ruben had pointed out she might find out where Willem's regiment had been fighting and what had happened to him. Thinking about Willem calmed her and she finally slept.

Chapter 13:

"How long has this hospital been here?" asked Gloria as she and Anneke set out early the next morning.

"The Wilhelmina Hospital is the largest medical complex in the Netherlands," Anneke said proudly. "It did suffer bomb damage during the war but not so much to shut it down."

Gloria stifled a yawn. It was going to take a while to become accustomed to getting up for an early morning shift. They walked in silence for several blocks.

"Are there other hospitals in the city?" asked Gloria.

"There are three," said Anneke. "One received quite a bit of bomb damage but the others were only slightly damaged."

"Isn't there some rule to say a hospital can't be bombed?" asked Gloria.

"I am not sure the Germans always knew where the bombs were going to fall," Anneke answered grimacing and shivering but whether from the cold or the memory of falling bombs Gloria didn't know.

"Here we are," said Anneke as they walked around a corner.

Gloria gazed at the building sitting well back from the sidewalk. It was a large house, made of dark brick, standing several stories tall with many windows on each floor. Unlike the shops in the centre of the city it was surrounded by a large lawn.

Anneke walked up the sidewalk and entered the building with Gloria following. They turned right immediately and went along a hall to an office. Anneke knocked and entered the room with Gloria on her heels. A woman wearing a white nursing veil over her short blonde hair was sitting at a desk and she looked up as the women entered.

"This is Gloria Spelt, the nurse I told you about," said Anneke stepping back and motioning Gloria forward. "This is Nurse van den Berg our head nurse." She waited while the two women shook hands.

"I must leave to get ready for my shift now." Anneke said to Gloria. "I will see you at lunch." With that Anneke left the office.

"Biel is one of our best nurses," said the head nurse in surprisingly good English. "She has worked here for many years. The doctors always speak highly of her. Come with me. I will show you where to put your coat and purse."

She stopped in front of the main desk and indicated that Gloria should put her belongings in the cloak room to the side. Then she motioned for Gloria to join her at the desk.

"Meijer, this is Nurse Spelt, from Canada. She will be filling in for Neman," she said.

Gloria smiled at the woman sitting at the desk. She looked to be older than Gloria and although she was thin she did not have the half-starved look so many others did. She appeared friendly as she smiled at Gloria and stood to shake her hand. Her hair was a reddish-brown pulled back in a single braid.

"You will find many of the nurses speak English," said Nurse van den Berg.

"I'm sure I'll manage very well," said Gloria. "I'm starting to learn Dutch too." The head nurse nodded but she was clearly more interested in showing Gloria to the ward where she would be working than chatting about language skills.

For the next several hours Gloria was busy tending patients. She'd been assigned to the children's ward where many of the children were suffering from malnutrition. Some had lost limbs due to frostbite and a few had been hospitalized with common childhood ailments.

"Is food for the hospital rationed?" she asked Nurse Meijer.

"It is," Meijer replied. "Although not as severely as for everyone else. We get powdered milk and powdered eggs. The taste is not very good but at least it is more nutritious for the children."

She tucked a blanket around a little boy. Gloria glanced at him and when he favoured her with a smile she walked to his bedside. As she stood there listening to Nurse Meijer she noticed his little hand sticking out from under the blanket.

She instinctively reached towards it and as their hands met he gripped her fingers. His hand was surprisingly warm but it felt light and undersized. Gloria was touched by the gesture. He held her hand for a minute before loosening his hold.

Just then another nurse entered the ward saying something to Nurse Meijer who turned to Gloria and said, "I will be right back."

Meijer followed the other nurse out the door and Gloria was left alone with the ward full of bed-ridden children. Many were sleeping but those who weren't looked at her as the little boy had done with big eyes and anxious expressions. None of them smiled at her. She had moved to the next bed when Nurse Meijer re-entered the room.

"Will you finish taking these temperatures?" she asked handing Gloria a clipboard. "I have to help on another ward."

Alone with the patients Gloria looked at the paper and saw the first name on the list was Pieter with a question mark. She looked to the corresponding bed and realized it was the little boy who had smiled at her.

She went to him and popped a thermometer in his mouth smiling at him as she took his thin wrist between her thumb and forefinger. He did not smile this time. His heartbeat was strong and rhythmic but he had the same air of resignation that she had seen in many adults.

She examined the bandage on his arm thinking that if her son had lived he would have been a year or two younger than this little boy. Finishing with the bandage she took the thermometer out of his mouth. His dark brown hair covered his forehead and without thinking she brushed it back. As she did so he flinched. His eyes widened in alarm and she heard his sharp intake of breath.

She pulled her hand back quickly but she could see the fear in his eyes and she patted his arm gently murmuring soothing words. As she tried to calm him she realized he must've lived most of his life in a country at war. She could only imagine what horrors he'd seen and she was sorry to have frightened him.

An unfamiliar sense of pity stole over her causing her to catch her breath.

She smiled at him again and nodded trying to encourage him to say something but he kept his mouth firmly closed. Even when she straightened his blanket he said nothing. He shut his eyes and this time they stayed closed. As Gloria moved on to the next patient she was puzzled by his actions and by her response.

Chapter 14:

During her lunch break Gloria sat at the long cafeteria table with Anneke and another nurse who was introduced as Mieke Clos. Gloria hoped no one would mind answering a few questions.

"Were there a lot of changes in the hospital when Holland was invaded?" she asked letting her gaze wander over each face turned her way.

"The upper management changed but that is all," explained Mieke. "Instead of being run by the government we had to answer to the German army. But everything else stayed the same. Our hospitals have always been very well run and the Germans did not want to change that. They had to use our medical services so they wanted them to function at top efficiency." Another nurse also spoke.

"During the war," she said, "The Netherlands were controlled by a German civilian governor who one-by-one got rid of non-Nazi groups."

"My father-in-law is a baker," Gloria said, "and he mentioned that bakeries, being non-political, were allowed to operate as best they could. They tried to keep up the production of bread even if sweets were unavailable due to a shortage of sugar."

Several other nurses murmured in agreement as they began eating. Conversation stopped while everyone was busy with food but when Gloria finished eating she had more questions.

"How are you coping with shortages?" she asked taking a sip of her tea. She'd gotten it from the large pot set up on a side table after observing others doing the same. The teapot sported a home-made tea cozy. Many of the cups were stained or chipped but the tea was hot.

"Of course, we have the same difficulties that way as everyone else," said Mieke. "We have to make do as best we can. During the last war I remember my mother saying there were hardships even though we remained neutral. War is hard on everyone."

"It is," said Gloria. "I feel especially sorry for the children. I noticed one patient whose name is Pieter but his last name wasn't listed. Does his family come to visit him?"

"Is he the little boy with the broken arm?" asked Mieke.

"Yes, I changed the bandage and it looks like it was infected." Gloria replied.

"A soldier brought him here. His arm was broken and it did become infected," said Mieke. "We do not know where he came from or where his family is. He does not talk about what happened."

"How old is he?" Gloria asked.

"We are not sure," said Mieke shaking her head and pausing to take a sip of tea. "Like so many of the children he did not eat so much for the past year but we think he might be six or seven. When he arrived, he repeated the name 'Tonny' over and over. It might be his brother's name. He was with a boy who died before he could be brought to the hospital."

"In Canada," Gloria said, "we didn't learn about how you were suffering until after the war ended." She folded the paper she'd wrapped her sandwich in and put it in her purse so she could reuse it.

"No one knew what was happening here," said Anneke, "until after the German army left. They did not want to broadcast what they were doing. But we knew and we helped others if we could. A friend who worked with mentally handicapped people told me that the staff kept a 19-year-old man who was not sick at the hospital to prevent the army from picking him up and taking him to work in the German factories." Another nurse sitting further down the table joined the conversation.

"And there were always little newspapers being passed around," she said, "to tell the real news not just what the German army wanted us to believe. Or people would change road signs to confuse the enemy soldiers. We kept our radios hidden so the German soldiers could not take them and we listened to the BBC in secret."

Gloria shook her head. How could anyone live like that? No wonder people were dejected and listless. Could that explain the little boy's behaviour or was there more to it than that? She hoped she could get him to talk about his family. She turned her attention back to the conversation at the table.

"After the war," Mieke was saying, "the Dutch people were so filled with hatred for the Nazis that they turned against those Dutch citizens who had worked with the enemy during the war." She switched into Dutch her words coming faster. After a minute she stopped talking and sat with her arms crossed her mouth firmly closed.

Anneke told Gloria that the inhabitants of a farmhouse had been dragged out and shot as sympathizers in May as soon as the German soldiers had left. Mieke had just learned their identity – her cousin and his wife.

"He would not work with the Germans," Mieke stated firmly nodding her head once. "They should not have killed him but no one tried to find the truth."

"You mean they didn't question them first?" asked Gloria. She looked at Anneke in amazement. If that was the case perhaps Mieke had just cause for feeling bitter. Gloria knew how easy it was in wartime for dislike to escalate to hatred having listened to her father's war stories from the Great War. Shooting people because they'd worked with the enemy seemed extreme however and it disturbed her.

"The neighbours would have known what he was doing," Anneke continued. "They would have said he was a sympathizer."

"He was not!"

"Many people worked with the Germans. You cannot know for sure," Anneke said softly. Mieke sat slightly turned away from the table and refused to say more. In the sudden silence another nurse told a story she'd heard about a Canadian soldier and the Dutch liberation.

"The soldier arrived in a village in North Holland," she said. "He began telling the villagers the war was over and they were free. He was alone; no other troops were with him. He handed out chocolates for the children and everyone was very happy. They all started dancing and singing but finally he had to admit that he was lost — he did not know where the rest of his regiment was. He had to ask to be directed back to the main road so he could rejoin his unit."

She laughed after finishing her story and several others joined in. The story didn't seem that funny to Gloria but perhaps their laughter was more at the joy of being liberated than at any humour in the telling.

"All Dutch people are very grateful to the Canadian army for liberating them," the nurse added as the smiles faded. "We will never forget the sight of those tanks rolling into the towns and villages and the kindness of the soldiers driving the German soldiers out and bringing us chocolates and biscuits."

The nurses at the table all nodded in agreement and a few added their own liberation stories. Gloria was proud to be a Canadian at that moment. The conversation shifted to more mundane matters and after a few more minutes she left to prepare for her next shift.

The head nurse gave Gloria her instructions and she set off towards the children's ward to check on her little patient. He opened his eyes as she approached his bed but his face remained expressionless.

"*Goedendag*," she said in greeting.

He stared at her without speaking.

"Do you speak English?" Gloria asked.

He nodded his head slowly watching her intently as she took his temperature and checked his pulse. He didn't speak and closed his eyes while she examined the bandage on his arm. She wondered about that but she didn't have time to pursue the matter. Her mind was soon on other matters as she completed her shift but she spent the time walking home at the end of the day thinking about the little boy.

As she started to drift off to sleep that night she found her thoughts were still with the little boy. She felt they shared a bond and she wanted to find out more about him and re-unite him with his family if that was possible.

Chapter 15:

It was not to be – the next day she was assigned to a different ward – surgical, post-operative. Gloria was momentarily distressed by this but then she realized that working on this ward would give her an opportunity to talk to soldiers. She headed to the ward with a spring in her step.

She entered the ward and surveyed the beds – about twenty in all. Each of them was occupied. Some men were asleep; some were awake but lying still and a few were sitting up leaning against the wall. As she checked each man's wounds and took his temperature she exchanged pleasantries with him in Dutch as much as she was able. Three of the men looked at her blankly. Perhaps they were unable to understand her accent. She was undaunted and smiled as she approached the next patient on her list. He seemed especially eager to talk and he knew some English although he spoke with a heavy accent.

Gloria was able to ascertain that his regiment had landed with the Canadian army to liberate Holland from the south. When she asked him if he knew a Willem Spelt he put his finger to his bottom lip. His eyes got a far-away look in them.

"That name is familiar," he said finally. "Spelt – I knew a Spelt but I do not think it was Willem."

Gloria was so excited she almost dropped her tray and she took a moment to compose herself setting the tray on a nearby table. The patient had lain down again but he was looking at her anxiously. She looked around the room and didn't see anyone else who needed her attention immediately. She took a few minutes to tell the patient whose name was Stefan why she was asking about Willem Spelt.

"Is Spelt a common name?" she asked.

"*Nee*, not in Amsterdam. More in the north," he said slowly, lying back and resting with his eyes closed. After a minute he opened his eyes. "Harrie? Could it be Harrie Spelt?"

"Oh," said Gloria startled momentarily. "His brother," she said eagerly. "He has a brother Harrie. I wonder if it's him." She thanked him for his help as she collected her tray. She was starting to turn away when Stefan caught her skirt.

"Another thing," he said hoarsely. "There were Dutch troops with the Canadians landing on Juno Beach in Normandy." He paused to get his breath.

"Were they the Queen's Own Rifles?" Gloria asked anxiously. "That was my husband's regiment." Stefan lay back and closed his eyes.

"I do not know," he said softly turning his head side-to-side against his pillow.

"Thank you for telling me this," she said kindly. "I am sorry to trouble you. Rest now."

He nodded and his face relaxed. When Gloria had time during the remainder of her shift she thought about what she had learned from Stefan. She needed to discover if the Queen's Own Rifles had landed at Normandy. And she might have word of Willem's brother!

After lunch Gloria was pleased to discover she'd been assigned to the children's ward again. She was excited by the prospect of seeing Pieter but her eagerness turned to unease when she found him more distant. When she asked him if he'd had enough to eat he replied that he hadn't had lunch. She thought that sounded strange and checked with the head nurse. He'd been fed an hour earlier along with the others in the ward. She returned to his bedside but he was crying and she didn't want to confront him about the obvious lie. He refused to tell her why he was crying. She checked his bandage and took his temperature but was unable to comfort him. She patted him awkwardly on the arm before she left the ward.

When her shift ended she met Anneke who was going off-shift as well. As they walked together Gloria told her what she had discovered.

"Stefan said he thought he remembered the name, Harrie Spelt. Do you think it could be Willem's brother?" Gloria asked eagerly.

"Spelt is a common name," Anneke said slowly modifying her pace as she thought. "So, it might not be him. But it would be very good news for the Spelts if it was." She paused, glancing at Gloria. "Do you mind if I tell them?"

"Please do," said Gloria happily. "I wish I knew if the Canadian troops who landed at Juno Beach were the Queen's Own Rifles."

"Hmmm," Anneke mused. "I could ask my father. He kept up on things like that even though he wasn't in active service during this war." Gloria turned to look at her excitedly.

"Oh Anneke," she said doing a two-step, "that would be swell!"

For the next week Gloria's shifts alternated between the surgical ward and the children's ward. Caring for the adults she listened to tales of bravery and courage. Many of the men joined her in laughing at her pronunciation mistakes and grammatical tangles as she tried to speak Dutch but no one had further information for her. Since Stefan had been discharged the day after their conversation she couldn't question him again.

Her interactions with Pieter varied according to the kind of day he was having, but even when he was uncommunicative she found she was spending much of her spare time thinking about him. She wanted to help him but more than that she wanted to protect him and to return him to his family so he could be happy again.

One day a couple of weeks after she'd started working at the hospital she was surprised when Pieter smiled at her as she approached. She took advantage of the moment and asked him his name.

"Pieter," he said. "Pieter Zweers."

"Who is Tonny?" she asked remembering the name he'd repeated after arriving at the hospital. She immediately regretted her bluntness.

Pieter's eyes filled with tears and his bottom lip trembled. He shook his head and closed his eyes. As much as she hated upsetting him this was the only way she could help him. She sat beside him patting his back and willing him to start speaking again. After a minute he spoke but it was so soft that she had to ask him to repeat it. Bending closer she heard him talking Dutch but when she didn't respond he repeated it in English.

"My brother died. I let him die," he said softly his voice unsteady.

"Your brother died because he had been without food for too long," Gloria said gently her throat tight with unshed tears. "But that was not your fault; you were lucky not to have died as well." She put her hand on his shoulder as a tear rolled down his cheek. He sniffed but still refused to cry.

"I not want him to die," he said in a small voice.

"Oh honey," said Gloria tenderly. "Nobody wants people they love to die. I'm sure you did everything you could to keep him alive but sometimes no matter what we do people die." She felt tears stinging her eyes as she smiled. "You are safe now. I am sorry your brother died but we will take care of you."

He looked at her solemnly as his eyes closed. She adjusted the blankets around him thinking how she'd had her mother to comfort her when her baby had died but Pieter hadn't had anyone to comfort him when his brother died. It strengthened her resolve to find his family.

When Gloria entered the children's ward to start her shift the next day she heard loud young voices and a quieter more mature voice. When she reached the commotion Mieke had her arms around Pieter as he stood beside his bed. His face was red and his hands were clenched at his sides. His body fairly hummed with anger. The boy in the neighbouring bed was cowering against the wall his eyes wide in terror.

Mieke and Gloria exchanged a look. When Mieke nodded slightly Gloria sat on the bed and as Mieke dropped her arms Gloria gently tugged Pieter into hers leaving Mieke free to comfort the other little boy.

"Pietje," said Gloria fondly, using the childhood form of his name. She'd heard one of the other nurses call him that and it had calmed him.

"What's the matter?" She rubbed his back to help calm him further.

"Hans stole my bread," sobbed the little boy. "I want to get it back." He relaxed against Gloria's chest and she hugged him tighter. Behind her she heard the other boy's protest stifled by Mieke who was trying to get him back to bed.

"I'm sure he didn't mean to," murmured Gloria soothingly. This habit of Pieter's of telling untruths worried her. She helped Pieter back to bed and when both boys were settled she followed Mieke to the far side of the ward where they could talk quietly but still keep an eye on the patients.

"What was that about?" Gloria asked in an undertone.

"These children were taught to lie during the occupation if their parents were hiding Jews from the Nazis. Most often the lies centred on food," said Mieke. "It is hard for them to break the habit. Today it is Pieter but it could just as easily have been Hans."

"I caught him in a lie one other time," said Gloria, "when he claimed he hadn't been given his lunch but he had." Mieke shook her head sadly.

"It will take time for all Dutch people to learn to live in peacetime," she said. "I fear it is especially hard for the children. They have suffered so much."

"I hope to find Pieter's family for him," said Gloria. "Once he's back with them and feeling secure again he'll be able to start acting like the little boy he is."

"I am sure he will," said Mieke nodding. "My nephew is a couple of years older and he acted in a similar way even at the end of the war but he does not do it so much now."

It was not only the children who had to adjust to post-war conditions. In the morning *Mevrouw* Spelt was unable to get out of bed and Gloria didn't know why. She made her mother-in-law a cup of tea and took it to her bedside but when she inquired if there was anything else she could do – even trying to say a few words in Dutch – *Mevrouw* Spelt ignored her. The woman looked well enough and didn't have a temperature. Gloria patted her on the shoulder before leaving for work. Perhaps *Mevrouw* Spelt only wanted to be left alone – a feeling which Gloria could understand.

Chapter 16:

Gloria was glad she could work at the hospital because it kept her busy and didn't allow her time to fret about the state of her marriage. She was frustrated by her inability to actually do anything concrete to look for Willem but she realized that simply being in Holland to be there when he came home was perhaps all she could expect. When the nurses congregated for their lunch break the others were interested in hearing about life in Canada.

"Did you have enough to eat?" asked one nurse.

"Yes, we did," said Gloria almost apologetically. "Coupon rationing for sugar, tea, and coffee was introduced in 1942 and eventually included butter and meat but the amounts we were allowed were very generous. We never went hungry.

"Before the coupons started there were periodic food shortages," Gloria continued, "and foods that had been available suddenly became very expensive but it was nothing compared to what you experienced in this country."

Another nurse whose name Gloria didn't know spoke up.

"We had to endure many hardships," she said in a grumpy voice. "It is hard for others who were not here to imagine. When we walked home from work we never looked at the German soldiers. We kept our eyes looking straight ahead. We did not want to give them any reason to ask questions because then they might turn our words around and make a reason to arrest us. We always had to be so careful." After she stopped talking everyone was silent for a few minutes but then another nurse further down the table started talking.

"The German soldiers could be very cruel too," she said sadly. "One time I saw a Jewish man in a wheelchair. He was crippled; he only had one leg and the German soldiers kicked at his chair until he fell out. He crawled trying to get away but they kicked at him more. When he curled into a ball and refused to move they picked him up and threw him onto the truck as if he were a bag of laundry. It was horrible just horrible." She covered her face with her hands and her shoulders shook for a minute but gradually she regained control of herself. She took a deep breath and bit into her bread. A nurse sitting several seats over clearly felt a change of subject was needed.

"The cheese factory a mile or so outside Amsterdam has just reopened. I hope my boyfriend can finally get a job," she said. She flashed a grin and continued. "If we both save our money we can get married next year." Other nurses near her nodded.

Gloria excused herself from the table and went to get ready for her afternoon shift. For the rest of the day as she was changing bandages and checking temperatures part of her mind was still thinking about the stories she'd heard at lunch. Most Dutch citizens hated Germans and these stories helped to explain why. It saddened her and she wondered if there'd ever come a time when Dutch and German people could be friends again.

Walking home at the end of her shift Gloria passed an empty lot where a few boys were kicking around a soccer ball. The ball was partially deflated and had seen better days but what really caught her attention what caused her to stop and watch was the fact that all the boys were wearing *klompen*, wooden shoes, with no socks. She couldn't imagine anything more uncomfortable but the boys were running around taking aim at the ball and kicking it in the same way a Canadian child wearing sneakers would. When the boys stopped for a break after scoring a goal she waved at them and walked on.

§ § §

On her day off Gloria met Maartje downtown. They'd not seen each other since the day they'd gone to the Red Cross office and Gloria filled her in on what she'd been doing at the hospital. Maartje had been working at her father's *apotheek* stocking shelves with the few new items that had come in and working on the books. Since her father had not needed her for the afternoon she'd gone to the Spelts' apartment hoping that Gloria would be free.

"I found out Pieter's last name," said Gloria as they walked. "It's Zweers." Maartje looked at Gloria and raised her eyebrows.

"Zweers is a common name in Friesland where my uncle's farm is," she said. "I'm planning to go to visit my aunt and uncle next week. Do you think you could come?"

"That's a swell idea Maartje. If his parents are still living there they must be so worried about him. I'll talk to Nurse van den Berg about having time off."

"I can hardly wait to see my aunt and uncle," said Maartje. "I visited with them often when I was growing up. My brother spent the final two years of the war there…" She stopped talking as she watched a couple walking towards them. Gloria followed her gaze; the people looked familiar but she couldn't quite place them.

"Oh look," said Maartje, "It is Gregor and Beatrix from the ship."

Gloria was surprised to see them — the last she'd heard they'd been going to visit with their son in Rotterdam. The four stopped to greet each other.

"Hello Gloria, Maartje," said Gregor formally inclining his head. "How are you?" Beatrix barely glanced at them and didn't say anything.

A café had put a few chairs out on the sidewalk and Gloria suggested they sit. Beatrix looked as if she might refuse but Gregor accepted for both of them and propelled her to a chair before she could voice an objection.

"How are things in Rotterdam?" asked Gloria while Maartje went to the counter to order a coffee for herself and a tea for Gloria. Gregor and Beatrix didn't want anything. Beatrix sat with her nose in the air although with an aura of sadness rather than her usual haughtiness. Gregor looked at Beatrix and opened his mouth to answer when Beatrix suddenly burst out crying. Gregor handed her his handkerchief and patted her arm saying "Shh-shh-shh."

"It was horrible," said Gregor as his wife gulped noisily and blotted her eyes with the piece of linen. "Last May the RAF mistakenly bombed the Bezuidenhout quarter of Rotterdam," he paused and glanced at Beatrix before continuing. "Our son and daughter-in-law were killed."

Maartje returned with the beverages in time to hear his statement. Setting the beverages on the table she glanced quickly at Beatrix and almost spilled the cup of coffee in the process.

"They've been dead for six months and we didn't even know," whispered Beatrix. Gloria looked at Gregor in surprise.

"They bombed it?" she repeated. "By mistake? How could they do such a thing?" Her gaze travelled from husband to wife and back again. Beatrix sobbed silently into her husband's handkerchief.

"The RAF were trying to destroy an installation of V-2 rockets in Haagse Bos Park," Gregor stated evenly, "but there were navigational errors and the bombs fell on a residential part of the city." He glanced at his wife before adding, "Such mistakes happen now and again but it is not often reported."

"I'm so sorry Gregor," Gloria said. "What a shock that must have been. And I'm sorry for you too Beatrix." She rested her hand on the older woman's arm but when Beatrix stiffened she withdrew it hastily. Beatrix brought herself under control and tried to look haughty once again straightening her hat and readjusting her gloves but the effect was ruined. She returned Gregor's handkerchief to him and stood.

"Thank you," she said touching her husband's arm. "Come Gregor we must go. We do not want to keep our friends waiting." She lifted her chin and looked at Maartje speaking a sentence in Dutch before walking away. She made a point of ignoring Gloria.

Gregor got to his feet and scrambled after her. He mouthed a "thank you" to Gloria and Maartje as he left. Each woman lifted a hand in a goodbye gesture to Gregor. After the couple had moved away Gloria grinned.

"Beatrix must have intended that comment as a final slight to me," she said, "speaking Dutch so I wouldn't understand but I think I caught the gist of it. They're staying with friends until they leave to go back to Curacao, aren't they?"

"Yes," said Maartje smiling.

"What a strange couple," Gloria said. "Beatrix really dislikes me, doesn't she?"

"It appears so but perhaps she is jealous because Gregor seems to like you," said Maartje. "They are an unusual couple. Gregor did not seem too upset by his son and daughter-in-law's death but I was surprised when Beatrix broke down like that."

"I wonder how they ended up married to each other since they seem so different," said Gloria. She drank her tea in silence pondering the question. Finally, she added, "I guess it does take all kinds as my mother always says."

"It does," said Maartje putting her empty mug on the table. "But that's what makes the world go 'round. Isn't that what some song says?"

"Something like that," said Gloria.

That evening for supper *Mevrouw* Spelt made gravy to eat with their vegetables. Unlike the gravy Gloria's mother made this gravy was thin and watery. Since tea was rationed it was only drunk at lunch and gravy counted as the liquid at the evening meal. As she stood and cleared the dishes it occurred to Gloria that while she had come to Holland because she'd wanted to Dutch citizens especially the children hadn't had that choice. They had to live in these conditions for as long as it took to get the country back to normal and heaven only knew how long that would take. She added the dishes to the ones stacked beside the sink. Dishes were only washed once a day in the evening when hot water was available.

After she helped *Mevrouw* Spelt with the dishes Gloria went into the living room to sit with Meneer Spelt. He had turned on a light since it was after five p.m., or *vijf uur's avond*, which Gloria had figured out meant five o'clock in the evening. She'd noted that one or the other of them might sit in near darkness and not turn a light on until the magic hour.

She studied her father-in-law as they sat in the living room together. Like his son, *Meneer* Spelt was content to sit quietly without feeling a need to talk to fill the empty air. Gloria had found Willem's quietness nerve-wracking at first. At the time she'd thought it was because he had not wanted to be in the army.

"When Willem and I first met he told me he didn't like being in the army," she said. *Meneer* Spelt raised his head before replying.

"In Holland all men have to be in army for a year," he said. "I tell Willem and Harrie do it before war start."

"He didn't tell it that way," said Gloria. "He only said that he was doing his conscripted duty when the war broke out." When *Meneer* Spelt looked at her steadily without saying anything she wondered if he hadn't understood. She waved her hand to indicate it didn't matter.

"I should not tell them that perhaps," said *Meneer* Spelt. He hung his head and pulled his handkerchief from his pocket. Gloria reached over and patted his arm.

"Don't be too hard on yourself," she said softly. "You couldn't have known it would lead to this." She stood and turned the light on beside his chair.

"I'm sure we'll find Willem," said Gloria smiling in what she hoped was a reassuring manner, "and then perhaps he and I can try to find Harrie." *Meneer* Spelt nodded several times.

Chapter 17:

Part of the Dutch army had been integrated into the Canadian and British armies. Those armies didn't keep track of foreign fighters which meant Gloria was unable to check registers to discover where her husband had been fighting. Talking to her patients as much as she could she'd been unable to add to Stefan's information. Anneke's father had confirmed that the Queen's Own Rifles did in fact land at Juno Beach but after a week of learning nothing further she felt she must swallow her pride and return to the Red Cross.

She was wary as she entered the office but a younger man sat behind the desk and he smiled as she approached. The name plate on the desk indicated his name was *Meneer* de Groot. She sat down smiling uncertainly as she told him of her plan to find her husband. They also discussed her work at the hospital since his wife was also a nurse, but at a different hospital. However, after consulting the latest reports of soldiers who were killed or missing he had no news to report.

"I'll check back in a day or two," said Gloria heartened by his friendliness.

"Please do," said *Meneer* de Groot pushing his glasses onto his nose. "I am receiving more names every day." Gloria thanked him. He stood and gave her a half bow as she left.

She began dropping in every few days when her shift allowed it. One day he grinned as she entered the office. He waved a piece of paper at her as she sat in her usual chair.

"Apparently there was a soldier, Willem Spelt, who was captured and sent to a POW camp in Germany. That might be your husband?" he asked his eyes crinkling as he smiled.

"Oh my," she said, patting her chest. "I hope it is. Do you know what happened to him? Has he been freed? Why hasn't he come home?"

"There is more," he said. "Several prisoners escaped from the camp just before it was freed and one of them was killed. Spelt was not found by the liberating army." He put the paper down his eyes on hers. Her mind was racing as she processed the news.

"So, if he wasn't at the camp," she began tentatively, "he must have been one of the ones who tried to escape. Do you know which POW camp he was in?"

He told her the name of the camp and where it was located. She jumped to her feet and put on her sweater preparing to leave. She knew she was on the right path now. She offered her hand to *Meneer* de Groot.

"Thank you for your assistance," she said feeling more optimistic than she had in many months. She wanted to show her joy by dancing out of the office but she restrained herself until she was out on the street. Then she did a little jig not caring about the looks she got. As she walked to the hospital she replayed the good news in her head. The other possibility occurred to her so suddenly that she stopped mid-step almost tripping herself. The man walking behind her had to double-step to get around her but she was unaware of his glare. She put her hand to her mouth. The horrifying thought took shape in her mind — what if Willem was the one who'd been killed?

That thought stayed with her during the remainder of her walk to the hospital. She entered the building filled with dread and the first person she saw was Anneke. Not wanting to show her feelings Gloria took a deep breath and tried to calm herself.

"Hello Anneke," she said as they approached each other in the corridor. "Are you just going off shift?"

"No break time; I am going outside for a cigarette," said Anneke stopping and looking at Gloria intently. "Is something wrong?"

Gloria was surprised Anneke had noticed but she didn't want to have to explain. She took another calming breath before answering. "I'm early for my shift. I'll come outside with you."

Anneke nodded and Gloria followed her outside. They sat together on a low wall surrounding the garden and Anneke pulled a cigarette out of her hand bag. It was wrinkled and one end was pinched; she'd obviously smoked part of it before.

"What is wrong?" Anneke repeated. There was no real warmth in her voice but Gloria couldn't hide her feelings any longer. She repeated the news she'd just received at the Red Cross office about the POWs escaping and finished by asking, "Do you think Willem would've tried to escape?"

"Why did you marry him if you know him so little?" asked Anneke rather than answering the question. There was no malice in her tone just puzzlement. "Was it because of the baby? Is that why you got married?" Gloria was surprised at Anneke's directness and she hesitated before answering.

"No," Gloria said finally. "I believed then and I still believe now that we got married because we love each other." She paused but when Anneke didn't say anything she continued. "But it's been over two years since I've heard from Willem. Some days I forget that we married for love, that when he asked me to marry him I said yes." She felt herself blush because that wasn't how it had happened at all. Anneke sat quietly puffing on her cigarette.

"The Willem I knew would have tried to escape from the POW camp," she said, "but he may have changed. War changes people. Do you think he was one of the ones who escaped?" She turned to look at Gloria blowing the smoke out of the side of her mouth.

"Yes," Gloria said with relief. "That's what I think too. I'm so glad to hear you say that."

Anneke had taken her cigarette out of her mouth and she looked at it her mouth turning down in distaste.

"This is foul-tasting tobacco," she said. "They are the only cigarettes not rationed though. I wish I could get some better-tasting ones through the black market." She pinched the end of the butt to make sure it was out and put it in her pocket. "I'll take this home for *Meneer* Spelt."

Gloria nodded grimacing slightly. Her father-in-law used any tobacco he could find to roll into smokes of his own. Personally, she thought it was disgusting but it seemed to be accepted as normal behaviour. Perhaps other people did it as well.

Anneke and Gloria stood and entered the hospital together. Gloria went one way and Anneke the other. Neither said good-bye. Gloria waved but she didn't think Anneke had seen it. Her fears about Willem receded for the moment. She hung up her coat and went to get her duties for the day. She was on the children's ward again.

§ § §

With a sense of guilty relief, she left the hospital when her shift was over and walked to Maartje's apartment. She took the steps two at a time and knocked on the door. Maartje opened the door inviting her to enter.

"Maartje," she said panting and trying to get her breath. "Is your uncle's farm near the border?"

"Not really. Although Holland is so small, no place is that far from the German border," she said leading Gloria into the living room. "Why? What is wrong?"

They sat facing each other and Gloria told her what she had learned at the Red Cross office ending with her fear that Willem might be dead.

"Since he wasn't freed from the camp he must have been with those who escaped," Gloria explained, "but what if he was the one who was killed? I couldn't bear it! I've come this far to find him and he might have been killed a few months ago? It wouldn't be fair!" She put her head in her hands.

"Shh-shh-shh Gloria. You cannot lose hope now." Maartje held out her hands and Gloria, raising her head, grabbed them like a drowning person grabbing a lifeline. "All this time you have been so sure that Willem was alive. You have to hang on to that belief." Maartje moved to sit beside her.

"Yes, you're right." Gloria said softly. "I must hold onto the belief that he's still alive." She ran her hands through her hair as she sat straighter.

"It was shocking to hear that and then to realize it might've been him…" her voice faltered, "who was killed."

"*Meneer* de Groot wasn't even sure it was my Willem." Gloria added in a stronger voice. "Is Willem Spelt a common name?" She paused before answering her own question.

"No," she said decisively. "I have to believe that it is my Willem and he is alive. I must believe that. I must." She pounded her fist into her palm.

"*Meneer* de Groot said the escaped prisoners might've tried to make it over the border," she continued, "maybe some place near Emmen. If your uncle's farm is near there perhaps I can get more information from the hospital or the church when we're there next week."

"*Oom* Henk's farm is a two-hour drive from Emmen but I am not sure he will have time to take us," said Maartje. "If he does not perhaps we can get information another way. Can you be ready to leave in two days?"

"I should be able to but I'll have to ask if I can be away from the hospital for a week," said Gloria nervously. What would she do if Nurse van den Burg said they couldn't spare her? Her first solid clue and she might not be able to check it out? She would be devastated.

Chapter 18:

Gloria stood in front of Nurse van den Berg's desk feeling like a school girl called to the principal's office.

"I was wondering if I could take a week's holidays," Gloria said her hands clenched at her sides. The head nurse looked at her and smiled.

"Nurse Spelt," she said. "I was going to call you down. Nurse Neman is ready to come back to work so I'm afraid we're going to have to let you go. I suppose it is good timing in this case." She stood and extended her hand to Gloria.

"We have appreciated your help and wish you luck in the future."

Gloria grasped the other woman's hand.

"Thank you for the chance to work here," she said. "Can I just go and say good-bye to Pieter in the children's ward?"

"You can work your shift today on that ward and leave your apron in the cloak room when it is over. Thank you."

The news was bittersweet — Gloria was glad she would be able to accompany Maartje but she would miss the people she had gotten to know at the hospital. As she approached the ward she met Anneke. After telling the Dutch woman that her stint at the hospital was over Gloria was surprised to find Anneke was genuinely distressed.

"What will you do now?" she asked anxiously. Gloria told her that she planned to accompany Maartje to Friesland.

"You may be able to get news of Willem that way," Anneke replied. She turned to walk away but Gloria stopped her and asked about Pieter's arm.

"Is it healing properly?"

"He needs more antibiotics and we do not have any," said Anneke. "We may get more supplies next week. Otherwise he seems to be doing well." She turned away, paused, and turned back to Gloria. "If I do not see you before you leave I hope you have a good trip."

"Thank you, Anneke," said Gloria. "I'll let *Mevrouw* Spelt know as soon as I can if I get any word of Willem and I'm sure she'll share it with you."

"Good," said Anneke before walking down the hall.

Gloria continued to the children's ward thinking about the lack of medicine for Pieter. On the other hand, he was warm and dry – that was something at least. She crossed the ward to Pieter's bed.

"Hello Pieter," she said touching his shoulder. He turned over to look at her and instinctively she felt his forehead briefly to determine if he was feverish.

"I'm not going to be working here from now on. Nurse Neman is returning and she will take good care of you," Gloria spoke gently watching his reaction. Would he be upset?

Pieter put his hand on hers and stared at her solemnly but didn't say anything. She was feeling sad that she might not see him as often. She wondered if he felt sad too. Did he think she might not come to visit him?

"I'm going away for a few days and I won't be able to come to visit you but after I come back I'll visit you every day," she said. He continued to stare silently at her.

"My friend Maartje is going to Friesland," said Gloria, "and I'm going with her. I hope to get information about my husband." Gloria paused when she noticed a tear rolling down his cheek. She wiped it from his face.

"Bad people," he said so softly she almost missed it.

"What did you say, dear?" she asked bending down.

"Bad people," he repeated. She waited for him to say more but he closed his mouth and shook his head. She straightened up.

"Who are the bad people?" Gloria asked taking him in her arms. He was trembling. Was he afraid? Clearly she didn't know the whole story if just the mention of a region in Holland produced such a reaction. She sat on his bed holding him and murmuring soothingly until she felt him relax. She asked him again who the bad people were but just as he started talking a nurse rushed over and he stopped.

"Please I need assistance with this child," the nurse said on her way to another bed. Gloria hated having to leave Pieter when he seemed willing to talk but she had no choice. She released the boy gently and followed the nurse. After the two nurses worked with the other child and he was breathing normally again, Gloria went back to Pieter's bed but he had rolled over and was facing the wall.

She sat on the bed beside him and rubbed his back. As his breathing became regular she stopped her hand movements but she remained where she was thinking about her feelings for the little boy. He was obviously afraid of something but at the same time there was a sense of dignity in him. She knew he felt he had failed his younger brother. Could that be it or was there more to the story?

Walking home Gloria was torn between feeling concern for her little patient and being happy about receiving word of Willem. Pieter's mention of 'bad people' brought to mind what a few friends had said when she was planning her trip to Holland.

Several people had cautioned her, saying "be careful who you talk to and what you say." She'd thought it silly at the time — the war was over and no one would suspect her of working with the Germans since she couldn't even speak Dutch — but now she wondered. Perhaps there still were 'bad people' around. The neighbours of Mieke's cousin had killed him because he had worked with the Nazis. It was a chilling reminder that passions had been running high as the war ended. Perhaps they still were.

"*Mevrouw* Spelt," she called as she entered the apartment, "I've had word of Willem." Her mother-in-law looked at her expectantly.

"Villem?" she said with a puzzled frown.

Gloria was tongue-tied trying to think how to word it so *Mevrouw* Spelt would understand. She eventually was able to say enough in Dutch that *Mevrouw* Spelt understood. Gloria's excitement was contagious and the two of them made so much noise that *Meneer* Spelt came out of the bedroom rubbing his chin. His hair was standing on end in places. *Mevrouw* Spelt spoke to him in his native tongue.

"Is he alive?" *Meeneer* Spelt asked quickly.

"I don't know for sure," said Gloria, "but I hope so." She explained her plans to him and he repeated it to his wife in Dutch.

"*Goed,*" Mrs. Spelt said. She returned to the kitchen with Mr. Spelt following her.

Gloria went to her room to figure out what to pack. Thoughts of her husband were uppermost in her mind but there was a sense of dread as well. She knew that soldiers who were in POW camps during the Great War had suffered. That experience plus seeing their fellow soldiers killed in battle had traumatized many of them. If Willem had been in such a camp would it have affected his wits? What if he was not in his right mind and he didn't love her any longer or even remember her?

She sorted through her clothes lost in thought. What should she take? She was cold constantly so she wanted to take as many warm clothes as she could cram into the small suitcase *Meneer* Spelt had given her. She'd noticed that if the temperature rose it rained making it feel colder. However, since it was winter a sunny day was cold as well. People had told her this was the coldest winter in a long time. Not even the weather was helping the Dutch people — their country had been ravaged by war causing fuel shortages and it was colder than ever.

Gloria wanted to find out about Pieter's family but she also wanted to discover where her husband was and Harrie, if at all possible. A lot was riding on this trip. She returned to the kitchen almost too excited to eat. Was this the beginning of the end of her journey – a journey where she'd find Willem? She took a few steadying breaths as she sat at the table.

Slow and steady wins the race she told herself; slow and steady.

Chapter 19:

Gloria turned over and snuggled deeper into the covers trying to ignore the morning light flickering through the curtains. Not wanting to leave the warmth of the bed she reviewed her situation. She'd been in Holland for more than a month and was able to conduct a simple conversation in Dutch. With Maartje's help she was taking her first real step towards finding Willem which was both exciting and scary. The thought of finding him was exciting but what if he'd changed? And if he was a different person would she want to stay married to him?

In retrospect it occurred to her that perhaps she and Willem had married too quickly, without giving their love a chance to grow into one that would last a lifetime. She spent a few minutes puzzling over that but soon gave up – reflecting on such possibilities was making her head spin. She needed to stay focused. She had to believe that she would find her husband and that they would still love each other. Hearing sounds coming from the other room she dressed quickly and joined her mother-in-law in the kitchen.

She poured herself a cup of tea knowing that *Mevrouw* Spelt had used a bit of their horde especially to make a cup for her as she started her journey. Sitting at the table she looked bleakly at the bowl of porridge *Mevrouw* Spelt had placed in front of her. Gloria's mother had always fed her porridge because it would "stick to her ribs" and keep her from getting hungry at school. Dutch people had a different association with it. She remembered the story a nurse at the hospital had recounted.

Nurse Meijer and her younger brothers had eaten porridge with no sugar for breakfast, lunch, and dinner during the last months of the war. To make the cereal she and her mother had scavenged from farmers, gathering wheat kernels from the fields, which they ground in a coffee grinder to make oatmeal. Even after war's end they'd had to eat porridge for several weeks only gradually adding other food to their diet until their stomachs could accept a full diet.

Another story Gloria had heard about conditions during the war involved two women getting food past the German guards. In the early days of the war two women went shopping and on their way home they'd been stopped at a checkpoint. The first woman approached the gate and the guard asked her to step aside. He suspected her of wearing the large coat to hide items she was smuggling. She opened her coat to reveal…nothing. She was merely a fat woman and she needed to wear the large coat to cover her girth. The guards were very embarrassed and let the second woman pass without comment. The two women continued on their way home where the second woman took several cans and other goodies from the pockets on the inside of her coat to share with her friend.

As Gloria ate she reflected on such tales and what some women had done to feed their families during the war. It certainly put things in perspective. She finished her porridge with greater appreciation. Her hunger pangs satisfied for the moment she carried her suitcase from the bedroom to the front door to await Maartje's arrival. *Mevrouw* Spelt bustled about the kitchen clearing the breakfast dishes. Gloria sensed her apprehension.

"Don't worry *Mevrouw*," she said. The form of address was used alone sometimes. "If I get word of Willem I'll let you know as soon as I can." She spoke slowly repeating a few words she knew in Dutch hoping the older woman would understand.

"*Ja* and take care *je zelf*," Mevrouw Spelt said in reply.

Gloria went to the window, looked out, and spotted a truck she recognized. When Maartje knocked on the door a few minutes later Gloria was ready to go. She hugged her mother-in-law good-bye and followed Maartje out the door. Theo helped them load the suitcases in the truck for the short trip to the train station. There was a delay before they could board the train but finally they were ready to begin their journey.

"This is so exciting," said Gloria as they settled into their seats. "I love travelling on a train. When I was studying to become a nurse I travelled from Stratford to Toronto weekly on the train."

Gloria relaxed against the seat and looked out the window which had no glass – it had been blown out during the war. There was no way to keep warm; she was chilled to the bone and her feet felt like blocks of ice. How different this was from riding the train in Canada!

The train stopped in Utrecht allowing them to change trains to go north. When they were settled on the next train Gloria took her mitts off and rubbed her hands together in an attempt to warm them. Even though these windows were intact it was not any warmer. Maartje was wearing her warm duffel coat but she kept her hands in her pockets.

"Where was Pieter before he arrived at the hospital?" she asked.

When her friend spoke Gloria imagined she could see the words crystallized in the air and she smiled inwardly at her fancy.

"The soldiers who brought him to the hospital found him on a road just outside Amsterdam," said Gloria. "Pieter was trying to wake a smaller boy but that boy died before the soldiers could get him to the hospital."

"We can ask *Tante* Lucie and *Oom* Henk if they know a Zweers family living in the area with at least two sons," said Maartje. "That will be a start."

Gloria agreed. She looked out the window at the passing countryside. In all directions it looked flat as a pancake. Leaning her head back against the seat she thought of her hometown, Stratford. The terrain there was flat as well but within a few miles there were gently rolling hills interspersed with stands of trees. In this country the flatness stretched for many miles but was dotted with windmills, most still stationary.

Her thoughts returned to her husband. Could she get to the German border where he might have been? Even if she made it to that area would she get word of him or would it turn out to be a wild goose chase? Gloria was back to feeling excited and scared yet again. She moved her knees so Maartje could look out the window as the train approached the station.

"There they are!" Maartje squealed pointing out the window.

Gloria looked in that direction and saw a crowd of people including a man and a woman waving their arms. As she followed her friend off the train she was feeling anxious again but Maartje's aunt and uncle greeted her warmly dispelling some of the anxiety. Maartje's uncle stood back while his wife welcomed Maartje with tears and hugs. They ushered the girls into a car which looked fairly old — the body was a patchwork of rust spots and the back seat, where Gloria and Maartje sat, was missing a few springs. Gloria wasn't sure it would survive on the rough roads but *Oom* Henk drove with care and after a while she got used to the shaking. He mentioned that he was lucky to have gas for it.

"I borrow gas from my neighbour," he said. "We have gas now but during war I use the car as wagon hitching horses to it. It not work the best but better than nothing," he added shrugging his shoulders.

During the drive to the farm *Tante* Lucie brought Maartje up-to-date on what had happened to her cousins and to various friends and neighbours. Gloria knew Maartje was anxious to hear how her relatives had fared. The two Dutch women spoke quickly and *Tante* Lucie had an unfamiliar accent so Gloria was unable to understand any of the conversation. Since she didn't know the people involved she was content to let the voices roll over her and she studied Maartje's uncle as he drove.

He was a solid man with fair hair and a large mustache. When she met him, she'd noticed the same air of resignation that she'd seen in many Dutch people as if the years of war had taken the joy out of their life. And perhaps in his case it had. Two of his sons had been killed; only their middle son and two daughters had survived.

"The war years were very hard on us," said *Tante* Lucie, switching to English, "but at least we not lose the farm." She half-turned to look at Gloria in the back seat. "Maartje says you want to find your husband."

"Yes. Apparently, he was in a POW camp in Germany," said Gloria, "but he escaped just before the war ended. The camp was close to the Dutch border. The nearest friendly hospital if they needed one would be in Emmen."

"Yes, Emmen is near the German border," *Tante* Lucie said after a pause. She turned to look at her husband. "Could we take the girls to Emmen, Henk? My sister, Carla, lives there and she would like to see Maartje."

"*Ja*," he said slowly. "I can maybe go this week. I have not used all my ration of gas. I can maybe get some more."

He sighed as if it was a hardship but as he glanced at his niece in the mirror Gloria caught the twinkle in his eye – Maartje was likely a favourite niece. Gloria leaned forward.

"That would be swell," she said. "Thank you very much."

He smiled and nodded but his attention was on his driving. Another car was approaching. It was the first traffic Gloria had noticed and both vehicles slowed down as they passed. The road was narrow as well as not being in good repair.

Maartje and her aunt continued talking about those friends and neighbours who had survived the war. After a few minutes *Tante* Lucie switched to English.

"My friend Atty who lives in Amsterdam came to our farm with her parents last winter. We had told her she must if things got too bad in Amsterdam. They held off as long as they could but when they realized no more food was available even if they have money to buy it they made their decision. They have to cross the Zuider Zee, a lake, to get here. A fisherman made them lie in a boat. He put their bicycles on top of them and covered everything with a tarp. The Germans were used to seeing him going out in his boat so they did not question him." *Oom* Henk picked up the story.

"The fisherman rowed them across the zee and let them off at an empty dock," he said. "They continued on their way knocking on farmer's doors begging for food and a place to sleep. They were happy to sleep in the barn with the animals if that was all there was. It took them a week or more to make the journey."

"How far is it?" asked Gloria, wondering what an empty dock was. Then she realized he must mean an abandoned dock. That made sense.

"It is not that far," replied Uncle Henk. "By car driving around the lake it would only take…oh…one or maybe one and one-half hours."

"My goodness," said Gloria, "how lucky for her."

"Oh yes very fortunate," said *Tante* Lucie. "There was not so much death here. One friend told me so many dead bodies in Amsterdam last winter the morgues quickly filled up and they had to pile the bodies in churches."

Gloria couldn't think of anything to say. There seemed to be no end to the pain and suffering the Dutch people had endured and few words left to express her reaction to it.

§ § §

"Many people use bicycles in Holland," said *Oom* Henk. "But during the war factories that made bicycles were closed and there was no rubber to make tires. In order to continue using their bicycles people have to use garden hose or wood if a tire wore out. And of course, all petrol was used for army vehicles; there was none for cars." As *Oom* Henk fell silent, *Tante* Lucie spoke.

"Many of our neighbours hid Jewish people to keep them away from the German police," she said. "One family hid a Jewish family with a backward daughter. She was simple-minded I mean. She could not talk but if she were upset she would call out. They have to be very careful when she was hidden in the room trying to keep her quiet."

"Did the Germans find her?" Gloria asked anxiously.

"There was one time about a year ago when two German soldiers came to their house," *Tante* Lucie said. "The family was in the hidden room. The soldiers searched the room where the hidden door was but luckily did not find it. They left but one of the soldiers hung back and he heard the girl calling out. Since the sound came from behind a wall it was muffled. The soldier stopped and looked at my friend's daughter. She pretended she had called out."

"Goodness," said Gloria, leaning forward. "What happened? Did he discover the family?"

"No," said *Tante* Lucie. "She said the soldier almost smiled at her but then he left quickly without saying anything. Both families lived in fear for many months but the German police did not return."

Gloria relaxed against the back seat. Hearing the story about a German soldier's compassion was a welcome respite from all the tales of woe she'd heard recently. It helped to restore her faith in humanity. She covered her mouth as she yawned. *Tante* Lucie turned to look at her.

"You should sleep," she said. "It has been a long journey."

It had been a tiring day and Gloria was happy to doze off. She woke as the car was slowing down. Peering out the window at a large farmhouse she wondered how long it would be before she discovered where her husband was.

Or if she would, whispered that little voice of doubt in the back of her mind.

Chapter 20:

Gloria awoke to the smell of frying bacon — what a delight! She dressed quickly and hurried to the kitchen. Maartje was seated at a large wooden table in the middle of the room. Her aunt was standing at the biggest stove Gloria had ever seen, but neither the stove nor the table looked out of place in the spacious kitchen. *Tante* Lucie served Gloria a plate of eggs, bacon, and toast. It was delicious and Gloria savoured each mouthful with a new appreciation.

"It's too bad neither your aunt nor your uncle know Pieter's family," she said to Maartje between mouthfuls. They had asked *Tante* Lucie and *Oom* Henk the previous evening if they knew such a Zweers family but they did not.

"We knew starting out that it would not be that easy," Maartje said. "I want to walk to town and show you around. Perhaps we will see someone I know who can help us."

"Oh yes," said Gloria enthusiastically. "That would be swell."

After breakfast *Oom* Henk showed them around the farm. As he talked about what life had been like before 1940, Gloria was struck by his matter-of-fact attitude.

"Before the war," he said, "this part of the country was a large agricultural area and on this farm we grew vegetables such as tomatoes, carrots, and turnips." He indicated the fields to either side of the barn. "Besides growing crops, I raised cattle and one of my neighbours raised sheep."

Gloria spotted several cows, black and white Holsteins, in the field beside the barn munching contentedly on grass oblivious to their surroundings.

"Now my herd is smaller," continued *Oom* Henk, "because there was not so much for them to eat during the war. My neighbour's sheep also died off. It will take time but soon both of us will be able to buy more livestock."

"Are other farmers in this area managing the same as you are?" Gloria asked. She took note of the new door on the barn and the recently painted building. *Oom* Henk sighed.

"Not all of them. Some have lost too much. Others have moved to the city to try to find work there. My neighbours and I are working together to get the windmills going again and to buy grain." Gloria followed his gaze to the right. In the distance she could see windmills but the blades were not moving.

She looked around trying to imagine what it would look like when it was restored to a fully functioning farm again. Perhaps in a few more months the windmills would be working. And, as *Oom* Henk had said, when the windmills were turning and providing irrigation they could begin to grow crops to feed the animals. When the farm was completely back to normal Gloria imagined there would be a dog and perhaps several barn cats. It could be a happy place again.

Her thoughts turned to Pieter wondering what it would take to make him happy again. She wondered if he'd been sent to this part of the country during the last winter of the war when food was so scarce in Amsterdam.

And if he had why hadn't he stayed here? She brought her mind back to the conversation at hand; Maartje was suggesting they start their journey into town. The two women waved good-bye to *Oom* Henk and turned to walk down the laneway.

Sloten, the nearest town, was two kilometers from the farm. Gloria had to ask how many miles; she wasn't used to the metric system. As they turned onto the main road Gloria noticed the elm trees growing along the sides of the road. Maartje's uncle had explained that the trees acted as a barrier to the winds that swept across the open fields. The land on either side of the road was uneven and Gloria assumed the craters were a result of the bombing. After they'd walked for a quarter hour they came to fields that had not been damaged at all. One of the fields had crops planted in it but others were bare. As *Oom* Henk had said it would take time to get the farms working again.

Gradually the fields gave way to buildings. There had not been any traffic while they were in the country but as the town came into view Gloria saw the occasional car. The women walked along the main street noticing that a few shops had opened. Gloria was aware of hope and despair existing side by side — one shop was open but the next one or two were closed.

"Allie! Allie de Jong!" Maartje called out. A woman on the opposite side of the street waved her arm in response and crossed the street.

"I wondered if I would see you while I was here," Maartje said in English as the other woman joined them. She introduced the two women and explained to Gloria that she and Allie had played together as youngsters.

"*Hallo* Maartje," Allie said, putting her hand out and clasping her friend's. "I am glad to see you." She wore her brown hair short but it looked like she'd cut it herself. When she smiled her teeth were straight and white. "I heard you were in Canada for the war years."

"*Ja.* I have been back for a month or so," said Maartje, her smile changing to a look of concern. "How is your family? Are your parents well?"

Watching the two women Gloria was struck by the difference in Maartje. She appeared more relaxed and even happy in spite of the bad news she'd been receiving. It must have been stressful for her having been so far away while her country was experiencing such tragedy.

"I am living with my parents for now," said Allie. "They survived the war, but their business is gone."

"I am sorry to hear that," said Maartje. She turned to Gloria. "Allie's parents owned a bookshop here," she said. "It was the only one in the village and had many children's books that I enjoyed reading when I was a child."

"My family also survived," she said to Allie, "but my boyfriend Mathias did not."

"I am so sorry," said Allie putting her hand on Maartje's arm. "There has been so much death but it does not make it easier to accept."

"I will miss Mathias. We had been friends since we were children but I had heard nothing from him since before the war," said Maartje. "I do not know if he would still be my boyfriend even if he had lived. Does that sound mean?"

Allie stopped as Maartje turned to enter a café.

"I cannot go in here," said Allie. "I have no money."

"*Tante* Stein gave me money before I left Canada," said Maartje tugging gently at Allie's arm. "I can treat both of you. I do not mind."

They must be really good friends if Allie was able to be that honest with Maartje, thought Gloria as she followed the other two into the shop. It was dark and they paused to let their eyes adjust. A counter ran along the far wall. There was a man standing behind it reading a book since there were no customers. There was one poor light beside him and Gloria wondered how he could see.

To one side were two small tables with two chairs at each. Maartje pulled one chair to join the others at one of the tables. The homemade menu board indicated only tea and coffee and a few baked goods were available.

An older man came in behind them and sat on a stool at the counter. His hat was pulled low on his forehead. He and the owner were soon engaged in a quiet conversation. Maartje went to the counter to order three cups of tea. When she returned to the table Allie responded to Maartje's earlier comment.

"No," she said. "I do not think it is mean to say that you and Mathias might have grown apart. It is realistic."

"I don't think it's mean either," said Gloria. "It's just the way things are. Life plans can change. But change doesn't have to be bad. It's better to try to make the best of whatever happens."

"That is true," said Allie. "I am a librarian and I worked in Amsterdam before the war. During the war Dutch libraries were one of the few institutions that the Nazis allowed to remain open but the German army removed books that they considered offensive. At the end of the war there were far fewer books in the library. Until the library can replace the books it lost and until more people are using the library it is not as busy and the library can operate with fewer staff. I agreed to take time off so I can help my parents.

"Although some days my father says it is not worth it. He has lost almost all interest in trying to get the bookstore running again," Allie continued. "He would like to retire but he cannot afford it. Once I get back to work I will be able to send my parents money and perhaps then he can retire. Meanwhile they are dealing with the same problems as so many others. We wait for businesses to start up again so we can work and make money. Or we wait for stores to re-stock the shelves so we can purchase the things we need. Slowly, slowly our lives are returning to normal."

The owner acting as waiter brought three mugs of tea over and set them on the table. He didn't offer milk or sugar and no one asked for it although Gloria had noticed Maartje took milk in her tea occasionally. Her tastes likely depended on whether milk was available.

Allie asked Maartje what the war years had been like in Canada and Maartje explained how she'd lived with her aunt and attended school in Canada. She mentioned that she and Gloria had met on the ship and encouraged Gloria to tell of her romance with Willem. Gloria gave her the condensed version and finished her story by telling about how she had met Pieter.

"His last name is Zweers," she added. "I'm trying to discover if his family was from this area. Maartje's aunt and uncle don't know the family."

"There are certainly Zweers living in this area," said Allie. "But I suggest you talk to vrouw de Bruyn. She is an older woman who is acquainted with or related to nearly everyone in this area."

Gloria noticed that the two men had stopped talking and seemed to be listening to what she and her friends were saying. When Allie stopped talking the proprietor leaned forward and spoke to Gloria.

"*Ben je Nederlands?*" he asked wondering if Gloria was Dutch.

"*Nee, Ik ben Canadees,*" she replied telling him she was Canadian and feeling quite proud that she was able to understand him and reply in his own language.

The proprietor nodded to the other man and said something in Dutch. Gloria wasn't able to follow the conversation and she looked to Maartje.

"They had a bet about whether you were Canadian. This man," she said, indicating the customer, "won."

The proprietor put a cookie on a plate and brought it to Gloria. He presented it to her speaking a sentence in Dutch.

"He wants to give you this to say thank-you," Maartje said. "You are Canadian and Canadians freed our country from the Germans." She paused and added in a softer voice, "This is a gingerbread cookie which we call *spekulaas*. It is a favourite in our country."

Gloria was deeply touched by the gesture. She stood and shook the owner's hand. He bowed to her saying *"bedankt, bedankt"* before returning to his place behind the counter. The three women talked for a bit longer but when several customers came into the shop they paid the bill and left.

Chapter 21:

Since *Oom* Henk was not ready to go to Emmen the next day Gloria was anxious to visit *Mevrouw* de Bruyn. Maartje had found out where she lived; Gloria and Maartje could walk there directly after breakfast. When they knocked on the door the Dutch woman was hesitant about letting them enter. Maartje explained who she was and *Mevrouw* de Bruyn finally opened the door completely.

The woman in the doorway looked old and disheartened as so many people in this country did. She led the younger women into a small room with dingy floral-printed wallpaper and indicated two hard-backed chairs for Gloria and Maartje. When they were seated Maartje introduced Gloria. After shaking Gloria's hand in greeting *Mevrouw* de Bruyn returned to the kitchen. Gloria wondered if the older woman was getting refreshments. She remembered what it had been like in her house when she was growing up.

When company came even if her mother was not expecting guests Gloria's mother had always served tea or coffee and a biscuit. Gloria's task as a youngster had been to count the number of people and put a corresponding number of napkins on the table.

But when *Mevrouw* de Bruyn returned she carried only a wooden chair. Upon reflection Gloria realized that in this country, having suffered through five years of occupation, social niceties were not important. *Mevrouw* de Bruyn placed the chair facing Gloria and Maartje, sat on it, and stared at Maartje.

"I know you," she said finally.

"I used to come to Sloten when I was a child," said Maartje, "to visit my aunt and uncle."

"Is your aunt Lucie de Wit?" *Mevrouw* de Bruyn asked pulling her glasses down her nose and peering at Maartje.

"Yes."

"Ja," said the old woman, speaking Dutch, "You look like your aunt." She sat back with a satisfied expression on her face.

"Do you think I look like my aunt?" Maartje asked Gloria in English, turning her head so Gloria could see her profile. Gloria looked at her friend.

"You do, but I never noticed before," she said, nodding her head. Gloria asked Maartje to tell *Mevrouw* de Bruyn the reason for their visit and Maartje began talking in Dutch.

"I speak *Engels*," the older woman said sharply.

Maartje switched to English. The older woman listened intently without interruption. When Maartje stopped talking *Mevrouw* remained silent for a few minutes.

"Zweers families are here," she finally said in heavily accented English. "En een family have two sons, Pieter and Tonny. Also two sons, ouder," she paused and raised her hand to indicate they'd been older, "killed when war start." Gloria glanced at Maartje before returning her gaze to *Mevrouw* de Bruyn..

"This must be his family," she said excitedly. "He said his brothers were dead. Can you please tell me more about the family?" she asked wondering if good manners would soften the woman's attitude. "If they still live here I want to reassure them that Pieter will survive his injuries." The old woman's unfriendly expression turned sad.

"You cannot," she said. "Family is gone, all gone. But I tell you." She settled back in her chair.

"Father's name Aert. Mother Anita. They very proud of four sons," she said.

Mevrouw continued her tale speaking English with occasional Dutch words thrown in or pausing frequently to search for the correct word. The two older boys had been quite a bit older than the two younger ones. The farm was prosperous – earning enough that one of the older sons had planned to marry his girlfriend when the war was over and to bring his bride to live on the farm.

Then Hitler had invaded Holland and the two older sons had joined the army making their parents proud. But that pride had quickly turned to despair when both sons were killed on the second day of fighting. After that tragedy the family had managed as best they could. Pieter was the next oldest but he was only three years old. He was still a baby but he'd had to grow up quickly. He looked after his younger brother to leave his mother free to help with the farm chores.

"The German army leave them alone for first two years of the war," said *Mevrouw* de Bruyn. She paused staring into space. "I think it was then German army told them to grow grain to feed German people. Aert planted grain but he and Anita not happy. That fall Dutch Resistance asked Aert to hide downed Allied pilots." She looked at Maartje.

"You know about that?" she asked. Maartje shook her head.

"No. What do you mean?" she asked. *Mevrouw* picked a cigarette from an ashtray beside her chair. After lighting it she switched to Dutch and spoke rapidly to Maartje. Then she sat back and puffed on the cigarette while Maartje talked.

"When Allied planes were shot down over Holland," said Maartje, "and the pilots were able to parachute out safely, the Underground needed safe houses to hide them. The Underground provided papers and clothing for the pilots but it was up to the families living in the houses hiding the pilots to make sure they weren't discovered. The families had to smuggle in extra food and they had to act natural when the houses were searched by Germans soldiers."

"It would have been difficult for children to pretend there was no one other than family there," said Gloria thinking about Pieter and his tendency to tell untruths. "Where did the pilots go? They couldn't have stayed until the end of the war." *Mevrouw* had finished her smoke and she answered.

"The Underground try to get the pilots back to England," she said. "If not, pilots go to Switzerland and get help there." Gloria knew that Switzerland had been neutral during the war.

"It was dangerous work," said *Mevrouw*, "but the Zweers not mind doing it. They were very bitter about their sons killed in war and they want to help end German occupation. They get many pilots back to England. Then suddenly, no warning, German soldiers raided farm and Aert and Anita taken to a concentration camp. Pilot sent to a POW camp."

"Oh, my goodness," said Gloria in astonishment. "And the two boys?"

"At first they disappear and we thought Germans took them," the woman said, looking uncomfortable. She went into the kitchen. A minute later Gloria heard the water running and *Mevrouw* de Bruyn came back carrying a glass of water. She didn't offer anything to the younger women.

"A few days later the boys, Pieter and Tonny, living with neighbour," she said resuming her seat and continuing her tale. "He have two sons but not much food and fuel. Still he let boys stay. Then a rumour started that he was the one to tell the authorities what Aert was doing. It was his fault farm was raided. His neighbours began to shun him and he took it out on the boys treating them like unpaid workers giving them only a little food and a place to sleep. He was not kind to them. The boys were very unhappy and ran away but after a few days a policeman brought them back. A few months later one of the neighbour's own sons starved to death.

"Then the war ended. Everyone was so happy. We all celebrated but that farmer and his wife not join in so much. They still grieved for their son and they remembered that their neighbours suspected them of betraying Aert. Pieter and Tonny ran away once more and the farmer did nothing." *Mevrouw* de Bruyn stopped talking and took a sip of water.

Gloria thought about what she'd heard – surely this must be the little boy's family! It explained why Pieter felt responsible for the death of his brother. The fear that haunted him could have been worry that the farmer would try to find him and his brother and punish them. Were they the "bad people" he had mentioned? She waited until the older woman put the glass down before questioning her again.

"What happened to Pieter's mother and father after they were sent to the concentration camp?" she asked.

"The liberating forces found the mother in a camp but she was too weak to save," said *Mevrouw* sadly. "She died in a soldier's arms. Her husband died two months before."

"And what happened to the neighbouring farmer, his wife, and son?" Maartje asked. "Did any of them survive?"

"When the liberating forces arrived, they put them in a hospital. They are all home now but the farmer cannot work. He has never accepted the betrayal of his neighbours," said *Mevrouw*. "The mother and remaining son are trying to get the farm going and there are a few neighbours trying to help but it is not good."

"Does Pieter have any other relatives living in this area?"

"Aert's mother lived in Amsterdam," said *Mevrouw* de Bruyn. "I hear she died in the war. Aert and Anita not have family here."

"When Pieter ran away I wonder where he was going." Gloria mused.

"To his grandmother?" the older woman suggested. "I do not know."

"Why did none of the neighbours try to find the boys after they ran away?" Gloria wondered aloud. To herself she wondered why this woman had not been more concerned. Why had no one tried to find two lost little boys?

"It is hard for you to understand I am sure," the woman replied patiently, her tone sad. "The whole country was in turmoil. Soldiers were everywhere. Canadian soldiers ask me to work in a… pretend…hospital," she paused and finished her thought in Dutch.

"*Mevrouw* worked in a make-shift hospital," Maartje said taking over the tale in English, "treating the people who were coming out of hiding and trying to reunite them with their families. She feels badly now that she did not try to find the boys, especially since Tonny died."

Gloria did not think *Mevrouw* looked sorry but Gloria had not lived through the horrors this woman had and she did not know how she might have reacted in a similar situation. If this had been peacetime there might have been an agency like the Children's Aid Society to notify. Two little boys lost and alone might have been noticed and something could have been done. However during wartime she discovered different rules applied. The villagers must have been so concerned with Individual survival that no one remembered two boys who were on their own. Did self-preservation take precedence over altruism in such a time of upheaval?

"I can tell the nurses what happened to his family at least," Gloria said. "I suppose this means Pieter is an orphan. What will happen to him? In Canada, I know that each province has a Children's Aid Society to look after runaway children and arrange adoptions. Does Holland have such an organization?" *Mevrouw* answered in Dutch speaking to Maartje.

"Before the war Holland had very good social service agencies," Maartje repeated it in English. "The government looked after old people and those less fortunate. They took care of everyone. But during the war much of that was abolished. The German army told the Dutch people what they could do, where they could go, and who they could visit. They had no choice in the matter. When the boys ran away the Dutch agencies had not been re-established."

"Right now, Pieter is still in the hospital in Amsterdam," said Gloria, "but when he recovers what will happen to him? Is there an orphanage he can go to?" The old woman laughed though it sounded more like a snort.

"We do not have such places here," the woman said. "The Church will find a family to take him if he is lucky." Gloria didn't want to think what might happen to him if he wasn't lucky.

"We are going to Emmen tomorrow," Maartje said after a moment's silence, "to follow up on a clue Gloria received from the Red Cross. Tell *Mevrouw* about it Gloria."

Gloria did as she was told explaining what she had learned at the Red Cross office.

"I hope you will not be too disappointed, if you do not get word of your husband," said *Mevrouw*. "Or if he is there you will find him different from what he was before. All is changed after the war. It is not good." Gloria was startled at the woman's assertion.

"I won't be disappointed," she said although she wasn't sure if that was true. "I think there's a good chance of finding out something. I have to go and check at least."

"I hope we'll be able to go to Emmen tomorrow," said Gloria as she and Maartje walked home. "Regardless of what *Mevrouw* said I feel hopeful."

Maartje didn't respond.

Chapter 22:

The next day dawned sunny and cool – a perfect day for travelling. The car was no more comfortable this trip but once again Uncle Henk was content to drive at a reasonable speed which minimized the shaking but made the journey that much longer.

To pass the time Maartje and Gloria compared notes on how their respective countries celebrated Christmas.

"We usually celebrate Christmas on December six and we call it St. Nicholas Day," said Maartje. "But during the war no one in Holland observed the holiday. Years ago, my brother and I used to put one shoe each at the back door the night before, the night of December five. In each shoe we put an apple and some hay for Sinter Klaas' horse. Before going to bed we sang Sinter Klaas songs and in the morning we rushed to the door to see what Sinter Klaas had left in our shoes. The treats for the horse had been replaced with a candy or a small present."

"My family in Canada will be celebrating Christmas soon," said Gloria, "on December twenty-five. When my sister and I were young we would be very excited on Christmas Eve. If we'd had a fireplace we would have hung our Christmas stockings on the mantle. Since we didn't we put them on the couch in the living room. Because we believed in Santa we put milk and cookies out for him." She shifted on the seat trying to get comfortable without being too obvious about it but then she noticed Maartje moving in a similar fashion.

"Did your parents tell you to be good in the months leading up to Christmas Day or St. Nicholas Day because Santa was watching?" asked Gloria with a smile. "Mine did. We were told Santa Claus kept a list of who'd been naughty and who'd been nice. Santa's elves made toys at his workshop at the North Pole and on Christmas Eve Santa delivered them to all the good children around the world." Maartje smiled.

"We were told that Zwarte Piet, or Black Peter, kept a record of all the things we had done in the past year," she said. "Good children received presents from Sinter Klaas but bad children found a piece of coal in their shoes, left by Zwarte Piet. I liked it when Sinter Klaas left me a *kruidnoten*, a gingerbread cookie, but my brother preferred getting a chocolate letter."

They talked of particular Christmases each of them remembered because she'd gotten a special present. Gloria mused about Willem's childhood. He'd likely put out a shoe containing treats for Sinter Klaas' horse too. Had he liked getting chocolate or a cookie in return? She knew so little about him. Maartje turned slightly to look out the window.

"I know I said it before," she said turning to sit properly on the seat, "but it is good to be home even though things aren't completely back to normal yet. I missed my country." She sighed happily.

Gloria thought again how relaxed Maartje looked. She was returning home and expected that her life would continue as it had been before the war. Gloria wondered what these journeys – the one to Holland as well as the one to Emmen – signalled for her. Would she find Willem and would they be able to continue their life together? Or would he have changed as *Mevrouw* de Bruyn had suggested? More importantly, if he was physically injured how would they manage? What if he couldn't work? She had no skills to earn money to provide for herself let alone her and Willem.

"I can't help but think of Pieter," Gloria said to Maartje after they'd travelled a while without speaking. "What he must've gone through after his parents were taken away and how frightening it must've been. Perhaps he was trying to get to his grandmother in Amsterdam as *Mevrouw* de Bruyn suggested. All this time I've been hoping to reunite him with his family and now I find he has no family."

"The church will take care of him," said Maartje. "I know that much. When I was young I went to school with a girl who had a sister come to live with her. We never thought anything of it at the time but later I realized it was an orphan girl who had come to live with them."

"Did the family adopt her?" asked Gloria.

"I do not know," said Maartje. "My friend referred to her as a 'sister'. I never thought about whether she actually was or not."

Gloria refused to let the idea that was starting to form take shape in her mind. She had to find Willem first. She had to know if he wanted their marriage to continue because without that she had nothing to offer Pieter. She also didn't know what her parents would think if she unexpectedly announced she had a young son, even if she was married.

After two hours of driving *Oom* Henk stopped the car so they could have a rest. Gloria was glad of the chance to get out and stretch her legs. Maartje followed her out of the car.

"What's growing in the field over there?" Gloria asked, pointing to a meadow of short green plants.

"That is peat," said Maartje. "After it is cut and dried we use it for fuel."

They walked around talking and looking at the country-side but hurried back when they noticed *Oom* Henk waving at them. As they climbed into the backseat they grimaced at each other. Gloria could tell her friend felt the same way she did: happy that the trip was almost over.

When they arrived at Emmen *Oom* Henk dropped Gloria off on the main street near the hospital. Maartje and her aunt were going to visit another aunt while *Oom* Henk went about his business. Before separating they agreed on a meeting time and place. Gloria waved as the car drove away.

She took a deep breath and found the air was clean and fresh. Being on her own in an unfamiliar place was a new experience for her. She'd gone from living with her parents to living with her husband to staying with her in-laws. Living a solitary life held no appeal for her but right now as she took what might be the first step to finding her husband it felt good to be on her own.

She rounded a corner and found herself in front of the hospital, a big house similar to the hospital in Amsterdam. She walked up the sidewalk, climbed the stairs, and pushed open the heavy door. The smell that assaulted her nose was familiar — not unpleasant, just slightly antiseptic and it brought with it a sense of foreboding. The uneasy feeling might have been exacerbated by the lack of light. The windows were high and looked like they needed a good washing. The only illumination came from a single light bulb hanging from the ceiling over the main desk.

Gloria approached the desk and asked to speak to the head nurse. She spoke Dutch and the nurse responded in kind, telling her she would have to wait. The nurse smiled pleasantly and motioned to some chairs along the wall. Being glad of a chance to sit and collect her thoughts Gloria relaxed into a chair. Fifteen minutes later another nurse approached speaking a sentence in Dutch. Gloria tried to respond in Dutch but faltered halfway through a sentence and finished it in English. The nurse smiled as she held out her hand.

"My name is Ilse van der Bijl. I am the head nurse," she said in English. "My office is this way."

Gloria followed her down the hall. When they were seated across the desk from each other Gloria began her explanation.

"If my husband was one of the ones who escaped from the POW camp," she said, "they might have tried to cross the border near here. Perhaps they needed to see a doctor and..." she stopped talking when she saw the look on the Nurse van der Bijl's face.

"In fact," the nurse said, "three soldiers were here after escaping from a POW camp and one was named Willem."

"He was here?" Gloria shrieked. Her hands flew to her cheeks. She started laughing but stopped abruptly.

"I'm sorry," she said. "It's just such a relief to know that he's still alive. Can you tell me anything else? Was he injured? Was he sick? How did he look?" She stopped talking and lowered her hands clasping them in her lap.

"He had received a gunshot wound in his leg," Nurse van der Bijl said in a straight-forward manner which helped to calm Gloria, "and he was weak when they first arrived. The other two were in pretty good health but they were all dehydrated." Gloria sat forward in her chair listening eagerly.

"Willem's wound had become infected," Nurse van der Bijl continued, "so he needed more care. We were surprised that he had been able to make it this far. He needed antibiotics but we did not have much to spare. He never complained though; he became quite a favourite with the nurses." Gloria blushed.

"That sounds like him," she said, tucking her hair behind her ear. "How long was he here?"

"Several months," the nurse replied. "It took a while to mend. And he left before it was completely healed. He was very anxious to get to Amsterdam to see if his family was still alive. Come with me to the common room. I will tell you all I can remember about him and we will see if we can figure out where he is."

Gloria followed her along the hall trying hard not to skip for joy. To think that her husband had been in this very building and only a short while ago! She could hardly believe it! Would her adventure have a happy ending after all? She closed her eyes briefly offering a small prayer of thanks.

Gloria followed the head nurse into a small room with two tables and several chairs. A large pleasant-looking woman wearing a nurse's uniform sat at one of the tables.

"Hello Lottie. Do you mind if we join you?" the head nurse asked politely.

In reply Lottie stood and pulled another chair over. The head nurse procured two cups of coffee and placed one in front of Gloria before sitting. Gloria usually drank tea but she was so excited she didn't notice what she was drinking.

"Lottie, you cared for Willem Spelt did you not?" the head nurse asked. "Remember — those three soldiers who arrived from the POW camp at the end of the war. Willem was the one with the gunshot wound in his leg." The nurse had been frowning but as Nurse van der Bijl spoke her brow cleared.

"Yes. I remember. He was so anxious to leave. We had a hard time keeping him in bed. When he was barely well enough to stand on his own he took off intending to walk to Amsterdam. He was especially worried about his brother but he also wanted to get word to his wife in Canada." The head nurse patted Gloria on the arm.

"This is his wife. She came here to find him." she said.

During this exchange Gloria had been stealing glances at Lottie. She seemed familiar.

"The other soldiers were ready to leave in a few days," said the head nurse speaking to Gloria, "and they left to join up with other Canadian soldiers who were here. But Lottie got to know Willem because he was here longer. I have to leave now but Lottie can stay for a few minutes." She left and Gloria turned to the other nurse.

"Would Willem have been able to walk to Amsterdam?" Gloria asked. "How badly injured was he?"

"His leg was in bad shape but he might have made it," said Lottie, "if he did not have any set-backs. But it has been so long." She sounded worried. "And you say he has not been there?"

"I stayed with his parents and they knew nothing of his whereabouts. They did not even know that he had gone to Canada or that he was married." Gloria stopped talking as several possibilities sprang to mind. "What if he was taken ill and died somewhere between here and Amsterdam?" she cried.

"There, there," said Lottie. "Try not to think of the worst. If you want to stay in the area to get more information, you are welcome to stay with me. My name is Lottie van Dyk and I live two streets over."

Gloria gulped several times before she was able to answer. She tried to clear her mind and concentrate on what Lottie was saying.

"That is so very kind of you," Gloria said hesitantly. "I would like to do that, but I have to meet my friend and let her know first." Lottie gathered her things and stood up.

"I have to get back to work," she said. "I will meet you here when I get off. Will that give you time to check with your friend?"

Gloria nodded dumbly and watched as Lottie left. She took several deep breaths before walking out of the room and making her way outside.

Chapter 23:

Gloria was back at the hospital in an hour and found a place to wait until Lottie had finished her shift. She was recovered somewhat from the shock of discovering Willem was alive but again the joy she wanted to feel was missing; something didn't feel quite right.

Sitting in a hard-backed chair with her head leaning against the wall she closed her eyes. Maartje had been skeptical about Gloria staying at first.

"This is the first time I've spoken to someone who actually saw Willem," Gloria had argued. "I can't leave until I check it out. He may still be in this area. I can stay with Nurse van Dyk but if that doesn't work out I can stay with your *Tante* Carla." That argument had finally won Maartje over.

Tante Lucie had explained to Gloria that her sister, Carla, was a member of the Dutch Reformed Church and while *Tante* Lucie did not agree with her sister's religious beliefs she did admire her and the other church members for the work they'd done during the war. The congregation had believed they were fighting a holy war because the Nazi propaganda was anti-Christian. Many church members worked for the Underground finding a sense of family even among those people who weren't members of the church because they were all working to achieve a common goal.

Gloria visited with Maartje and her aunts for half an hour and while she was getting ready to leave, to return to the hospital, Maartje put her hand on Gloria's arm.

"If you need money," Maartje said shyly, "I can give you some. As you know my aunt made sure I had plenty before I left Canada. I have enough to share with you if you need it." She lifted her eyes and Gloria could tell she was embarrassed. She thanked her friend assuring Maartje she had sufficient funds at present.

§ § §

On her way back to the hospital Gloria's mind had returned to the question of why Lottie seemed familiar. After finding a chair to sit on while she waited for Lottie she reviewed the people she'd spent time with recently and it suddenly occurred to her who Lottie looked like — Mieke Clos, one of the nurses in Amsterdam.

Gloria opened her eyes and sat straighter as she heard someone approaching.

"I am ready to go now," said Lottie, as she neared Gloria. "I have tea at home to warm us."

Gloria nodded her agreement. The dampness had felt cold going straight through her fur coat as she'd walked outside. She got up and followed the other nurse out of the building.

"Are you related to Mieke Clos who works as a nurse at the Wilhelmina Hospital in Amsterdam?" Gloria asked abruptly as they walked along the street.

"Why yes. She is my niece," Lottie said looking at Gloria in surprise.

"Oh my goodness," said Gloria suddenly. "It was your son," she stopped talking as she made the appalling connection.

"Yes," the woman said sadly. "My son and daughter-in-law were killed. Fortunately, they did not have children. I am too old to think about raising a family." Gloria felt miserable.

"I am so sorry to have mentioned it," she said. "I had just started working at the hospital when Mieke heard the news and she was very upset. She didn't think her cousin would have worked with the Germans."

"My son, Michel, fell in love with a girl from a German background," said Lottie with a slight shrug. "He married her quickly just before the war started. Perhaps that is why they worked with the Germans during the war. We will never know."

Gloria followed Lottie into the apartment feeling discomfited at the memories she'd raised.

Chapter 24:

It was two days before Gloria found someone else who had known her husband. The first day it had rained and she'd only had time to walk around the market square before it was too wet to continue. A large church that had been built in the Middle Ages stood in the square but she didn't take time to go in. On the second day the weather was drier and she'd taken the opportunity to enter the building.

Being in the sacred structure calmed her and strengthened her conviction that her husband was alive. She wondered if he might have come into the church after he left the hospital to give thanks for having survived the war. Willem was not particularly religious but as the saying goes there are no atheists in fox holes.

It was dark and cool in the church. As she walked around the outside of the pews she pulled her jacket tighter. She stepped to the side as the church custodian went past sweeping the stone floor. He glanced at her quickly but then stopped and spoke in Dutch. Gloria assumed it was an offer to help. She smiled nervously but was able to say in Dutch that it was a beautiful building. The custodian nodded and continued to talk in Dutch at which point Gloria had to admit that she couldn't understand him.

"*Ik ben Canadees*," she stammered.

The custodian nodded pleasantly, smiled at her, and walked away. While they'd been talking another man had approached.

"Can I help?" he asked in heavily accented English.

Gloria stepped back and looked at the newcomer, a man dressed in a black cassock, obviously the pastor. His blond hair was thinning and his glasses framed friendly eyes. She gave a sigh of relief and started her story. The padre listened patiently nodding occasionally. When Gloria finished he was silent for several minutes.

"I have not seen anyone like that around here," he said and Gloria's spirits fell. "But I was only recently appointed to this parish. A few older men, soldiers from this war and the last one, often gather at the post office in the morning. Perhaps they could help you."

Gloria thanked the padre. She turned away feeling dejected. When she left the church to walk to Lottie's she was passed the post office. It was a grand building though not as old as the church dating from only the beginning of the century. There was an empty wooden bench in front of the building and she could imagine an old soldier or two sitting on it talking about the "good old days." She'd return in the morning to see if they had materialized and if they had any pertinent information. It raised her spirits slightly.

Already feeling gloomy, her fear that Willem had started the journey but had fallen ill returned. That thought was followed by another which knocked all others from her mind. No one had mentioned anything about a baby! Had Willem not mentioned that he was a father? The nurses had said that Willem had wanted to get to Amsterdam – to find his family and to find her. But he'd replied to the letter she sent telling him there was going to be a baby. It made no sense that he would not mention it. She didn't know what to think.

When she reached the van Dyk's apartment no one was home. Gloria found a fairly comfortable rock to sit on while she waited for Lottie to return. She closed her eyes and let her head fall forward onto her chest.

§ § §

"Gloria! Have you been here long?" The voice jerked Gloria awake and she shook her head to clear the cobwebs.

"No no. Just a few minutes," she said quickly. She stood and followed Lottie up the steps and into the apartment.

After Lottie left for work the next day Gloria walked to the post office. No one had materialized on the bench but Gloria found a place nearby to sit. After half an hour an old man, wearing a worn jacket open at the front and pants held up by a rope, shuffled along the path. Wooden shoes covered his bare feet and he held a cane in his right hand.

He passed Gloria without acknowledging her. His attention was on another man similarly attired walking towards him. The second man didn't have a cane but he too wore wooden shoes, the once colourful pattern now faded and barely visible. He sat on the bench and indicated his friend should join him. Gloria eavesdropped since they seemed unaware of her presence. She could hear bits and pieces of what they were saying and she understood enough to know that they were talking about farming. She approached them, knowing it would be a test of her language skills.

"*Goedendag*," she began tentatively. They turned and smiled at her giving her confidence to continue. She managed to stammer a few sentences in Dutch explaining that she was looking for her husband, a Dutch soldier. One of the men knew a few English words and he was able to finally understand what she was saying. He said something quickly to the other man and then motioned for Gloria to follow him, saying "*Mijn zoon spreekt Engels.*"

Gloria had exhausted her knowledge of Dutch but she understood that he was inviting her to go with him to talk with his son who could speak English. They left the other man and walked slowly along several streets before coming to an apartment building similar to the one where Lottie lived. The man walked to a door at street level and went into an apartment.

The living room was small but tidy. He indicated Gloria should sit on the sofa while he went along the hall to another room. After a brief pause during which Gloria heard voices that she was unable to comprehend the old man wheeled his son out in a chair. It was cumbersome and difficult for him to manoeuvre but after a few minutes Gloria and the young man were sitting close enough to talk.

The son didn't meet her eyes while his father spoke introducing him as Ernst Visser. After his father stopped talking Ernst fiddled with the rug covering his legs rather than offering to shake hands. From the way the blanket lay, it was obvious his left leg was missing. His father left the room and Gloria waited for Ernst to say something. When he said nothing, Gloria spoke.

"I am looking for my husband, Willem Spelt," Gloria began. She was going to say more but Ernst jerked his head to look at her. He lowered his eyes immediately and Gloria was unsure if she saw hatred or fear in his eyes.

"He was with the Queen's Own Rifles, landing at Juno Beach," she continued. "Do you know him?" Ernst was silent for so long she was afraid he was not going to answer.

"My father will take you to the kitchen," Ernst said. He called to his father and spoke to him quickly. The father led her into the kitchen and pulled a chair out from the table motioning her to sit in it. Then he left the room.

Gloria tried not to listen to the conversation in the other room but it was hard to ignore. She couldn't understand the words but she could tell Ernst was angry. Was he annoyed because she was a girl and he was crippled? She wished she'd thought to tell him she was a nurse and that she'd seen many men in a worse state. She thought of all the soldiers she'd nursed in the hospital in Amsterdam. Quite a few were missing an arm or a leg. She recalled one soldier who'd lost both his legs.

The older man appeared at the doorway and motioned for her to follow him. She sat in the chair she'd recently vacated. Ernst looked at her without smiling. She could feel his hostility but if he was willing to talk to her that was all that mattered. He didn't have to like her. She assumed a pleasant expression as she waited for him to begin speaking.

"The name Spelt is familiar," he said. Gloria waited expecting him to say more but he stayed silent, clenching and unclenching his hands in his lap. Beads of sweat appeared on his forehead.

"The nurses at the hospital said Willem planned to walk to Amsterdam," Gloria said when it was obvious he wasn't going to say more. "Do you know which road he might have taken?" Ernst stayed silent for so long that Gloria was on the point of repeating her question.

"I can guess which road he took," said Ernst, wiping his face with a cloth. He called for his father and when he appeared Ernst said something in Dutch. His father started to roll him away but Gloria reached out and touched the side of the chair.

"Which road would he take?" she asked. Ernst held up his hand and his father stopped moving the chair. He said a couple of words that Gloria didn't quite hear and then lowered his hand indicating his father could move the chair.

Gloria waited until the older man reappeared. She stood and thanked him. He accompanied her to the door but didn't say anything. As soon as Gloria was outside she took a deep breath. It had been a very strange encounter and she was glad it was over.

"Emmaveg" was what she thought the name of the road was, and "Dommolenar", the name of the farm. Thoughts of Ernst faded. She hurried back to Lottie's apartment intent on finding out where that road was. She needed to find the farm to ask if Willem had stopped there.

After talking to Lottie that evening two misconceptions were straightened out: the road was "Ermerweg" and the name was likely a first and last, "Dom Molenaar," not just one name. Lottie pointed the road out on a map which she then gave to Gloria.

Getting into bed that evening Gloria's excitement mounted as she considered she was closer than ever to locating Willem. Her enthusiasm was tempered when she recalled where she'd gotten this last clue. Could she trust what Ernst had said? He'd been quite angry talking to his father, she was sure, even though he had seemed reasonable enough talking to her. She fell asleep dreaming of Willem.

She was still happy the next morning eating toast for breakfast and not noticing there was nothing to put on it. She sipped her tea as she contemplated the next leg of her trip. She had only kept a few things with her, letting Maartje take most of her belongings to Sloten. Her friend would then take Gloria's suitcase with her to Amsterdam. Gloria knew she was imposing on Maartje but she had to take advantage of this opportunity and Maartje had quickly reassured Gloria that she did not mind.

"I will be on a train and the suitcases will be in the baggage car," she'd said. "I will not be carrying two of them myself. And you cannot take a suitcase with you while you walk. It is more important that you find Willem. Theo will meet me in Amsterdam and we will drop your suitcase off at the Spelts' apartment. Then I can tell *Mevrouw* Spelt what is happening."

Lottie entered the kitchen. She was working an afternoon shift and had slept in. Gloria acknowledged her with a smile and a nod of the head as she took another sip of tea. A few trains were running now but there wouldn't have been any running when Willem had first set out. Gloria was unsure why he had decided to walk but since he had she felt obliged to do the same.

She set her mug beside the sink and looked out the window at the drab weather. There was a light snow falling but it couldn't dampen her enthusiasm. She was sure she'd have answers soon. Lottie gave her a map and Gloria stood in front of her hostess as she put the map in her pocket.

"Thank you so much, Lottie," she said, gripping her friend's hand. "Will you get in touch with Mieke? She was so upset. I'm sure she'd like to know how you are doing."

"I will," the older woman said. "I am glad you told me. I hope you find your husband but if you need to come back it is fine with me."

Gloria hugged Lottie impulsively before turning to walk away. She remembered how the shopkeeper had given her the cookie to say thank-you for the Canadian soldiers having freed Holland. Perhaps good works were performed in a circle and if you couldn't always pay back your Good Samaritan doing a good deed for someone else counted. These people had been good to her and she would remember.

She held onto that thought as she walked through the city eventually leaving the buildings behind. Once she was in the country she found herself relaxing and almost enjoying her outing. It might take her the better part of a day to reach the farm she was seeking but at least the snow was holding off.

On both sides of the road were fields undamaged by bombs and seeing the unspoiled landscape put her in a good mood for the start of her journey. She kept walking even when she felt like resting waiting for her second wind to kick in. After passing several farms but none with the name Molenaar her spirits flagged. There were no signs either, telling her how far she was from Emmen, but Lottie had explained that many sign posts had been removed during the war and replacing them was not a priority.

Each time the dreadful thought that Willem might have started out and then been taken ill resurfaced Gloria suppressed it. She would not think bad thoughts until she was forced to do so. As long as there was a small chance that Willem was alive she would hold fast to her dream.

She met a few people and smiled at them but most didn't even look at her. Those who glanced in her direction averted their gaze quickly when their eyes met. There were no vehicles. She wanted to sit and rest but the ground was covered with snow. Not as much as there'd been in Canada before she left but enough to saturate her clothes if she sat on the ground. Sitting on a rock if she could find one would mean she'd be drier but she would get very cold. She trudged on singing to herself to keep her feet moving.

A horse and buggy approached and it slowed down as it came towards her. She raised her hand to the couple sitting high on the seat but then looked away willing it not to stop. The man acknowledged her but didn't stop.

She turned to watch it turn into a laneway on the opposite side of the road. People lived along here – that was a promising sign.

It gave her renewed hope and she picked up her pace. She'd finished the third verse of "Oh when the saints…" and she judged it was late afternoon when she rounded a corner and a farm came into view. A wooden sign with the name Molenaar stood at the end of the laneway.

As she started walking towards the farmhouse excitement replaced her tiredness. She knocked on the door. Voices on the other side stopped and she heard footsteps approaching the door which was opened a crack as the footsteps stopped. A face peered out, a young woman with freckles and blonde hair pulled back off her face. The woman held the door in such a way that Gloria couldn't see into the room.

"*Ja?*" the woman said. Unlike many of the people Gloria had met thus far this face looked welcoming and she was heartened by that.

"Hello. My name is Gloria Spelt and I'm from Canada," she said starting her prepared speech. She stopped talking when she heard a cry and uneven footsteps coming from behind the door. The door was pulled open by a skinny young man who then leaned against the door breathing heavily, slightly off balance.

"Gloria!" he exclaimed.

Chapter 25:

Gloria stared at the man without recognition. She realized her mouth had fallen open and she closed it as her brain finally made sense of what her eyes were seeing. She struggled to speak.

"W-Willem! Oh Willem," she breathed. Her first impulse was to rush forward to hug him but something in the young woman's posture caused her to hesitate. The woman had moved only enough to allow Willem to use the door for support.

"Come in," the woman said to Gloria before turning and assisting Willem to a chair. He sat awkwardly and Gloria did rush forward then. She knelt in front of him, took his hands in hers, and clasped them to her cheeks. Closing her eyes, she stayed in that position until she felt Willem moving his hands. When she opened her eyes they were alone; the woman had left.

"Gloria," said Willem tenderly his hands cradling her face. "Gloria," he repeated.

He began stroking the back of her head. After a few minutes when Gloria was sure she wouldn't laugh or cry she stood up. There was another chair close by and she pulled it over so she could sit facing her husband. Her eyes roamed his face taking in how gaunt he was. His hair was long and rather wild and he had a beard. But he was her dear Willem!

His right hand moved to his thigh and began massaging the bandaged area. A grimace of pain crossed his face but his eyes never left her face.

"You're hurt," she said unnecessarily. "Do you want to lie down?"

She got to her feet stepping back from the chair. He stood awkwardly shifting his weight.

"No. I do not need to lie down," he said, "just give me a minute." Another spasm of pain crossed his face but he flexed his leg and relaxed.

"Jenny," he called. "Come back. You must know who this is." He put his arm around Gloria's waist drawing her to him as the young woman reappeared.

"I guessed," she said smiling. She offered her hand to Gloria. "I am Jenny Molenaar. My husband Dom and Willem were in the army together. When he turned up on our doorstep we persuaded him to stay until his leg improved."

Willem sat and turned to Gloria so suddenly that she knew the one moment of their reunion she'd been truly dreading had arrived.

"The baby…" he said with a question in his voice.

Gloria sat in the other chair and looked at his eager face. She took a deep steadying breath trying to remain calm. She lowered her eyes before she began speaking.

"There…" she stopped, swallowed, and started again. "There is no baby."

When Willem didn't say anything, she gulped and continued.

"He died before he was born."

In the ensuing silence Gloria heard Jenny leaving the room. She folded her hands in her lap her eyes still downcast bracing herself for what was to come. This was it. Her marriage was over. All her feelings of certainty, her belief that they were meant to be together – it was all gone. She could hear him breathing and she raised her eyes to watch him. His face was serious, his eyes were on her.

"He?" he asked expectantly. "It was a boy?"

"I think so," she said in a small voice. She got out of her chair and knelt before him, encircling his waist with her arms, staying away from his wound. Willem stroked the back of her head again. They stayed like that for several minutes. Finally Gloria sighed, got to her feet, and moved to the chair. Overcome by emotion all the worries she'd refused to acknowledge came tumbling out.

"Are you disappointed?" she asked her eyes downcast. "You must be disappointed. This means we didn't need to get married. Do you want me to leave? Are you sorry you married me? I can go back to Canada." She took a breath to say more but after glancing at his face she stopped. He had tears in his eyes but he was smiling – a small, sad smile.

"Gloria. Gloria. No, I do not want you to leave," he said reaching to hold her hands. "I am very glad you are here. While I was in the POW camp I did not hear from anybody. I began to fear that you were all dead – you, the baby, and my brother. But here you are!"

Gloria moved her chair tight beside his and put her arm across his shoulders in a one-armed hug. She leaned her head close and squeezed his shoulder.

"Oh Willem I'm so glad I've found you. Perhaps your brother is not dead either. I will help you look for him. As soon as you are well enough we can start searching for him." She gave his shoulders another squeeze. "I told your father I would look for him." Willem's eyebrows shot up.

"You have met my father?" he exclaimed.

"And your mother and Anneke," Gloria said, laughing. "I have much to tell you and I want to hear what happened to you as well."

It seemed that her marriage was saved for the moment. They could work together to find Harrie and sort out their relationship after that. Her husband needed her and that was good enough for now.

§ § §

Gloria met Dom, Willem's army buddy, when he came in to eat supper. Rationing wasn't as strict in the country as it had been in Amsterdam but Gloria followed Jenny's example and let the men, especially Dom, eat more food. When Gloria finished eating she looked around and her gaze landed on the curtains. Jenny waved at them and grimaced.

"During the war," she explained, "we had to tape cardboard to the windows to comply with blackout regulations. Now there are no more blackouts but I cannot buy new curtains. These scraps of cloth are all I have." She shrugged her shoulders and Gloria was reminded of the other Dutch people she'd met recently. Gloria told Jenny about Maartje's Uncle Henk who was slowly getting his farm working again.

"He said it will just take time for farming to return to what it was before the war and I'm sure that's true for all parts of life," she added. "Soon you will be able to buy pretty curtains."

When they were sitting in the living room after the evening meal Willem wanted to hear how Gloria had come to be in Holland. Dom and Jenny stood but Gloria waved them to sit.

"You are wondering as well I'm sure," said Gloria. "I don't mind if you stay to hear the story. Willem?"

"It is fine with me," he said without hesitation. Dom and Jenny sat down again.

Gloria began by telling them how she had waited for a letter that never came. Words tumbled out of her with very few interruptions from the others. She told them of her belief that Willem was alive and how that hope kept her going but she didn't mention her fears about their marriage. That was for a private talk with Willem later.

Part way through her recitation Dom stood and fetched a stool for Willem to rest his foot on. Gloria stopped talking while Willem stood and flexed his leg. When they were settled again she resumed her story but by the time she finished she could tell Willem was tired.

"Do you have anything you can take for the pain?" she asked including Jenny in the question.

"He has taken all the aspirin I had," Jenny said. "It was not enough but we have been bathing it and Dom made a poultice to put on it. I have a recipe for a tisane from my mother. That provided comfort as well."

"It was not so painful," said Willem making a face as he said it. "I should have stayed longer in the hospital but I was so anxious to get to Amsterdam I did not want to wait. Now I am glad I stayed here where you could find me." He stood and opened his arms. Gloria moved into his embrace.

Darkness had descended. Jenny showed Willem and Gloria to a double bed.

"You two can sleep here. It will be more comfortable. Dom and I will sleep in the smaller bed," she said putting out the lights before departing. Gloria and Willem were left standing in the moonlight.

Gloria glanced up at Willem suddenly feeling very shy. Willem wavered and moved to sit on the bed. She sat beside him smiling to herself and feeling foolish. They were married for heaven's sakes, and with his sore leg he'd likely not be able to have marital relations. She helped him get undressed and into bed before doing the same.

As they lay together she remembered all the reasons why she loved him. His hand sought hers beneath the sheet and held it tight. She heard him take a breath and she turned towards him.

"I am sorry I was not with you when the baby died," he whispered.

"I know," she said softly. "I wish you could have been with me too but the baby still would have died. Nothing can change that."

"We can have another baby," he said in a low tone, "in fact it will be fun trying." He sounded more like her Willem than he had all evening which was a promising sign. She kissed his arm – the closest part of his body.

"Are you sorry you married me?" she asked in a whisper.

"No not at all," he stated emphatically but in a soft voice. "I am glad we are married. I just wish I could show you how glad but that will have to wait." He paused. "Are you sorry you married me?"

"No of course not; I'm glad we're married too. And I don't mind waiting until your leg has healed," she said squeezing his arm. They lay silently for a while until Gloria heard Willem snoring gently. She listened to his breathing for a long time scarcely believing they were together again. She felt happiness bubbling up inside her – something she hadn't felt for a very long time. Finally, she drifted off to sleep.

Gloria woke to hear rain spattering on the window. Since noises from the other side of the door indicated someone was already up she got out of bed without disturbing Willem. Jenny and Dom were both in the kitchen. Gloria got herself a cup of tea from a pot that was still warm to the touch.

"Willem seemed to be moving quite well last evening," she said. "I wonder if he will feel like beginning our journey to Amsterdam today. We'll have to walk back to Emmen to catch the train, won't we?"

"Yes," said Dom. "There is only the one train. But he should be all right if he takes it slow and does not try running." He paused and smiled to indicate he was joking. But then he turned serious again. "And you are a nurse so you can keep an eye on his wound." He stopped talking as Willem came out of the bedroom.

"*Ja*, she can look after me," Willem said, "but I do not think we should leave today in the rain. It may turn to snow; it is cold enough. Now that I have Gloria with me I am not in such a rush to get to Amsterdam." Dom poured Willem a cup of coffee and handed it to him.

"You are welcome to stay a few days," he said. "Do you feel like helping me work around the farm today?"

"Ja, if I do not move too fast. I may spend all my time watching you," Willem said, smiling. "I will be out as soon as I finish my coffee." Dom waved and grabbed a rain slicker before he went through the door. Willem sat at the table and picked up the paper Dom had left. The newspaper had only recently started printing again.

Chapter 26:

"It looks like we'll be staying for another few days," Gloria said to Jenny. "I'd like to rinse out a few undergarments if I may."

"Of course," said Jenny, "if you're finished here we can do that now."

In response Gloria went into the bedroom to gather her clothes and followed Jenny to a back room. After hanging her clothes to dry Gloria spent the rest of the day helping Jenny with household tasks while Willem stayed outside with Dom. Gloria knew that Dom wouldn't let Willem do too much and risk re-injuring his leg. In fact, the odd time she glanced outside she saw Willem sitting on a stump or a rock talking to Dom who was moving some wood and then fixing a fence. The men only came in at mealtimes and after the evening meal they stayed in since the light was fading. That evening as the four of them were relaxing Gloria asked Willem what he'd done after he left England.

"Jenny and Dom have heard this before," Willem said in apology.

"I do not mind hearing it again," said Jenny hastily while Dom added, "I can make sure you tell it right."

Willem went quickly over their landing on Juno Beach and the push into France. Dom nodded in places agreeing with Willem's account.

"A month after landing four of us were captured and taken to a POW camp in Germany. We were there for," he passed a hand over his forehead, "I do not remember how long. It felt like years. Finally the four of us made a plan to escape and we would have made it except an officer showed up and the guards shot at us," Willem said with a grimace. "If the officer had not been there they might have let us escape since they were running out of food and fewer prisoners meant more food for the guards."

He swallowed and a look of sadness crossed his face.

"Ken was killed, poor chap," he said. "Hit in the head. We knew he was dead as soon as he hit the ground. I took a bullet in the leg but I was able to keep going with Simon tending to it. We got lost and wandered around quite a bit. We knew the general direction we wanted to go but we weren't sure where we were until we met some Canadian troops.

"The soldiers helped us get to the hospital at Emmen," he continued. "We were all pretty weak by then. After a few days Eric and Simon left with the Canadian troops to get back with their own regiment but I stayed longer. The medicine I needed was in short supply and my wound took a much longer time to heal."

When Willem stopped talking Jenny got him a mug of water. He drank deeply wiping his mouth with the back of his hand when the cup was empty. While he was drinking Gloria told the three of them the part she had omitted the night before – her visit to the Red Cross.

"At the Red Cross office in Amsterdam I learned that one soldier had been killed," she said, "but I didn't know if it was Willem or not until after I arrived at the hospital in Emmen. The nurses there gave me the good news." She reached over and grasped Willem's hand and they smiled at each other. She turned to Dom to ask him where he'd been during this time.

"I stayed with the Dutch army in England and did not go with the unit that went to Canada but I met up with Willem again when he returned to England in '43. We were together for the landing at Normandy. After Willem and the others had been captured I fought with the troops through to Falaise, in France. From there we joined the other Allied forces to liberate the Netherlands." He rubbed his hands over his face.

After a few minutes of silence Gloria asked if either of the men remembered a soldier named Ernst Visser, the soldier in a wheelchair whom she'd met in Emmen. Willem shook his head immediately but Dom got a strange look on his face. He looked away for a minute before admitting the name was familiar. When he didn't elaborate Jenny stood and gathered the mugs. Willem and Dom resumed the conversation while Gloria helped Jenny tidy the kitchen. When the women joined the men, no mention was made of Ernst Visser. The four of them talked about more pleasant topics until it was time for bed. When they were alone in their bedroom Gloria asked Willem if he thought he'd be able to start the journey to Amsterdam the next day.

"We can stay here for a day or two," he said. "My leg is feeling better every day but I think a few more days rest will help. Once we start as Dom said you will be with me to tend to my leg if it is necessary."

§ § §

New Year's Eve was traditionally celebrated in Dutch households with treats such as *oliebollen* or deep fried doughnut balls and *appelflappen* or apple turnovers and with champagne to drink. The night of 1945 becoming 1946 was observed in a more modest way for many Dutch revellers but it was completely ignored at the Molenaar farm having been eclipsed by the joy of Gloria and Willem's reunion.

A few days into the New Year Gloria and Willem decided it was time to leave. They'd been unable to get word to Willem's parents in Amsterdam informing them that Gloria had found Willem. Gloria hugged Jenny and shook hands with Dom while Willem pocketed the sandwiches Jenny had made for them. Gloria stood to the side while Willem said good-bye to the couple. After expressing their thanks once again they set off.

The first half hour of walking passed quickly but then Gloria called a halt. Willem's face was pale and he was perspiring. They found some rocks to sit on. Gloria encouraged Willem to lean against her or to lie down but he refused. Glancing at him Gloria remembered that he could be stubborn at times and she didn't press the issue. They started walking again but after another hour of walking in a comfortable silence Gloria asked Willem why he hadn't told her Harrie was his twin brother.

"When I arrived in England," he said, "Harrie was not on the boat. I expected that he would get another boat but no other boats arrived. After a few weeks when I realized that the Germans had invaded France and Germany as well as Holland I began to wonder if he was dead. I volunteered to go to Canada so I would not have to think about it. There was no point in saying anything to you." He stumbled and a look of pain cut across his face. Gloria put out a steadying arm. Willem ignored it but motioned to a dilapidated barn a little ways off the road.

"We can find a place to rest in there," he said. When they were both seated Gloria took his hand.

"I was so surprised to hear that your brother," she said, "was in fact your twin. That's why you wanted him to be your best man, wasn't it? I wondered if there was another reason you hadn't told me." Willem frowned as he looked at her.

"What other reason?" he asked. Gloria shifted her weight. This all seemed so silly now.

"Perhaps you didn't tell me because you didn't think we were going to stay married," she said softly. "It was me that asked you if you remember."

"Telling you or not telling you that I had a twin brother had nothing to do with me wanting to marry you," he said sitting on a pile of wood. "What a ridiculous idea." Gloria sat beside him.

"You were gone for so long," she said leaning her head on his shoulder. "By the time the war ended I'd had a lot of silly notions. I tried to remain positive but when I didn't hear back from you at the end of the war I was afraid you'd changed you mind about wanting to be married. If you'd only married me because of the baby…" her voice trailed off.

"We did rather rush into marriage," said Willem, "but I am sure we would have gotten married after the war was over." He smiled at her and squeezed her hand indicating with a nod that he was ready to go again. By the time they were on the road again the sun was shining.

Gloria sensed a slight reluctance on Willem's part to discuss the issue. As she thought about it she realized that while she'd been living with the knowledge of their baby's death for three years, Willem had just found out about it. She would say no more about it until Willem indicated he was ready to talk about it.

They continued on their way without talking for a while listening to the sounds of nature. When Gloria noticed Willem's pace slowing again she suggested they stop to eat. While they were eating she told him about her conversation with Ernst Visser.

"Ernst Visser was angry but I'm not sure why," Gloria said "He spoke in Dutch to his father which I couldn't understand. It might've been about me — perhaps he was angry with his father for allowing me to see that he was injured."

"But you're a nurse," said Willem quickly. "Did you tell him?"

"I didn't," said Gloria hanging her head momentarily. "I was more interested in getting information about where you were."

Willem patted her hand reassuringly but didn't speak. Gloria finished her sandwich before speaking.

"Ernst suggested I take the road past Dom's farm," she said. "I'm not sure why he was helpful like that if he was angry at me. It doesn't make sense."

Willem didn't answer. He was quiet for so long that Gloria wondered if he'd fallen asleep. When she looked at him she saw he'd found a dry piece of ground and was lying down staring at the sky. Not wanting to disturb him she lay beside him and closed her eyes.

§ § §

"I hope to be able to visit Holland sometime when the flowers are blooming everywhere again," said Gloria lifting her face to the sky. "Maartje said Holland would not be Holland without the flowers." She had been observing Willem as he walked and she thought he was moving more easily after his rest.

"Tell me about Maartje," said Willem.

"She always understood that I was missing you," Gloria said smiling in memory, "and she kept my hopes up especially after getting the news from the Red Cross office. Her brother Theo has a good sense of humour. He likes to laugh and that helped me to stay hopeful too."

"There have not been so many reasons to laugh recently," said Willem. "But being reunited with you has made me very happy." He paused before adding, "If we find Harrie too that will increase the happiness." Gloria grabbed his hand.

"I'm sure we'll find him," she said. "And then we'll have a reason to celebrate." They walked in silence with Gloria silently delighting in being with her husband. As they rounded a corner in the road Willem slowed and finally stopped.

"I have to rest," he said looking up, "but I do not like the look of that dark sky. We will have to walk faster after our stop if we want to make it to Emmen before it begins to storm."

"I don't think we should walk any faster," she said scrutinizing Willem rather than gazing heavenward. His colour was still good but his face was creased in pain. "You don't want to take a chance of re-injuring your leg."

There was a dry area just ahead where they could sit for a few minutes. When they were seated, Gloria examined his wound and suggested removing the bandage.

"I'm glad this road is deserted and no one will see you lowering your pants," she said in a teasing voice as she removed the dressing. She believed letting a little air get to the wound would be good for it. His long pants still protected it.

"I can go again," said Willem standing and starting to walk. Gloria scrambled to her feet and caught up to him. They had not gone far when Willem started talking.

"I remember a game that Harrie and I used to play with our friends when we were children," he said in a wistful voice. Willem had not talked about his brother while he was in Canada and Gloria was intrigued to hear what Willem had to say.

"One person was the sheriff and he would cover his eyes. Everyone else would hide. The sheriff would have to search for each person until he found him and escort him to the place we had chosen as the jail. If the other kids could get back without being seen they could free the ones in jail and all of them would hide again. The sheriff would have to start looking again."

"My sister and I played a similar game with our friends," Gloria said, "but we called it hide and seek. One person would be 'it' and they covered their eyes while everyone else hid. We'd try to get home before the person who was 'it' found us. If we all got home free we would hide again and the person who was 'it' would have to start looking all over again."

"I guess all children like to play the same kinds of games," said Willem. Gloria nodded in agreement reaching for Willem's hand. She was glad to hear that Willem had happy memories from his childhood. Maybe they just needed time to get to know each other better and time for Willem to accept the death of their baby. She looked forward to this being a time of courtship. This was what they'd missed in those years between their meeting and their marriage. They walked in silence swinging their clasped hands.

As buildings came into view Gloria began to recognize the outskirts of Emmen. She stopped briefly trying to remember the way to Lottie's apartment but then set off walking confidently. They strode along several streets with Gloria stopping at each corner and looking around before deciding which way to go. Halfway down one block she stopped and turned in a complete circle.

"Hmmm," she said. "I could've sworn…" A man was walking towards them. She waited for him to reach them before speaking.

"Do you know where Allee Street is?" Gloria asked in halting Dutch.

"*Allee Straat?*" he questioned. Without waiting for an answer, he proceeded to give directions in Dutch. Since Willem was listening intently Gloria didn't bother telling the gentleman she couldn't understand what he was saying. Willem thanked him for his help. As the stranger turned to leave Gloria added her thanks in Dutch. After they'd walked half a block Gloria looked at Willem.

"Thank you for not laughing at me when I couldn't find the street," she said smiling sheepishly.

"You're welcome," he replied his lips twitching.

Chapter 27:

Five minutes later they turned onto Allee Street and Gloria saw a familiar apartment building.

"I hope Lottie is home," she said as she and Willem climbed the steps. At the top Willem hung back while Gloria knocked on the door. It opened and a familiar face peered out.

"Gloria! It is good to see you," Lottie said. She frowned. "Is anything wrong?"

"Lottie! I'm so glad you're home," Gloria said stepping to the side and pulling Willem forward. "I found Willem! He was at his army buddy's farmhouse. That's as far as he got."

"You were right." Willem said, grinning sheepishly. "I did leave the hospital too soon but Dom and Jenny took care of me and my leg is feeling much better now."

Lottie invited them into her apartment.

"Can we spend the night with you?" Gloria asked. "We'll take the train to Amsterdam tomorrow."

"Of course. Of course," said Lottie. "I am just having supper. Please join me."

Any misgivings Gloria might have felt at imposing on her new friend disappeared immediately at Lottie's gracious greeting. After they'd finished eating Gloria caught Lottie up on what had happened since they'd last seen each other. They discussed other topics of mutual interest but Gloria noticed Willem was sitting with his eyes closed.

"I think poor Willem is going to fall asleep right here," said Gloria patting her husband on the arm. He opened his eyes.

"I will give you two my bed," said Lottie. "I will sleep on the floor." When Gloria protested Lottie waved her hand airily.

"My bed is only single size; it will not be so comfortable for you," she said taking a sheet and blanket from the closet and handing them to Gloria. Lottie left, closing the door. Willem removed his pants and when Gloria looked at his leg more closely, she realized the wound was weeping. Since Lottie was a more experienced nurse she called her in to take a look.

"I have some antiseptic powder. I'll get it," Lottie said after examining the wound.

"Perhaps I should let you sleep in the bed by yourself and I'll sleep on the floor as well," said Gloria. "What do you think?"

Willem hesitated only a moment before nodding. When Lottie returned with the powder Gloria told her of the change in plans.

"I think that makes a lot of sense," said Lottie. "I was hesitant to suggest it myself." She sprinkled some powder on Willem's leg and handed Gloria some cloth before saying goodnight to Willem and leaving.

"Is your leg very sore?" Gloria asked as she bound his leg.

"Not very," he said stretching his leg and flexing the muscle.

"You don't mind if I don't sleep with you?" she asked.

"I will miss having you close," he said, "but I think it will be better for my leg." He touched her cheek with his knuckles and pulled her close for a kiss.

§ § §

It took Gloria a few moments to realize where she was when she awoke in the morning. She blinked several times and turned her head. Then she remembered – she and Lottie had talked far into the night. Lottie did not talk easily about what had happened to her husband, who had worked for the Resistance, but had had to pretend to be a collaborator. After the war ended a neighbour had tried to kill him before it became known that he hadn't been a traitor. Lottie visited him in the hospital but he would likely be crippled for the rest of his life. Gloria wondered if Willem's night on the bed had been more comfortable than hers on the floor.

"*Goedemorgen,*" said Lottie as Gloria entered the kitchen. Gloria returned the greeting as she accepted a cup of strong tea from her hostess. It was darker than she usually drank it but fortunately Lottie had milk. Gloria poured a little into her mug.

"How did you sleep?" asked Lottie. "It was not very soft, I am sure."

"No, it wasn't," said Gloria truthfully. "But beggars can't be choosers." Lottie looked at her wide-eyed.

"Beggars? Choosers?"

"Oh, sorry," said Gloria with a faint smile. "It's an expression we have in Canada. In this case it means that if someone is taking you in and giving you a place to sleep you shouldn't complain if it isn't very comfortable." Lottie was silent for a minute her brow creased. Finally, her face cleared.

"Oh, I see," she said smiling.

"It doesn't matter," said Gloria with a wave of her hand. "I'll go see how Willem is."

No sooner had she finished speaking than the door opened and Willem emerged fully clothed.

"How do you feel, dear?" asked Gloria.

"Better," he said. "Much better." He crossed the floor and gave her a hug. "Thank you for letting me sleep in the bed." He stepped back and looked at Lottie. "Thanks to both of you. I won't ask how uncomfortable it was on the floor."

"Good," said Lottie pouring a cup of coffee and handing it to Willem. "Then we won't have to fib." She smiled at him to soften her words.

"Now," she said in the brisk manner Gloria remembered, "I have to go to work. Here is the key. Please lock up and leave the key under the mat. I am so glad you found Willem." Gloria stood and impulsively gave her a hug.

"Thank you, Lottie, for everything. I've really enjoyed getting to know you. I'll write after we get to Amsterdam."

"Please do that," said Lottie, shaking Willem's hand. She gathered her things and left the apartment with a final wave. After the door closed Willem looked at Gloria.

"That was an abrupt departure wasn't it? Was she upset about something?" he asked.

"She may have felt a little uncomfortable after last night," Gloria said. "We talked for quite a while and she told me about what happened to her husband during the war. I don't think she finds it easy to talk about that or what happened to her son." Gloria explained how Lottie's son had been killed because he had worked with the Germans during the war.

"Lottie feels disgraced because of her son. The fact that her neighbours thought her husband was a traitor too only adds to her shame. Some neighbours still don't believe he was actually working for the Resistance." When Gloria fell silent Willem shook his head.

"I volunteered to go with the unit that went to Canada and there were times when I missed Holland," he said. "But it was difficult for those who stayed here as well. If Harrie survived in 1940 I wonder where he spent the last five and a half years." Willem put his dishes by the sink and went into the bedroom to collect his belongings.

"There's no way of knowing what Harrie's chances of survival were," Gloria called to him. "We'll just have to press on hoping that he is alive." It even crossed her mind that maybe just maybe Harrie would be in Amsterdam to greet them. She voiced that thought.

"No," Willem said finally. "I do not think that is likely. I fear it will be more complicated than that. It is just a feeling I have."

"If you and Harrie have a special connection because you are twins," Gloria said. "Can't you tell whether he's dead or not? Don't you feel it in your bones?"

"I have never felt a connection to my brother because we were twins," said Willem, "and I do not know what you mean – a feeling it in my bones. All I know is that if the German army captured a Dutch soldier they would not treat him well."

"Perhaps he found another way to survive during the war," she said.

"Perhaps," he said softly ushering Gloria out ahead of him. She stopped to take one last glance, checking that they had left things in good order. She let Willem carry her bag into which all of her things and his few possessions were crammed.

Chapter 28:

Gloria left Willem sitting on a bench and approached the ticket counter. She'd seen the pain in his face and knew his leg was bothering him more than he was admitting. Once they got on the train he'd be able to rest his leg. She opened her purse and took out her wallet. She hoped she'd have enough money to buy the tickets. Worrying about that it took her several minutes to realize that the noises coming from behind where she was standing in line were associated with her husband.

Turning around she saw four youths talking loudly in Dutch and pointing to Willem. She glanced around at the others nearby but no one seemed inclined to interfere. Expelling her breath in disgust she abandoned her place in the line and strode over to the ruckus. Willem was standing with his back against the wall and he was arguing with the youths.

"What's going on?" she yelled. "Willem?" she said in a quieter voice trying to get his attention. She'd put her wallet back in her purse and she slung the strap over her head to free her hands.

Willem and one of the youths were standing toe to toe and Gloria tried without luck to insert herself between them. The youth yelled something in Dutch and pushed Willem who yelled a retort as he regained his balance.

Others in the station were paying attention now and the youths had regrouped. They were making movements of attacking Willem when a loud authoritative voice spoke. At another command from the officer the youths turned and left. One glared at Willem and said something as they were leaving.

"Thank you, Officer," said Gloria politely although she wasn't sure he understood what she was saying. "I don't know what I would've done if you hadn't intervened."

The officer barely glanced at her before turning to Willem and engaging him in conversation. After a few minutes he clapped Willem on the shoulder and left. The loudspeaker announced the next train and Gloria had barely enough time to purchase two tickets before joining Willem in the line to board. Willem limped onto the train grimacing in pain his hand rubbing his thigh. She helped him to get comfortable before asking questions.

"What was that all about?" she asked finally.

"They thought I was Harrie and they called me a traitor," he said through clenched teeth. "Harrie cannot be a traitor."

Gloria sensed his conflicting emotions but he couldn't really know whether his brother was a traitor or not, could he? War changed people and when faced with torture or death surely even a true patriot could've betrayed his country.

"One of them said something as they were leaving," said Gloria. "What did he say?"

"He said he'd get me next time," said Willem wearily, "because no one likes traitors."

Willem leaned his head back and closed his eyes. Gloria rested her head on Willem's shoulder and closed her eyes. After she and Lottie had stopped talking the night before she'd been unable to sleep and had only dozed, waking every time Lottie moved. It had not been restful. But soon they would be back in Amsterdam back to the apartment on Griftstraat. She wondered if she would be able to catch up on her sleep then. Would Willem's parents be upset when they heard the accusations against Harrie?

§ § §

"Lead the way," said Gloria as she followed Willem off the train. "I'll follow. I have no idea where to go."

Willem shook his head but didn't say anything. He offered to carry Gloria's bag since it contained his things as well but she refused.

"It looks like a purse and you would look silly carrying it," she said slinging it across her chest. There were more people here and after their experience with the youths in Emmen, she didn't want to attract undue attention.

"I'll take your arm though," she said putting her hand in the crook of his arm. They walked along streets and over bridges. Going up the slight incline of a bridge crossing the canal Gloria slipped on the cobblestones but Willem caught her before she fell. She smiled her thanks as she tightened her grip on his arm. Finally, even Gloria began to recognize landmarks. Eventually they turned the corner onto Griftstraat. Willem slowed and finally stopped. Gloria slipped her arms around his waist and rested her head on his shoulder.

"It's not going to be any easier if we wait," she said gently. "We'd better just go in." Willem rested his chin on her head.

"*Ja*," he said indicating Gloria should precede him.

At the apartment Gloria knocked on the door but opened it and went in before anyone responded. As she crossed the kitchen she thought she heard someone crying softly.

"Gloria!" Meneer Spelt cried as he rose from his chair. Then his eyes travelled past her. Gloria stopped walking and let Willem come to her side.

"Willem, Willem, Willem," Meneer Spelt switched from one name to the other without hesitation. Gloria stopped as her father-in-law rushed past her and engulfed his son in a hug. Looking into the living room she could see Mevrouw Spelt was sitting in the living room, holding a piece of cloth to her face.

"Willem?" she said in a soft voice lowering her hands. She repeated his name in a louder voice and rose from the chair hurrying towards the two men. They broke apart and her arms went around her son with her husband encircling them both.

Gloria checked in the cupboard for tea, found there was some, and put the kettle on the stove her mind working furiously. There seemed to be more happening here than just joy over Willem's return. Why had Mevrouw Spelt been crying?

Willem and his parents stepped back from one another and they all began talking in Dutch. Meneer Spelt held up his hand. He ushered them all, including Gloria, into the living room and started speaking before anyone had a chance to sit.

"Willem," he said speaking English. "We are glad you are home but we have sad news. Harrie is dead."

Chapter 29:

"Harrie is dead," Willem repeated sinking into a chair. He leaned his head back and closed his eyes. Harrie oh Harrie. I have failed you in the worst way possible. Harrie – his childhood friend and playmate. His co-conspirator. His comrade in arms. Harrie was dead. And Willem hadn't known!

Scenes from his childhood flicked by: He and Harrie skating together; he and Harrie playing tag; he and Harrie in school – responding to each other's name and trying to confuse the teachers. And more recently: he and Harrie as soldiers fleeing the country. But Harrie hadn't made it out of the country. Had Harrie had been dead for five years? And Willem hadn't known!

His mind wandered to the scenes of his dream – the one he'd had in the POW camp. He saw the soldier beating Harrie and he saw Harrie sprawled on the ground, lying still. Harrie was dead. And Willem hadn't known!

Another part of his dream jumped into his mind – Gloria wailing in grief with their dead baby in her arms. His son was dead! What about Gloria? He opened his eyes.

No, she wasn't dead. There she was – her eyes bigger than usual above her hand which was covering her mouth. She sat in the chair to his right.

The pale afternoon sunlight had gone; it was dusk. His hand sought Gloria's other hand squeezing it briefly before releasing it.

"How do you know?" he asked looking at his father his voice hoarse.

"A message came," Pa muttered in a gruff voice. "Some papers…." His voice trailed off. Willem sat straighter and took his handkerchief out of his pocket.

"Who was the message from?" he said wiping his face. His father switched to Dutch.

"The police found a report that the Germans had missed in their clean-up before they left," he said. "A man, Dirk Simmt…"

"I know that name," Willem interrupted. "He's the watch maker, isn't he?"

"Was," Pa said. "The report was of his death but there were two bodies found. One was Dirk's and the police believe the other was Harrie's."

"Why would they think that?" asked Willem impatiently leaning towards his father. His father shrugged his shoulders but didn't say anything. Gloria looked at Willem in confusion. She hadn't understood the conversation.

Willem translated what he and his father had said for Gloria's benefit and then he slumped in his chair. Simmt, a watchmaker from Germany, had opened his business in Amsterdam in 1934 or 1935. He and Harrie had gone to the shop often because Harrie had been fascinated with the process of making time pieces. On a particular day just after Harrie had told his brother he was attracted to men rather than to women, the two of them had gone to the shop. Willem hadn't noticed anything between the older man – he must've been in his 30s – and his brother until just as they were leaving. He'd seen a strange look on Harrie's face and Simmt had been acting odd. A few days later Harrie told him he'd gone to the shop alone.

Harrie hadn't said why and Willem hadn't asked. Gloria leaned forward and touched Willem on the arm.

"Why would Harrie be living there?" she asked softly. "Why wouldn't he come to live here if he was in Amsterdam?" Willem shrugged his shoulders.

"I do not know why he was living with Simmt," said Pa in Dutch. "The police did not say." Willem repeated it in English for Gloria.

"I did not like Simmt ten years ago," said Willem angrily, "and I doubt he has changed. I do not trust him one bit."

No one spoke in the silence except for soft sobs from Mevrouw Spelt. Gloria suddenly jumped up and ran into the kitchen. Willem heard cups rattling and he remembered that Gloria had put the kettle on. She must have made tea. She made two trips getting all four cups into the living room. The tea had milk added to it which wasn't how any of them usually drank it. It must have steeped too long and she'd added milk to make it more palatable. Willem smiled weakly as she handed him his cup. Nothing could make the news they'd just received more palatable.

He looked at his mother who dried her eyes and was trying to smile. He patted her hand. She'd just received news that one son was dead but her other son, whom she'd feared dead, had returned. Joy and sadness. Hope and despair. So similar to the country itself.

Willem began telling Mamma what he had been doing since leaving Amsterdam in 1940 but he paused and turned to his wife.

"Have you told Mamma about our wedding?" he asked. After a pause he added in a lowered voice, "and the baby."

"I told your mother," said Gloria, "I don't know if your father knows." Willem nodded and continued talking. He talked quickly and earnestly looking from one parent to the other.

"Now I have arrived home," he said in English finishing his tale, "only to find that my brother is dead."

§ § §

No one wanted to eat dinner. Mamma and Pa went into their bedroom and stayed there. Willem went to bed early and Gloria followed soon after.

"All my life," Gloria said to Willem as she got into her nightgown, "I have tried to look on the bright side, to remain optimistic against all odds, and to be hopeful even if a situation looks hopeless. But I can't do that now." They got into bed. "I can't find anything positive in any of this."

"For the past five years," said Willem, as they lay together, "I have tried not to think that Harrie was dead in the hope that not thinking about it would keep it from being true. It seems that did not work. This is further proof of how badly I failed my brother." Gloria put her arms around her husband.

"You did not fail him," she said. "It is not your fault he died." After a moment's silence Willem patted Gloria's arm.

"But if it is true that Harrie was living with Simmt," he said softly, "it is very bad news." Gloria looked at him and raised her eyebrows.

"I always suspected," he said quietly, "that Simmt was a homosexual. We do not talk of it but Harrie is one also. Simmt was so much older; he should not have been interested in Harrie. We were in our teens."

"Harrie is a homosexual?" she repeated. "Isn't that against the law?"

"Not in Holland," he said. "It has been legal since the 1800's for men over the age of twenty-one. Simmt was older than that but Harrie was not. That is what I find so wrong about it; Simmt should not have encouraged him."

"What do your parents think about Harrie being a homosexual?" asked Gloria.

"My parents know nothing of this," said Willem. "Do not say anything in front of them. Please. It will hurt them too much." Gloria nodded. Willem had his arm around Gloria as they talked quietly.

"If I had been here in Holland," he said, "I might have saved him. If I had been here when the police delivered the report I would have had some questions for them. I would have found out where he was killed and where his body is buried." Gloria murmured in agreement.

After a few minutes of lying in silence Gloria asked him how his leg was.

"Does it hurt?" she said.

"I have not even thought of it," he replied. "It is a little sore but not bad." He moved his hands.

"Willem, my dear, I have missed you so much," she said gently. His lips claimed hers forcing her into silence.

Chapter 30:

Gloria had been worried that the first time she and Willem were together after not having had marital relations for so many years it would be awkward but it hadn't been — not in the slightest. It had been wonderful. Surely this meant their love would grow into a happily-ever-after as she'd always dreamed. She lay in bed thinking dreamy thoughts of the night before when the memory of what they'd just learned slammed into her consciousness. Harrie was dead!

She slipped out of bed without waking Willem and donned her dressing gown. She sat at the kitchen table in the morning light unable to think of what to do. With half her mind she wanted *Mevrouw* Spelt to get up but with the other half she didn't. She wouldn't know what to say to her mother-in-law even if they'd been able to speak the same language. How could she comfort the woman who'd given birth to Harrie and loved him for more than twenty-five years?

The bedroom door opened and *Mevrouw* Spelt came out. She looked old and worn with circles under her eyes and her hair uncombed. As *Mevrouw* Spelt entered the kitchen Gloria rose and moved towards her opening her arms. She put her arms around the older woman as they came together.

"I'm so sorry. *Het spijt me...*" Gloria's voice broke.

"*Ja ja*" said Mevrouw Spelt waving her hand as if to ward off the news. She hugged Gloria briefly, dropped her arms, and sat at the table. Not knowing what else to do, Gloria returned to her bedroom. Willem was still sleeping. She climbed into bed and curled next to him.

The rest of the day didn't improve. Willem spent the day in bed. Gloria only got out of bed when driven by hunger. Bread and margarine were all she could find to eat; she wasn't about to attempt to cook anything. She didn't see either of Willem's parents although she heard someone in the kitchen once. Pa had come home at 6 a.m. having been sent home and told to take the day off by his boss. No one – not even Anneke – came to visit.

§ § §

Gloria dragged herself out of bed at 8:00 a.m. and was surprised when Willem followed her into the kitchen. Both his parents were already there. Gloria sat at the table while the other three conversed. She looked out the window. It was cloudy and probably raining again. Willem turned to her and switched to English.

"Mamma and Pa are feeling better today," he said. "Pa will sleep most of the day so he can go back to work early tomorrow. Mamma will take it easy today but I want to talk to Meneer Salentijn. I have some questions for him."

"Who is he?" asked Gloria.

"He is a friend of Pa's. I have known him my whole life," said Willem. "During The Great War he was a spy for the Allies. He could ride a bicycle across German lines without arousing suspicion and he reported on German troop positions. One time he was stopped and searched very thoroughly," Willem lowered his voice for the last two words to give them added emphasis. Gloria shuddered not wanting to know what a very thorough search might entail.

"Fortunately, the German soldiers didn't search his bike." Willem continued. "He'd hidden a map of enemy troop lines in the handlebars and if the soldiers had found it they might have just shot him. Holland was neutral during the Great War but the Germans would not have looked kindly on him spying on them." When Gloria shuddered again Willem encircled her with his arms.

"Salentijn was one of the leaders of the Underground in this war," he continued. "He might know what Harrie did during the war. I want to know where Harrie was killed and where his body is buried."

They each kissed Mamma's cheek before they left. Gloria was glad of the chance to get outside after having spent two days doing nothing. Walking in silence beside her husband Gloria noticed more rubble had been removed the closer they got to the downtown section. She was surprised at how many bicycles there were. More bicycles than cars although there were very few cars.

"What will you do if this chap doesn't have the answers you want?" she asked.

"If he cannot offer proof that Harrie is dead," Willem said boldly, "I will look for a sign that he is alive."

"I will come with you," stated Gloria firmly.

Willem stopped to hug Gloria. They stood silently supporting each other for several minutes. Finally they broke apart and Willem stepped back looking around.

"That is how close a bomb came to destroying Salentijn's store," he said, pointing to a store that had sustained minimal damage. Beside it was one brick wall attached to a partial wall with one window in it. Two shutters were hanging crookedly on either side of the window. The rest of the lot was empty – the building was gone.

She followed Willem down a path alongside the building, through a door at the back, and up a flight of stairs.

Chapter 31:

After climbing the set of stairs Willem knocked. The door opened slowly and a gaunt face peered out. The old man held the door open only enough to allow him to see who his caller was.

"*Meneer* Salentijn!" Willem said. He paused and when the old man didn't respond he added, "It's Willem Spelt."

Salentijn smiled then and speaking in Dutch invited him into the apartment. Willem put his arm around Gloria and drew her forward.

"This is my wife, Gloria," he said proudly. "Gloria, this is *Meneer* Salentijn."

Salentijn ushered them into the kitchen before he and Gloria exchanged greetings. Salentijn had switched to English as Willem had known he would. The three of them sat on wooden chairs around the table.

"We have just found out that Harrie is dead," said Willem. "The police told my parents. Apparently there is a report. Have you seen it?"

At first Willem thought Salentijn was going to deny all knowledge, to pretend that he knew nothing. Salentijn had taken a breath but he released it without saying anything. Both men were silent for several moments. Salentijn squared his shoulders.

"I have not seen a report," he said finally. "But it would not surprise me to know that is what the police thought."

"What do you mean?" asked Willem.

"The police, the Dutch police, found the report stuck in a drawer," said Salentijn. "It was something the German army missed in the final clear-out."

"So, the report might not be true? Harrie might not be dead?" asked Willem.

"I have no reason to think the report is not true. Harrie could be dead. In fact it is likely he is," said Salentijn with what sounded like real regret in his voice. "The German army found two dead bodies in the building but they were only able to identify one. When the Dutch police resumed control they asked me who I thought the other body might be. I had sent Harrie to live at Simmt's house so naturally when I told them that they believed the unidentified body was Harrie's." He stopped talking again.

"But it could be someone else's body? Where is Harrie now?"

"Our last contact with Harrie," said Salentijn, "was in May. We have heard nothing from him since then."

"That's eight months ago!" Willem exclaimed. "How can you lose someone for eight months?" He paused. "Wait. Are you saying Harrie was working for the Resistance?"

"I suspected Simmt was spying for the Germans." Salentijn said. "We needed someone to be close to him but it had to be someone we trusted absolutely. I knew it would be dangerous but Harrie was willing to go."

"Was it more dangerous than any other job?"

"A few years ago Simmt told the German police about a Jewish family in hiding at his neighbour's house. The Nazis raided the house and took the Jews and the family to a concentration camp. Simmt never expressed regret for his actions. He felt it was his duty. Because of that he was not well-liked. He had lived in Amsterdam for many years and his neighbours hoped he would be sympathetic towards the Dutch," said Salentijn. "But he was not. We, those of us working for the Resistance, needed to know what other information Simmt was sending to the Germans.

"Towards the end of the war getting the information was even more important. Once the Germans realized they were losing the war we were worried they might try something." Salentijn rubbed his hands over his face and through his short hair making it stand in tufts.

Willem thought Salentijn looked sad but Willem could offer no comfort. He hadn't been here during those years. He hadn't known what it was like to live with an invading army in charge.

"When did Harrie contact you?" Willem asked the older man in an effort to piece together what his brother had done in the intervening years.

"Harrie started working with the Resistance in '42 in Friesland. I do not know what he did prior to that time. He was doing good work for us there living with a farmer and helping to get downed pilots back to England but he had to leave them suddenly in '43."

Salentijn got up and walked into the kitchen. Gloria looked at Willem. He raised his eyebrows but Gloria shook her head fractionally. Willem heard a tap being turned on in the kitchen and a minute later Salentijn reappeared carrying a mug of water. He sat and took a sip before putting the mug on the table.

"I have heard a rumour that Harrie was a traitor," Willem said. "How could it have started?"

"You were not here while the Germans were in charge. They could have started it," said Salentijn sadly. "Who is saying these things?"

"We met some youths in Emmen. They thought I was Harrie at first," said Willem, "and they accused me of being a traitor. They attacked me and would have injured me if Gloria hadn't stepped in and called an officer over. The youths ran off."

"Nothing anyone can say will ever convince me Harrie was a traitor." Willem added, his mouth set and his eyes hard. After a moment he softened his pose.

"It is not your fault," he said in a gentler tone. "You could not control what Harrie was doing."

"He did have a habit of dropping out of sight for a week or two at a time though," said Salentijn. "We would hear nothing for a week after an assignment had ended and then all of a sudden he would contact us and would ask for another assignment."

Willem remained silent. He didn't know what to think about that. He rubbed his hands over his face. Had his brother changed so much?

"There was time between his assignment with the farmer in Friesland," said Salentijn speaking slowly and choosing his word carefully, "and his going to Simmt's for him to travel around. Perhaps he was in the north of Holland for another reason." Salentijn raised his eyebrows and glanced at Gloria before looking back at Willem.

"Why were you in Emmen? What took you to that area?" Salentijn asked.

Willem explained that he'd escaped from a POW camp and had made it as far as the hospital in that city. He added Gloria's story about coming to Holland to find him. While he was talking he tried to figure out why

Salentijn had changed the subject. Did Salentijn know that Harrie was a homosexual? Was that why he had changed the subject?

When Willem made a move to leave Gloria stayed sitting.

"Before we leave," she said, glancing up at Willem. "I want to ask Meneer Salentijn something." As Willem resumed his seat she continued.

"The farmer that Harrie was with — was that Meneer Zweers? Near Sloten?" Salentijn turned to look at her.

"Yes," he said, startled. "He was there for a year or more. Why?"

"I know a little boy," said Gloria, "and I've just discovered that his father worked for the Resistance hiding downed pilots. I wondered if it was the same family." The old man nodded.

"And his neighbour betrayed him. It was sad," he said. His eyes brightened. "You say his son survived? I am glad to hear that. He is all right then?"

"Yes, his son is well," said Gloria not bothering to tell him only one son had lived. No point in adding to his pain.

"Who is Pieter?" Willem asked when he and Gloria were on the sidewalk.

"He's a little boy I met when I was working at the hospital." Gloria spent the next quarter hour talking about Pieter and her feelings for him.

"I hope you will like him, too," she added.

"I do like children," said Willem, "and I am certainly anxious to meet this little boy who has so captured your heart."

When they arrived at the apartment Anneke and *Mevrouw* Spelt were seated at the kitchen table. Both women had red eyes. Anneke jumped up as they entered.

"Willem!" she cried, choking on his name. She added a sentence in Dutch putting her arms around his shoulders. Willem returned the hug and released her.

"Harrie is dead?" Anneke asked stepping away from Willem. Her mouth was trembling and tears were visible in her eyes. She sniffed and got her hankie out of her pocket. The three of them joined *Mevrouw* Spelt sitting at the table.

"I am afraid he is," he said. "Salentijn said Harrie was living at Simmt's house. There is nothing to suggest the report may be wrong." He put his head in his arms on the table. Gloria put her arm across his back and rubbed gently. No one said anything for several minutes.

Anneke stood and put her hand on Willem's back as she walked to the door. Willem raised his hand in response to her goodbye pat. He lifted his head as his mother spoke to him in Dutch. When she finished speaking he translated for Gloria.

"My mother would like you to call her Mamma too," he said, a soft smile on his lips. Gloria stood and moved to where her mother-in-law was sitting. The older woman got to her feet and Gloria hugged her.

"I would be very pleased to call you Mamma," she said. Willem's father had already told her to call him Pa making her feel a part of the family. It was one bright spot in an otherwise dismal day.

Chapter 32:

Gloria had just finished her toast the next morning when she heard a knock on the door. Putting her plate in the sink she wiped her face with her hand and grimaced. Eating toast without having tea to drink was awful but she reminded herself not to complain. After answering the door Gloria was surprised to see Anneke standing outside with a shopping bag in her hand.

"I will go shopping with *Mevrouw* Spelt if she wants to go," Anneke said. Gloria invited her into the kitchen but Mamma was already on her way to the door with her jacket on and a cloth bag in her hand.

Pa had left for work at 3:00 a.m. and Mamma was going shopping. After a two-day hiatus life was returning to normal. The women had just left when Willem got up. Gloria and Willem talked about general things as he ate breakfast. She thought Willem seemed distracted but she didn't question him.

He departed without saying where he was going or when he'd be back. She'd seen the pain in his eyes – the grief for his twin's death – but she wasn't going to ask him about it. He'd always been her strong protector. What if he started crying? She wouldn't know what to do.

Gloria wandered into the living room. A letter from her mother was propped on the table. She picked it up and opened it. Her mother had written a chatty letter talking about what was happening in Stratford. The ladies auxiliary at the church had put on a tea and it had been well attended. A neighbour's son had succumbed to his injuries but it was perhaps a blessing, her mother wrote, for if he'd survived he'd have been crippled for life. Her mother ended her letter asking her if they were short of anything. Beryl's mother sends cigarettes and socks to her daughter and son-in-law and I'm sure I could do the same she wrote, talking about a girl Gloria had gone to school with who'd also married a Dutch soldier.

Gloria wanted to write back immediately. She found paper and a pencil and sat at the table to write asking her mother to send cigarettes, socks to fit Willem and Pa, and toilet paper. There was always the possibility that the cigarettes would be pilfered but Gloria hoped that her parcel would remain intact. After finishing that letter, she dashed off a quick note to Lottie informing her that they were in Amsterdam but not mentioning anything about Harrie. Willem had not returned by the time she finished so she walked to the corner store to buy stamps.

Gloria's parents had given her Canadian money for her trip and she had some of her own money. She'd been prepared to change it into Dutch guilders when she arrived in Holland but upon her arrival she'd discovered the country was not using guilders. The Germans had done away with the currency in each of the countries they'd occupied during the war and replaced it with another coin. Now that the war was over it was taking time to get the currency converted back to the national money. Instead of changing her money into guilders she'd had to change it into the ersatz money the country was using. On the way home she put the letters in the mailbox on the sidewalk.

Gloria had brought a book with her, Emma, by Jane Austen. She took it from her suitcase and for the next few hours was lost in 19th century England with a romance gone wrong. She was taking a break from her book when Mamma arrived home with Anneke right behind her carrying two bags of groceries. Anneke handed one bag to Gloria before leaving without saying anything.

When Mamma went into the kitchen Gloria returned to her book. Willem didn't return until after Pa was home. Gloria was half-way through her book but she put her bookmark in place as soon as she saw her husband.

"You're back," she said as Willem took off his jacket.

"I decided I needed to do something so I went to the police station," he said irritably. He was scowling. "But it was a waste of time. Adri was not working today." He stomped into the bedroom but after half an hour he came back out and apologized to Gloria.

"It is not your fault," he said speaking more calmly, "that I could not talk to Adri." He took a deep breath and smiled self-consciously at Gloria.

Mamma was busy in the kitchen. They both looked in that direction as Mamma called them to dinner.

"*Kom en eet.*"

Gloria exchanged a small smile with Willem as he indicated she should precede him into the kitchen. Dinner, such as it was, was served.

§ § §

Gloria awoke in the morning feeling well-rested. When she joined Willem for breakfast he said he'd had a better night's sleep as well. He spoke to his mother in Dutch saying something that held her attention. When he finished speaking Dutch he told Gloria he was going to invite Anneke to join the two of them in their apartment. A half hour later the three of them were gathered around the Spelt's kitchen table.

"I have explained to Mamma," said Willem, "that there is a rumour going around that Harrie betrayed his country and that may be why he was killed. We are all sad that he is dead but we cannot do anything to change that. We can prove that he was not a traitor though and that is what I intend to do." He looked at Gloria and Anneke in turn. "I would like both of you to help me. Will you?"

"Yes, I will," said Gloria. "What do you plan to do?"

"I will too," said Anneke nodding her head in emphasis. "What do you want me to do?"

"Dirk's sister, Ursula, came from Germany to live with Dirk and Harrie in 1944. We need to find out where she is," said Willem. "But before we do that I will go to the police station again and this time I hope to be able to read the report. I want to know exactly what it says."

Gloria and Anneke sat without talking while Willem spoke to his mother in Dutch again. When he finished talking Anneke stood and said it was time for her to leave.

"How is Pieter doing?" Gloria asked quickly.

"He is not at the hospital any longer," Anneke said. "His arm has healed and he has been sent to live with a couple from the Dutch Reform Church." Gloria sighed in relief.

"He was placed with a family then?" she asked. "I discovered that he is an orphan – his parents died in a concentration camp. Will that make a difference to what happens to him?"

"You can tell the family he's with now," Anneke said getting a piece of paper from her purse. "I will give you their address if you want to visit him."

Gloria handed her a pencil and motioned for her to sit at the table.

"Was Pieter glad to leave the hospital?" Gloria asked.

"I think he was not happy," said Anneke. "He cried when he had to go with the Mueller's. Before he left he made me promise to tell you where he was living."

"Willem and I need to go there," said Gloria. "It's time Willem met him."

She looked at her husband and he nodded. When they were getting ready for bed a few hours later Gloria reiterated her promise to take Willem to meet Pieter.

"I'm sure you'll like him," she said. "He's a very sweet kid and he's suffered so much."

"If you like him," said Willem, "then I am sure I will like him also."

Gloria snuggled closer.

Chapter 33:

Willem pushed the door and entered the police station. He'd been too upset the day before to notice the familiar smell. It brought back memories of him and Harrie doing their training before the war, leaving him grief-stricken and close to tears. As he struggled to contain his emotions he spotted Adri Bloom who had been a new recruit with him and Harrie.

"Adri!" he called extending his hand. The other man hesitated before gripping his hand. Adri looked different. He was thinner and he'd lost the spark of humour that had warmed his otherwise austere face.

"Willem," he said in a cool voice. "You are back in Amsterdam. What are you doing here? We are not ready to resume police training."

Along with his physical appearance his manner had also changed. It was not the welcome back Willem had been expecting. Adri had been one of his best friends when they were in training together.

"Is there some place we can go to talk?" Willem asked in Dutch looking around. A few of the other policemen were looking at him in an unfriendly way. Adri led the way to an unused room and motioned for Willem to go in first.

"I'd like to see the report of Harrie's death if I may," Willem said icily. He wasn't as good as Gloria was at understanding underlying emotions but even he recognized the hostility that was greeting his presence in the station.

"I doubt I can show you," said Adri. His face softened. "I was sorry to know Harrie had been killed at first," he said.

"What do you mean 'at first'?"

"Before I realized the reason why he'd been killed"

"Why was he killed?"

"Consorting with the enemy," Adri said. He paused before continuing. "Look Willem. I really liked both you and Harrie when we started our police training but the war changed everything. I didn't get out of Holland in '40 but I worked as a policeman during the war. If Harrie didn't get out when you did he could've worked here too. Even without finishing our training, there was still work to be done."

Adri moved behind the desk to sit. He indicated Willem could sit in front of the desk.

"Harrie would not have worked with the enemy," said Willem in a low voice enunciating each word. "And I will prove it. That's why I want to see the report. I want to know where he was killed and what happened to the body."

"It was probably buried or it may have been burned. There has been too much death to make sure all the bodies were buried properly," said Adri. "The one body was identified as Simmt's by the Germans. The other body was shot in the face and the Germans didn't even try to find out who it was." Adri got up and looked out the window, standing very still. He finally took a deep breath and turned back to face Willem.

"We showed the report to people in the Resistance," said Adri resuming his seat. "I think it was Salentijn who suggested it might have been Harrie because he was living there." He pursed his lips. Sensing a change in his attitude Willem asked again.

"Can I see a copy of the report?" he said softly, lifting his eyebrows.

"Wait here," said Adri as he stood. He left the room but didn't shut the door. Willem could hear voices in the hall but he couldn't tell what anyone was saying. The voices did not sound angry which led Willem to wonder if he'd been mistaken in his initial impressions. Adri returned after five minutes and placed a folded piece of paper on the desk.

"If asked," he said tersely, "you didn't get it from me."

Willem took the piece of paper and put it in his shirt pocket without looking at it. He nodded once and leaned back in his chair.

"How is the changeover going?" Willem asked referring to the shift in policing now that the war was over.

"It's getting settled," said Adri. "The Nazis left at the end of the war and it was absolute chaos until the Canadian and American soldiers took over."

"I had just arrived back in Amsterdam when my parents learned of Harrie's death," said Willem. "I may not reapply to work with the force here in Amsterdam. I got married while I was in Canada and my wife will want to move back to Canada as soon as we can."

"Will you work for the police there?" asked Adri.

"I'd like to get on with the police force in the town where my parents-in-law live," said Willem. The sounds from the hall had diminished and Willem judged it was time to leave. He stood and shook hands with Adri before leaving the room. In the hall an older man stepped in front of Willem. He jabbed at Willem with his forefinger.

"Your brother did not die in that fire," he said angrily. "I know what really happened." Willem was so shocked it took him a moment to respond.

"What do you mean? Harrie isn't dead? Where is he?" Willem's first response was to feel hope but one look at the man's face and he knew that wasn't the case. This man was angry, very angry.

"Harrie, the Nazi-lover, lived with that Nazi for years pretending to be loyal to the Dutch queen," the man said loudly his face getting red, "but when the Nazi was killed, Harrie helped his girlfriend get back to Germany."

"Vim, you don't know that for sure," said Adri trying to calm the older man. Another policeman came and escorted the older man away. Adri turned back to Willem.

"I'm sorry," he said. "That chap helps out in the office but he gets his facts mixed up."

"How many others think that way? How many others think that Harrie betrayed his country?" asked Willem looking at the man's retreating back. From the looks on the faces of those policemen near him there were several who believed what the man was saying. Willem looked at Adri.

"You don't believe Harrie was a traitor, do you?" Willem asked. Adri looked tired and suddenly Willem didn't want to know. If Adri thought Harrie was a traitor Willem didn't want to hear it. He turned and walked out of the building without waiting for Adri's reply.

§ § §

When Willem arrived at the apartment, Gloria was sitting at the kitchen table.

"I have the report," he said patting his pocket before hanging his jacket on a hook. Gloria stood to accept his hug and they each took a seat at the table. He pulled the paper out of his pocket and put it on the table. Gloria looked at it but it was written in Dutch.

"What does it say?" she asked.

"There were two male bodies," said Willem. "And one was definitely Simmt's."

"Does it say who found the bodies?"

"No. The other body was shot in the face. And the description of the body does seem like it could be Harrie. Black hair, medium build. Adri agreed with that conclusion."

"That's still rather vague," said Gloria. "It could've been someone else."

"Who else?" questioned Willem. "Harrie was living there. It was just as the war was ending. People would not have been going to visit their neighbours. We may have to accept that it was Harrie."

"There are those in the police ranks who do not believe it," Willem said slowly. "They believe that Harrie turned traitor and helped Ursula escape to Germany."

He put his head on his arms on the table. Gloria rubbed his back.

"Does your friend, the one you went to see, does he believe that also?" she asked. Willem raised his head.

"I do not know," he said. "Likely he does. I am afraid that is the prevailing attitude – that because Harrie was living with Dirk he was a Nazi sympathizer and after the sister, Ursula, came to live with them Harrie fell in love with Ursula and helped her return to Germany." After a moment's silence Willem continued.

"They do not know Harrie the way I do," he said in a stronger voice. "I doubt even Adri knows. It is impossible that Harrie could fall in love with Ursula. I will never believe that Harrie has changed so much."

"Did the police finger-print the body?" asked Gloria suddenly in a perplexed tone.

"They did not even try," he said. "I am not sure why they did not. Maybe the body was too badly decomposed." He took a deep breath and expelled it forcefully. Gloria put her hand on his arm and gave him a loving squeeze. She moved away from the table and when she sat at the table again he saw she had a pencil and a pad of paper.

"We need to decide what we're going to do to prove Harrie wasn't a traitor," she said briskly. She assumed the position of a stenographer – pencil poised over paper.

Willem gazed at her fondly. She obviously wasn't going to let him spend time becoming maudlin. There was something that needed to be done and she was going to find a way to do it.

"We need to talk to the sister," he said decisively.

"Great!" said Gloria. "How do we find out where she is? Didn't Mr. Salentijn say she was missing?"

"She is," said Willem. "But we know where she, Harrie, and Simmt were living. Maybe a neighbour knows where she went."

Gloria wrote: 'Find sister' on the paper and underlined it.

§ § §

"We likely would have gotten married whether there was a baby or not," said Willem. The conversation had drifted from talking about Harrie to talking about their marriage. "It was hastened by the war, of course."

"The war also brought us together," said Gloria, "if you hadn't come to Canada with the Dutch Army we wouldn't have met. We must remember that."

Willem reached over and patted her knee. He hoped she wasn't going to pressure him into making any decisions until after they'd cleared Harrie's name. He could not leave Holland until after he'd proved Harrie was not a traitor.

"That is true," he said aloud. "Hitler invading Holland brought one tiny spark of light amidst so much tragedy."

Chapter 34:

Gloria blotted her lips and put the tube of lipstick back in her purse. Her first disastrous experience with pancake make-up had caused her to stop using it altogether, but she did like to highlight her lips and she'd packed a tube of her favourite shade to bring with her.

Pancake make-up was all the rage in the 1930s. She'd wanted to try it when she was going to a dance in an effort to cover her pimples. Part way through the evening she'd chanced to see her reflection in a mirror and had been horrified to discover rivers of sweat carving gullies on her face. After that evening she'd vowed never to wear foundation cream again and she'd held true to her promise.

She surveyed her face in the mirror. Her hair had grown to shoulder length with a hint of natural curl at the ends. She was ready to go.

Gloria was taking Willem to meet Pieter. She hadn't seen the little boy for weeks and she was anxious to see how he was doing. The recent events around Harrie's death had eclipsed the rest of her life and she was feeling nervous about this meeting. She'd allowed herself to entertain the idea of adopting the little boy but she could only do that if Willem liked him too. If he and Willem didn't get along those hopes would be dashed.

The sun was trying to shine but it was still cool. Gloria was glad of the fast pace Willem set. In another couple of months it would be the one-year anniversary of the end of the war and she wondered if any of them would feel like going to the celebrations now that they knew Harrie was dead. Gloria felt pulled in two directions. She felt miserable about Harrie because she knew Willem and his parents were grieving. She regretted that she would never have a chance to meet Willem's twin brother. At the same time she was happy and excited that she'd found Willem and they were getting along well together.

When they reached the correct address, Gloria approached the door and knocked. A pleasant-looking woman answered. Gloria tried out her Dutch.

"Is this where Pieter Zweers is staying?" she asked only faltering once.

The woman in the doorway nodded. She was wearing the traditional Dutch garb of a long skirt and matching long-sleeved top with an apron. Wooden shoes peeked out from under the skirt. On her head was a traditional Dutch cap. She had just started to answer in Dutch when, through the doorway, Gloria saw Pieter and she waved at him.

"Nurse Spelt," he cried running towards her. "You are here!"

Pieter rushed forward past Mrs. Mueller and into Gloria's arms. She gave him a good hug but then released him.

"You know Pieter then. Come in, come in," the Dutch woman said. She'd pronounced the boy's name, "Payter." Gloria stepped into the hall and Willem followed shutting the door behind him. As Gloria began introducing Willem to Mrs. Mueller he stepped into the open and when Willem's face was visible Pieter gasped.

"*Oom*," he whispered in a soft voice. He added a sentence in Dutch. Gloria looked from Pieter to Willem. What did the little boy mean? She squatted down and gently turned Pieter so he was looking at her.

"Why are you calling him uncle?" she asked softly. Willem knelt beside Gloria and smiled at the boy.

"What do you mean it is too late?" he asked. "Too late for what?" Pieter stared at Willem intently.

"You have come back," he said in English, "but it is too late. Tonny is dead."

Pieter looked at Gloria with tears in his eyes. Gloria put her arms around the little boy while she tried to make sense of what he was saying. Another little boy came into the room and gestured for Pieter to go with him. At first Pieter ignored him but as the boy tugged at his arm he squirmed to get out of Gloria's arms. She watched the two boys run into the other room.

Her mind was working frantically. She thought back to what the woman in Sloten had told her about Pieter's family and then she remembered what Salentijn had said. Suddenly it made sense. She stood and looked at her husband.

"He thinks you're Harrie," she said to Willem. Mrs. Mueller motioned for them to precede her into the living room.

"No need to stand at door. Sit down, sit down," she said pointing to the chairs. They all sat.

"We owe you an explanation," Gloria said to the other woman in English speaking slowly and carefully. "We've just discovered that Willem's twin brother, Harrie, was at the Zweer's farm during the war. I suspect that Pieter thinks Willem is Harrie." Willem repeated it in Dutch although

Mrs. Mueller had nodded obviously understanding parts of what Gloria had said.

"Pieter come a week ago," said Mrs. Mueller in broken English. "I know nothing from before. Our church take in children with no family. We take Pieter."

"When I introduced Willem just now Pieter called Willem '*Oom*,'" said Gloria. "Is that what he calls your husband?" Perhaps Pieter called all men that he knew well 'uncle'.

Mevrouw Mueller looked at her blankly and Willem spoke swiftly to translate.

"Pieter call him Meneer Mueller," she said. "He is a *politieagent*." She added proudly.

"Is your husband with the Amsterdam Police force?" Willem asked.

There followed a conversation in Dutch that Gloria couldn't follow. When they finished talking, Willem indicated he was ready to leave. Gloria asked Mrs. Mueller if she and Willem could come to visit Pieter again.

"Always welcome to visit," said Mrs. Mueller nodding and smiling, "always welcome." She pronounced it "allus."

"*Danke*," said Gloria as she and Willem left. When they were on the sidewalk Gloria asked Willem what he and Mrs. Mueller had talked about.

"As she said her husband is a policeman," said Willem, "and she is very proud of the fact that he stayed true to the Dutch people when the Nazis came. Sometimes he received beatings because he did not whip the Jews as the Nazis commanded. He refused to harm Dutch citizens no matter what religion they were." They walked on in silence.

"That was very brave of him," Gloria said suddenly. "Do you think many policemen did that?"

"No," said Willem. "Mevrouw Mueller said that most of the policemen followed the orders of the German army because they couldn't risk being fired or worse."

Chapter 35:

Two days later Willem suggested they go to the apartment building where his brother had lived with Simmt. He wanted to get information about Simmt's sister Ursula. Gloria grabbed her sweater and followed Willem out the door into a perfect spring day that was considerably warmer than it had been.

"Do we need a cover story?" she asked as they rounded a corner. "To explain why we're there asking questions this many months later. Will she think it's odd to be coming around now rather than right after it happened?"

"Hmmm," he said slowing his pace. "I had not thought of that. I am no longer a policeman so I cannot be asking in that capacity."

Willem had gotten his discharge from the army but he had not signed up with the Amsterdam police force again. He thought it likely that he and Gloria would immigrate to Canada although they had not made a firm decision yet.

"Perhaps we could pretend to be reporters," she said, "researching what people need to re-start their businesses now that the war is over."

"That might work," said Willem. "I'll leave it up to you to decide if we need such a story."

Willem started paying attention to the numbers of the buildings they passed. He knew Simmt had lived at 4 Handelstraat, apartment #5 on the second floor. When they got to the right apartment building he led the way to the apartment directly below the one where Simmt had lived and knocked on the door. When a woman answered he stayed back while Gloria introduced herself.

"We have a few questions about Dirk Simmt who used to live in this building," she said.

The woman hesitated but then shut the door and loosened the chain before opening it again. The woman was holding a baby on her hip. She looked past Gloria to Willem and gasped.

"Harrie?" she said cautiously. As Gloria moved into the room with Willem right behind her, the woman caught a better look at Willem.

"I am sorry," she said shifting her baby to the other hip. "I thought you were someone else." She motioned them into the kitchen and turned to walk down the hall saying something in Dutch over her shoulder.

"She's putting the baby in his crib," Willem said softly to Gloria. They sat together on one side of the table and waited for the woman to return. Since she had obviously mistaken Willem for Harrie, it was pointless trying to defend their presence with a cover story. Their best bet was to tell the truth as much as possible.

"You have questions about Dirk Simmt," the woman said making it a question.

"We do," said Gloria, "As I said before my name is Gloria Spelt and this is my husband Willem."

"*Mij nam is Renate Fischer,*" she said extending her hand. Willem and Gloria shook it in turn. "You look so much like Harrie," she said. "At first I thought he had come back."

"Did you know Harrie and Dirk well?" asked Willem.

"I talk to them to say hi only," said Renate. "Then they move away without saying goodbye. That was strange."

 "When did they move?" asked Willem gently

"Let me see," said Renate. "Erik was born last May and I had to go into the hospital. My husband said one day he came home and they were gone. It was in June." She stopped talking, listening to baby sounds coming from down the hall.

"Why do you want to know?" she asked as she started to get up. "Wait a minute. I have to go to Erik."

While Renate was out of the room Gloria and Willem held a hurried conversation about how they'd handle the rest of the interview. They agreed Gloria would ask the questions. Renate returned holding the baby in her arms. She pulled up her sweater preparing to feed her baby.

Willem noted that Gloria looked the other way. Since Gloria was a nurse he thought she should be comfortable with women nursing their babies in public but perhaps she'd never encountered it before. He'd seen his cousin feeding her baby this way and it didn't bother him.

"Why do you want to know?" Renate repeated, starting to feed the baby.

"We are trying to find out where Dirk's sister is. She hasn't been seen since the end of the war. Could she have gone to her home in Germany?" Gloria asked.

"Ursula? Perhaps she did. I have not seen her. She was strange," Renate said. "I not like her at all. When it was just Dirk and Harrie my husband and I get along with them. But after Ursula came things change."

"How did it change?" asked Gloria.

"Other men started coming to the apartment," said Renate. "Many strange men with loud voices. Some men have short hair and look like soldiers. We were afraid to report them for being too noisy. One of my neighbours did that and the next day she find a dead mouse wrapped in a paper with her name on it. She not say more after that."

"Did you know that two dead bodies were found in the apartment?" Gloria asked.

"We knew something was wrong," said Renate, "from the smell. My husband finally called the police. He not want the German police to come; he want to wait for the Dutch police to be in charge again. But the smell was really bad." Renate repositioned the baby against her shoulder to burp him. "After soldiers take the bodies no more smell."

"Do you know who the dead people were?" asked Gloria.

"No one ever told us," said Renate, rubbing the baby's back. "We not have anything to do with it." She glared at Gloria, repeating that she and her husband weren't involved. The baby had fallen asleep and Renate stood holding the baby gently in her arms.

"I have to put him in his crib," she said leaving the room.

"I do not think I should answer more questions," she said in an unfriendly tone when she returned to the kitchen a short time later. "We did nothing wrong. Dirk and Harrie moved. Ursula is gone and I am glad. That is all I know."

Gloria snatched her sweater from the back of the chair before following Willem out the door. They didn't slow their pace until they were outside on the sidewalk.

"That was interesting," said Gloria. "I wonder what caused Renate to change so quickly?"

"When she put the baby in his crib," said Willem, "she had time to reconsider why we were asking these questions. Perhaps she was afraid we were going to accuse her of Dirk's death. From there it would not be difficult for us to think she had killed Harrie too."

"I guess," said Gloria. "Seems a stretch though. I thought she might accuse the other men of doing something – the ones who looked like soldiers. That would make sense."

"She's still afraid of those men," said Willem, "even this long after the end of the war. That might mean that something really bad happened and she hasn't gotten over it."

Chapter 36:

Gloria was awakened by Mamma shaking her shoulder. It was still dark and Gloria struggled to clear her head of the dream she'd been having. She and her sister were at the Bob-Lo Island Amusement Park on Bois Blanc Island in the Detroit River. They were on the roller coaster but something was wrong with the ride. It was going too fast. They were going to crash!

"Gloria," Mamma spoke in a soft but urgent voice. She shook Gloria's shoulder again. "Gloria! *Sta op!*"

Gloria pushed her hair out of her eyes as she sat. Mamma put her finger to her lips and beckoned. Reaching for her dressing gown Gloria thrust her arms into the sleeves as she followed the older woman out of the room. Two policemen were standing in the kitchen.

"Are you Mrs. Spelt?" one said. He was the taller of the two and he was standing slightly in front of the other man. Gloria nodded not taking her eyes from his face.

"*Mevrouw* Mueller asked us to contact you," he said. "Her husband, Constable Mueller, has been badly injured and she asked if you could take Pieter her foster son."

Gloria's mind was in a whirl. Mevrouw Mueller – the friendly woman who had accepted Pieter into her house – her husband had been injured? She looked questioningly at Mamma and raised her eyebrows in a silent plea. Mamma spoke to the officer in Dutch and he replied. They reached an agreement. Mamma looked at Gloria with a small smile nodding her head slightly. Gloria turned her gaze to the officer.

"When will Pieter come?" she asked. "What happened to Mr. Mueller?"

"We cannot tell you the details of the accident but Mevrouw Mueller is at the hospital with her husband," said the officer. After a pause he added, "The two little boys are at a neighbour's. Mevrouw Mueller's son will go to his aunt's but she cannot take Pieter too. Mevrouw said to bring him here, if you agree."

"Yes, of course bring Pieter here," said Gloria. The poor boy; he must be so frightened.

The officers thanked her and nodded to Mamma before they left. In the sudden silence Gloria suddenly remembered Willem's heart-breaking acknowledgement from the day before. She glanced at Mamma who looked drained and exhausted. As Mamma went back to her bedroom Gloria thought she moved more briskly – as if the thought of a child coming to stay had given her new energy. Gloria put the kettle on. She hoped there was tea but if not, she'd have a cup of hot water.

An hour later Gloria opened the door to admit a large woman, her blonde hair in two braids. She was dressed in a uniform and holding Pieter by the hand. She handed the bag she was carrying to Gloria. Gloria put the bag on the table and knelt to speak to the boy.

"Come in Pieter," she said gently starting to undo his coat. His eyes were red but the rest of his face was pale.

"You must be very tired," she said softly. "We have a bed for you to sleep in."

At the mention of sleep he suddenly burst into tears.

"No! No! I will not sleep," he cried. He put his arms out as if to hug her and then stopped and let them go limp. Gloria hugged him and as his arms went around her neck she stood and held him in her arms. The woman at the door handed some papers to Mamma and left without saying anything more.

Gloria carried the little boy towards her bedroom. When she opened the door, Willem was sitting on the bed his hair tousled and his eyes closed. His eyes flew open as he stood. Gloria walked into the room with the little boy in her arms. She didn't say anything but when Pieter saw Willem he cried out and reached towards him. Willem opened his arms.

"Oom," Pieter said sleepily as he relaxed in Willem's arms. "Oom."

Gloria helped Mamma spread a blanket on the floor and then she motioned to Willem to put the sleeping boy on it. He did so without waking the boy. Willem ushered Mamma out of the room ahead of him. Alone with Pieter in the room Gloria covered him with another blanket and tucked him in. But when Gloria tried to tiptoe away he cried out.

"No! Stay with me! Where is *Oom*?"

Gloria went back and knelt beside him so she could rub his back lightly. He lay quietly with his eyes open.

"I have to explain something to you, dear," said Gloria gently. "That man was not *Oom* Harrie. He is Harrie's brother, Willem." She wasn't sure Pieter heard her.

"I want *Oom* Harrie," he said in a sleepy voice. Gloria murmured softly and continued to rub his back. After a few minutes she began singing nursery rhymes that she remembered from her childhood. Pieter lay with his eyes open for quite a while but eventually his eyes closed and stayed that way.

She stayed where she was for a few more minutes not touching him or singing. When he seemed finally to be asleep she got up and left the room. In the living room Willem was sprawled in a chair. Mamma had gone back to bed. As Gloria approached him he opened his eyes.

"Is he asleep?" he asked softly.

"Yes," said Gloria. At the same time, she heard a cry from the bedroom.

"Come," she said turning and opening the door again. "We might as well go to bed too."

In the morning Gloria awoke before Pieter but lay quietly beside Willem. She was stiff from having spent a good part of the night on the floor. Every time she'd gotten into bed Pieter had cried out wanting her to stay close. Finally he'd fallen asleep and she'd been able to go to bed herself. As she lay there watching the little boy, Pieter opened his eyes. She put her finger to her lips and motioned for him to follow. When the two of them left the bedroom, Willem was still snoring softly.

Gloria and Pieter were just finishing their toast when Mamma came out of her bedroom. She caught sight of Pieter and her mouth started to curve into a smile. Pieter stayed close to Gloria while she introduced him to *Mevrouw* Spelt. When Mamma talked to him in his own language Pieter's eyes grew big. He looked from Mamma to Gloria and back again a smile slowly spreading over his face.

"*Je kan Nederlands spreken,*" he said excitedly. Mamma nodded and held out her arms.

Pieter went to her glancing at Gloria as he did so. She signalled yes encouraging him with a slight wave of her hand. Pieter held the older woman's hand as they went into the living room. Gloria sipped her cup of tea feeling almost happy. When she peeked in to see what was happening, Pieter showed her a train engine.

"Oma found this in a closet," he told her excitedly. "She said *Oom* Harrie used to play with it." He ran it along the floor. "It used to have tracks to go with it but she traded them for food," he added matter-of-factly.

Gloria smiled at him. She was glad Mamma had asked him to call her "Oma" or "Grandma." They were obviously feeling quite comfortable with each other.

Chapter 37:

Willem rapped firmly on the door and when it opened he stepped into the room.

"I have come alone," he said speaking Dutch and taking Salentijn by surprise. "I want you to tell me everything you can about what Harrie did during the war. You left something out when I was here with Gloria. What did you not want to say in front of her?"

Salentijn looked at him steadily for a minute. He invited Willem to sit in a chair with a wave of his hand.

"There were things I couldn't say in front of a lady," said Salentijn. He sat in a chair holding himself erect. "I think I know where Harrie went before we sent him to Simmmt's."

"Where did he go?" Willem asked quickly leaning forward.

"Harrie was with Zweers as I told your wife," said Salentijn. He took his handkerchief out of his pocket and wiped his face. "He did not contact us immediately after leaving Zweers. I would not have thought anything about that, except one of our members mentioned seeing him in Emmen in the company of another man. They were together." He emphasized the last word. Willem knew what he meant.

"You see why I couldn't mention it in front of your wife," Salentijn added.

Willem expelled his breath and leaned back in the chair. The two men sat facing each other across the kitchen table. Willem thought Salentijn had aged considerably over the past five and half years and he was sorry to have to distress him further. Salentijn shifted in his seat.

"A year or more after we sent Harrie to spy on Simmt," he said, "the sister showed up. Some of our members felt that Harrie was falling in love with her. I knew that was not happening but I couldn't offer proof without blowing Harrie's cover. Harrie was sending us good information and he was trusted. If any of our members felt a reason to suspect Harrie they would not have trusted the information he was giving us.

"We knew Simmt was German and we knew he had moved his business to Amsterdam in the early 1930's. Just before the war started we heard that his cousin, a German Nazi, had tried to recruit him as a spy. We didn't know if the Nazi was successful," Salentijn continued, "and we thought it was prudent to keep an eye on him, on Simmt. But if Simmt was a spy for the Nazis, that increased the danger for Harrie being there. Simmt's neighbours knew he was German and that he still had ties to Germany. To some people that branded Harrie as a traitor but Harrie knew the risks he was taking. We had discussed it.

"After we knew that the Germans were no longer using Simmt we tried to get word to Harrie, telling him to leave but we were unable to do so. The war was ending. The Allies and eventually the Dutch police were taking over control from the German army. Our lines of communication were in disarray. Then Simmt disappeared. And then his sister disappeared. Finally even Harrie was gone. We had no idea where he was. We would not know anything about Simmt's death except for that report."

Willem sat quietly trying to absorb what Salentijn was saying. He knew it had been a chaotic time from what Adri, at the police station, had told him. Did that account for the police and the Resistance losing track of Simmt and his sister and of Harrie? Was there something else Salentijn wasn't telling him?

"Where was the sister from?" asked Willem speaking more gently this time.

"I might have that information in my desk," said the old man getting up and crossing the floor. He returned with a piece of paper in his hands.

"Marl," he said simply.

"The sister was from Marl, Germany," repeated Willem.

"That's what this report says," said Salentijn. "I have no reason to doubt it."

Willem thanked his friend as they shook hands. He was glad to note that the older man's colour was better. Perhaps talking to Willem had been good for him. If this was one less thing the old man had to feel guilty about his trip had not been in vain. Willem heard Salentijn lock the door once he was through it.

Back at the apartment Willem filled Gloria in on what Salentijn had told him ending with the announcement that Ursula had likely come from Marl in Germany.

"So, if we want to question her about Harrie," said Gloria, "we'll have to travel there. Is that what you're thinking?" Willem nodded his head slowly in agreement.

"But we must remember what Renate, the neighbour, said too," he added. "She was very afraid."

"Perhaps she saw Ursula killing Dirk and Harrie," said Gloria. "That would certainly make me feel frightened if I were in her situation."

"Why would Ursula kill her brother and Harrie?" said Willem. "That doesn't seem likely."

The two of them were sitting at the table in the kitchen. Pieter was in the living room with Willem's parents. Willem could hear the three of them talking although he couldn't make out what they were saying. Pieter laughed occasionally.

How likely was it that Ursula had been the one to kill the two men? But perhaps it explained why Renate suddenly turned hostile.

"If Renate was starting to forget what had happened," said Willem, "and then suddenly we showed up and started asking questions that might explain the change in her behaviour." He drummed his fingers on the table. Did he want to take Gloria with him to question a murder suspect? Someone who perhaps thought she'd gotten away with it and was safe?

"If Ursula killed Dirk and Harrie and she knew that Renata had seen her do it, why not kill her too?" Willem said. Gloria rolled her eyes.

"Don't ask me," she said. "I don't go around killing people so I wouldn't know." Her voice had gotten louder and Willem turned around to look into the living room. He wanted to make sure Gloria's words hadn't upset Pieter but the little boy wasn't paying them any attention. He was playing with crayons that Pa had given him. Pa had also taken to his role as grandparent.

Willem took Gloria's hands in his.

"I am sorry," he said. "I did not mean to upset you. I am just trying to…" he paused and releasing one hand, made circles in the air with his free hand.

"Play devil's advocate," Gloria said. He nodded.

"I know," she said. "I'm not blaming you." She ran her fingers through her hair. "Not knowing is so frustrating."

Nothing was said about Harrie or Ursula or Dirk for the rest of the day. Willem and Gloria took Pieter for a walk that afternoon. The park area in which Willem remembered swinging on a set of swings when he was a child was bare. It was simply a patch of dirt but Pieter found a stick and used it to draw letters. It was warm and Willem was content to sit and watch the little boy playing in the dirt. His mind went over what Salentijn had told him and he tried again to make sense of it.

Had Harrie turned traitor? Had he fallen in love with Ursula and betrayed his country through her? Willem didn't think that was possible but he hadn't spoken to his brother for more than five years. Surely his brother, his twin, could not be so different from the man he used to be after only five and a half years! Willem could not think of any situation in which he would have betrayed his country. He could not imagine a scenario where he would be disloyal to his friends. And he had known his brother well enough as they were growing up to know that such an idea had been as abhorrent to Harrie as it had been to him. But then he remembered Gloria saying that war changes people. Willem did not know what his brother had coped with during the war; perhaps whatever had happened to him had changed him. He sighed and got to his feet.

Gloria looked at him as she stood and called to Pieter but she didn't say anything. The three of them walked home slowly. The adults listened to Pieter chattering about the war being over and being able to start going to school.

Shortly after they arrived home Mamma served dinner. True to her word Anneke had asked if the Spelts could be given extra food coupons to cover Pieter staying with them. Since he was a child they'd also been given extra milk vouchers. Their meals were not lavish but they'd improved in the short time Willem had been home. He knew many food items were still rationed.

Pieter slept in their bedroom on a cot which Maartje had loaned them. Willem recognized that Gloria was happy to have Pieter living with them. The boy was adjusting to his new life but Willem didn't feel as close a connection to Pieter as Gloria did. Willem liked him – he was an intelligent inquisitive child but Willem believed that raising a child was a big responsibility.

Since talking to Adri and Salentijn Willem's guilt about Harrie had returned in spades. It was his fault Harrie had not gotten out of Holland which meant it was his fault that Harrie was dead. If Willem couldn't look after his brother, how did he think he was going to be able to raise a son? He would be a poor excuse for a father.

Chapter 38:

Gloria was pleased that Pieter was settling in nicely and was no longer having nightmares. In fact he rarely even wakened during the night. She was surprised therefore when she received a message from *Mevrouw* Mueller asking Gloria to visit her, alone.

"I'm not sure," Gloria told Willem in an indecisive tone, "if going alone means without you or without Pieter but I think I should go without either of you." She looked questioningly at him.

"You should go by yourself. You will be fine," Willem said. "I am sure it is nothing. Perhaps she wants to check that Pieter is still doing well or maybe she wants to take him back."

"Oh, I do hope it isn't that," said Gloria with feeling. "He seems to be happy living here. I would like him to stay forever." She slanted a look at her husband.

"What would you think of that?" she asked. Willem stilled.

"Adopt him you mean?" he asked. At her nod he continued. "We can think about it. We do not know what is involved in adopting him but he can stay for now."

Gloria grabbed her coat and gave her husband a quick kiss before leaving the apartment. She was content to have Willem's agreement with that for now. She walked quickly trying to warm herself. Even with the extra warmth of her coat she felt the damp cold. When she arrived at the Mueller's apartment she nearly didn't recognize the woman who opened the door.

Mevrouw Mueller's hair was unwashed and uncombed. Her eyes were puffy and her complexion pasty. She tried to smile when she saw Gloria but was unable to and her mouth twisted in pain instead.

"Come in, come in," she said quickly in Dutch. She grabbed Gloria by the arm to hasten her entry. "You keep Pieter with you?" she asked switching to English.

"Pieter can stay with me for a while."

"No, no" said *Mevrouw* Mueller sitting in a chair at the kitchen table and motioning Gloria into the other chair. "You keep him. My husband sick. He will die."

Gloria looked closely at the woman and realized that *Mevrouw* Mueller was near her breaking point and in no condition to look after anyone.

"Where is your son?" Gloria asked slowly hoping the woman would understand although she seemed to speak English better than Gloria had originally thought.

"Ben is with my sister. He is all right. She look after him." *Mevrouw* Mueller fumbled with a pack of cigarettes trying to get one out. Her hand was shaking so badly she could not light it. Gloria took the match book from her and lit a match holding it to the end of the cigarette.

The woman smiled her thanks as she began puffing. She sat quietly calmer now but still watching Gloria.

"Someone from church will take Pieter if I ask but it is better him to live with you," *Mevrouw* Mueller said blowing smoke from her mouth and waving it away with her hand.

"What happened to you husband?" Gloria asked gently.

"Police not tell?" asked *Mevrouw* Mueller. "He step on bomb and it go off. He lose both legs. No medicine for pain."

Gloria was horrified and she murmured comforting sounds as the woman sobbed silently. *Mevrouw* Mueller took a deep breath.

"My sister help but not take Pieter," she said between sobs.

"I understand. I will take care of Pieter." Gloria stayed a while longer until *Mevrouw* Mueller's neighbour came.

"I come to help Greta," the neighbour said to Gloria.

"Greta," she said to *Mevrouw* Mueller, "How is Derik today?"

She marched into the kitchen and began making coffee. Gloria said goodbye to *Mevrouw* Mueller and told her not to worry about Pieter.

Gloria greeted Willem as she entered the apartment and sat in the chair beside his.

"*Mevrouw* Mueller asked me to keep Pieter," said Gloria after giving Willem a quick kiss on the cheek, "not just for these few weeks, but forever." She explained what the Dutch woman had told her.

"Why doesn't she ask the church to find another family to take him?" asked Willem.

"She could," said Gloria, "But she thinks he'd be happier with us." She paused. "I think she's right."

"You really do want to adopt him," he said.

"I do," said Gloria.

"Gloria," Willem said warmly taking hold of her hand. "I am fond of the boy and I think he should stay here for now." He released her hand and put his arm across her shoulders drawing her closer. "But adopting him is a big responsibility. We need to talk about it. Raising a child is a big decision and we do not want to rush into making the wrong choice. We want to do what will be best for Pieter and for us. But right now all my thoughts are of Harrie."

He dropped his arm and held his hands in his lap hanging his head. He took a deep breath. Gloria shifted her weight so she could hug him with one arm across his shoulders.

"I understand Willem," she said. "I truly do and I don't expect an answer right now. This situation, having Pieter live with us here, will do for now. I'll have to talk to someone at the church to find out what's involved in adopting him.

"For now let's turn our energies to finding Ursula," she said.

Chapter 39:

"Do you have the chap's address," asked Willem one evening, "the one whose father works for the government? We'll need his help if we're going to get into Germany."

"Piet Boswel," Gloria said supplying the name, "one of the guys I met on the ship. That seems like a long time ago." She patted his knee before getting up and going into the bedroom.

Willem recognized the irony in the situation. He and Gloria were travelling to Germany to find Ursula and by doing so they were either going to prove that his brother was dead or that he was a traitor. Gloria returned and handed him a piece of paper. He looked at it before putting it in his pocket. It was not far; they could walk there tomorrow.

The next morning was clear after a few days of rain. Willem and Gloria left when breakfast was over and were pleased to discover that Piet was at home.

"Gloria!" Piet exclaimed opening the door and inviting her into the apartment. "And this is Willem? You found him," he added opening the door further and extending the invitation to Willem.

The two men exchanged pleasantries as Gloria and Willem followed Piet into the living room. When they were seated Gloria explained what they were after. She and Willem had already decided what story they would use to explain why they wanted to go to Germany.

"We have learned that Willem's brother is dead," she said. "He died at the end of the war when he was living with people who had come to Amsterdam from Germany. We have some questions about how he died and we want to ask a woman who we think now lives in Germany. You said your father works for the government. Could he help us get the papers we'll need to travel to Germany?" Belatedly she noticed the older man sitting in a chair by the window.

"This is my father," said Piet, gesturing to the man in the chair. "Why don't you explain to him what you need?"

Gloria signalled for Willem to take over. He told Piet and *Meneer* Boswel the whole story starting with him and Harrie trying to get out of the country in 1940. He finished by recounting what he and Gloria had learned since returning to Amsterdam. When Willem finished talking Piet's father nodded several times.

"I will get you the papers," he said, "but it could take a week or more. Do you have a phone? Can I call you when I get everything straightened out?"

The Spelts did not have a phone so Willem had to return to the Boswel's apartment a few times. Gloria happened to be with him the day he was able to pick up the documents. Boswel handed him an envelope.

"Thank you, sir," Willem said extending his hand. After the two men shook hands Gloria stepped forward and offered her hand to the older gentleman. *Meneer* Boswel looked at her in surprise but he took her hand in his placing his other hand on top.

"Thank you from me too," said Gloria. "And thank you, Piet, for your help as well."

§ § §

With papers in hand they boarded the train. They'd been traveling for an hour or more when the train stopped. The train had been following a river and Willem wasn't surprised.

"The bridge was blown up during the war," he said to Gloria in answer to her question. "This is a Bailey bridge. It is made from wood and steel and doesn't need heavy equipment to put it together. They were used during the war and this one is being used here until they can build a new bridge."

Another woman had gotten off the train with them and she was also listening to his explanation. The three of them joined the other passengers as they climbed into the back of a truck waiting on the road leading to the bridge. It had obviously been a troop truck during the war – there were two benches in the back one along either side of the truck.

The woman sitting on the other side of Gloria was gripping the bench so firmly that her knuckles were white.

"This bridge is quite safe," Willem told Gloria. He noticed that the other woman, the one who was scared, was listening too. "I had to drive over several during the war. The bridge can handle a great weight."

Gloria relaxed and let go of his hand that she'd been gripping fiercely. The woman kept her gaze fixed straight ahead. When they were halfway across she turned to Gloria and spoke in a slightly accented voice.

"It really is not that bad after you get used to it," she said.

"No although I'll admit it's a little scary at first if you're not expecting it," said Gloria.

When the truck reached the end of the bridge there was more shaking. Gloria gripped Willem's hand again. He patted it absent-mindedly as the truck drove off the bridge. Willem descended from the truck and helped

Gloria off the truck. Another man had helped the other woman to get out of the truck and she'd gone the other way.

"She seemed a nice woman," Gloria said when she and Willem were seated on the train. "I'm sorry I won't see her again."

"Perhaps she is going to Marl," said Willem, "and you will see her again." Gloria shrugged.

Willem hoped they would meet her again. Gloria hadn't made many friends although her friendship with Maartje had proved beneficial in planning this trip. After getting help from Piet's father to obtain the necessary papers they'd had to find a place to stay in Marl. In talking to Maartje Gloria had discovered that she had another aunt who had moved to Marl just before the war started.

"Maartje said that if we stay with her aunt and uncle it might heal their family quarrel," Gloria told Willem.

"What family quarrel is that?" asked Willem.

"Maartje's Aunt Margriet married a German, Otto Lasker, in 1931," Gloria explained. "Her grandmother believed Otto was a Nazi and ordered the whole family to stop talking to her aunt especially after they moved to Germany. Maartje's mother and aunts obeyed the grandmother and stopped all correspondence but her brother continued to write to Margriet's son, Hans, who's the same age as he is. Margriet had been married before but her husband died. Hans is from her first marriage, but Otto adopted him so his name is Lasker as well. Theo only stopped writing to Hans when letters could no longer get through because of the war."

"And how will us staying with Margriet and Otto help?" asked Willem.

"If Otto is willing to help us that will prove he's not a Nazi, I guess," said Gloria.

Willem looked doubtful but he didn't say anything else about it. He leaned his head against the back of the seat. This countryside reminded him of his flight to freedom after escaping from the POW camp. He felt Gloria's hand reaching for his and he closed his fingers over hers grateful for the tactile comfort. He opened his eyes.

"When the four of us escaped from the POW camp," he said, "we travelled through countryside that looked very much like this. You never knew if the trees were concealing you from the enemy or if the enemy was hiding from you." He exhaled noisily but continued. "We talked about our plans for our lives after the war to help pass the time. Ken, the one who was killed, had wanted to become a vet. The loss of livestock angered him nearly as much as the human suffering."

"What about your other friends, the ones who lived?" asked Gloria.

"Simon was knowledgeable in first aid and his wish was to become a doctor," said Willem staring out the window. "Without his skill I might have lost my leg. I hope he's on his way to achieving his goal. Eric was British, but was hoping to go to Canada after the war to join the RCMP or the Mounties as they are called. When he knew that I was married to you he suggested I join too if you wanted to live in Canada."

"I would like to live in Canada," said Gloria. "But when we have more time we can talk about it. We don't need to make a decision now."

Willem squeezed her hand but didn't say anything. When the train slowed and stopped Gloria and Willem stood. He guided her with his hand at her back as they made their way to the front of the car and he followed her off the train onto the platform.

"I'll stay here," she said standing close to the building, "while you go to collect our bags."

Willem made his way to the baggage car. He knew that Marl was well-known for its coalmines and he was pleased to see the city had not received heavy bomb damage. Many buildings were standing tall and untouched.

"Do you have the paper with Mr. Lasker's address?" Gloria asked Willem after he returned with their suitcase.

"Hmmm," he said searching his pockets. He finally found it in his wallet. "Here it is. I was afraid I'd lost it when I gave the conductor my ticket," he said grinning self-consciously.

Since they had no idea which way to go Gloria suggested they stop at a shop to ask how to get to Gartnerweg, Garden Street. Willem's sense of direction had always been good and after talking to a shopkeeper he felt he'd be able to find his way without problems. It was late afternoon and the temperature was cool.

Chapter 40:

Gloria had butterflies in her stomach. They were in Germany! And the war was barely over. She glanced around as they walked along each street expecting to see "the enemy" hiding behind buildings. She smiled inwardly. What nonsense!

People here in Germany were similar to the people she'd just met in Holland. This was what made war pointless. People were the same everywhere; although she had to admit that perhaps it was a little different being in Europe rather than in Canada. Still she thought straightening her shoulders there was no one lurking in the shadows here wanting to do her and Willem harm. She hoped.

They turned a corner onto a residential street and Gloria spotted three or four boys kicking a soccer ball around. They halted the game if it could be called that — there was no net — and turned towards Willem when he spoke.

"Is one of you Hans Lasker?" Willem asked in German.

One of teenagers looked at his friends and after receiving nods of approval raised his hand.

"I am," he replied in English. "Who wants to know?"

"My name is Willem Spelt. I'd like to talk to your father if I may," said Willem. The youth looked around at his friends again before answering.

"You cannot," he said aggressively his hands balling into fists. After a pause in which no one spoke he added, "He is dead." He spoke English with a slight accent.

Hearing that, Gloria gasped and covered her mouth with her hand.

"I am sorry to hear that," Willem said putting his arm around Gloria. He waited for Gloria to get over her shock before introducing her to the boy. The teen nodded to Gloria but his hands stayed at his sides.

The others had been following the conversation without interest and when Hans moved off the field the boy holding the ball threw it to the ground. Hans grabbed his jacket and walked to where Willem and Gloria were standing as his friends started kicking the ball around.

"Your cousin, Maartje Smit, in Amsterdam is a friend of ours," said Willem in English since the boy seemed to understand it. "She suggested we contact your family. We have some business in Marl."

"I have a cousin Theo in Amsterdam," said Hans. "But we have not written in many years." Some of the bravado had gone out of him. When Willem didn't say anything he added, "I take you to mother."

Willem signalled to Gloria that she should follow Hans. Neither she nor Willem attempted to converse as they followed the teenager up the stairs of a nearby apartment building. The boy stopped on the fourth floor and opened the door calling to his mother. As soon as she appeared he left leaving Willem to explain why he and Gloria were there. Willem had barely started his explanation when another woman entered the kitchen from the living room. It was the woman from the train. She spoke a sentence in German to the German woman and then smiled pleasantly at Gloria and Willem.

Gloria had studied German in high school, listening to Herr Hitler's speeches on the radio in the early 1930s as a way of increasing her understanding of the language. Since her knowledge was quite limited she trusted Willem, who spoke German fluently, to tell her what people were saying.

After the three of them finished their conversation in German Willem indicated Gloria should take a chair in the living room. Once they were all seated the woman from the train introduced herself as Esmee Hofman. Gloria let Willem handle the introductions although she smiled at each woman.

"I have told Margriet and Esmee how we know Maartje," Willem told Gloria. He switched back to German and Gloria gathered he was telling the other women that she could not speak much German.

"I speak little bit Engels," said Esmee. "Margriet and I born in Holland and learn Engels but Margriet live too long in Germany – no speak Engels now."

As Willem and Margriet had a conversation in German Esmee leaned closer to Gloria and began talking softly in English. After a few minutes Esmee apologised to Margriet for interrupting them.

"Mij brother, Frederick," Esmee said in English, "live on second floor by himself. Willem can stay with him; Gloria can stay here." She repeated it in German for Margriet's benefit.

"Hans…" said Margriet.

"Of course," said Esmee, "Hans can go to Frederick too."

Gloria listened intently as Margriet spoke in German but she was unable to understand anything the German woman said. Willem started to repeat it in English when Margriet surprised them all by speaking for herself.

"What Maartje say? Is her mother want to write me?" she asked in heavily accented English. She leaned back in her chair an anxious frown on her face. Gloria looked at the woman in surprise.

"I think *Mevrouw* Smit would be very happy to hear from you," she said. "Did you know Maartje spent the war years in Canada with your sister?" Gloria added. Willem repeated the question in German.

"*Nein*," Margriet said. She asked Esmee a question in German.

"She wonders if you know how her sister is," Esmee translated.

"I do," said Gloria. "But it is not good news I'm afraid. Maartje says her aunt is getting frail and may not be able to make the trip again."

Esmee relayed the message to Margriet and they all fell silent. When Esmee asked Gloria about Canada Gloria was happy to talk about her hometown of Stratford. She finished with the story of how she had met Willem.

In the spirit of getting better acquainted Esmee shared that she and Margriet had been friends for many years. Because of that Gloria thought that her brother Frederick would be quite a bit older than Willem but when they went to his apartment an hour later Gloria was surprised to discover he looked to be nearly the same age as her husband. Esmee had accompanied them to make introductions. When they were seated in his living room Frederick asked how he could help.

"Willem and Gloria come to Marl from Amsterdam. They look for woman name Ursula Simmt. Willem want to question her," Esmee said. "You work for police. You can help."

"Perhaps I could," said Frederik in a surprisingly soft voice. "Why do you think she is here?"

Gloria hoped Willem would be discreet in telling him what they were seeking. Even though the people they'd met so far had been friendly and helpful they had to remember that the two countries, Holland and Germany, had been at war for five years and she and Willem were from the winning side. There might be animosity towards them because of that. He must've had the same thought because he said only that Ursula might know something about his brother Harrie's death.

Frederick looked sharply at Willem hearing that. Rather than commenting on what Willem had said Frederick voiced his disapproval of what Hitler and the Nazis had done during the war. Esmee agreed with her brother saying that many German people did not agree with what the Nazis did. They were victims too. Mothers lamented the loss of sons and wives of husbands no matter what side of the conflict they were on.

Gloria nodded sadly. She agreed whole-heartedly. Esmee turned to her brother.

"Can Willem stay with you?" asked Esmee, "and Hans too?" Frederick made a face and shrugged.

"Sure, I can put them up here," he said. "It will not be the most comfortable but we can manage. Hans often stays with me so he is used to it." He looked at Willem.

"It is fine by me. Thank you." Willem crossed the room to give Gloria a quick kiss on the cheek.

"I will see you in the morning," he said softly.

"Good night Willem." she said blowing him a kiss.

Chapter 41:

"Let's just walk around the town first," said Willem as they walked past a pub that was open for business although it was only ten in the morning. He wanted to get a feel for the place before he started asking questions. Frederick had said he would check for police reports about Dirk or Ursula Simmt.

The American military presence in Marl was evident with soldiers walking the streets and occasionally stopping citizens to ask for papers. In the few days he and Gloria had been in Marl, they had never been stopped. Rather than stopping them and asking questions a few passing soldiers had nodded to them. Willem wondered at that. Was it so evident that they were not German? Perhaps it was – by their dress and the way they walked. Or maybe it was Gloria who looked less European. Whatever it was, it reassured him. As they strolled by an old church Gloria grabbed Willem's arm.

"Let's go in and look around," she said impulsively. She tugged his arm gently as she turned and walked up the steps but he didn't resist. He pulled the door open for her to precede him into the cool dark building. She spoke to him over her shoulder after they were in the building.

"You've been very quiet dear," she said as they walked down the centre aisle. "What are you thinking?" Willem shrugged.

"We are in Germany now," he said, "but we are on a wild goose chase. We do not know where Ursula is. And even if we find her she may not want to talk to us. In fact, if we accuse her of murdering Dirk and Harrie we can be guaranteed she will not want to talk to us!"

"We can ask Ursula how Harrie died," said Gloria, "without accusing her of murdering him. We'll just tell her we are trying to clear his name and remove any suspicion that he might've been a traitor." Willem patted her arm as they strolled.

This whole mess was his fault. If only he'd made sure Harrie was on the boat to England before it left France – then this would never have happened. Finding Ursula and questioning her was one way to atone for that. If he could clear Harrie's name Mamma and Pa could have a memorial service for him and perhaps in time they would not feel such shame even though they would always grieve for him.

"Let's sit here," said Gloria speaking in a whisper and moving into a pew. Willem followed her and they sat together facing the front of the church. Other people were milling about but all voices were hushed. He closed his eyes waiting to feel a sense of Harrie's death but there was nothing. It wasn't unexpected - he had never had that sort of connection with his brother. Even when they were children living in the same house they had never experienced that kind of bond.

Harrie had fallen while skating once when they were teenagers. He'd broken his leg but Willem hadn't known about it until his mother told him what had happened. Another time Harrie had had an accident with his bicycle and Willem had known nothing until Harrie told him. Willem would have to use more practical means to discover what had happened. He was a policeman – he could use the skills he'd learned in his training.

"If the American soldiers are keeping an eye on Ursula –" said Willem opening his eyes and raising his head, "and they might if she's a Nazi or a Nazi sympathizer – then we need to talk to them."

Willem wasn't sure how to go about getting them to talk to him. If he had information they wanted perhaps he could swap them for information about Ursula but he was sadly lacking in the information department.

They sat in silence for several more minutes. Gloria put the kneeler down and leaned forward. Willem thought she might be saying a prayer since she was more religious than he was. She'd sung in the church choir in Stratford and she'd attended a church group for girls when she was a young girl. She'd still been going to Sunday services with her parents when they'd met. But since it hadn't been his custom to go to church they hadn't attended one recently. Willem exited the church hand in hand with Gloria. When they were on the sidewalk she spun around to face him. Her face was flushed, her eyes big.

"What if Harrie fell in love with Ursula?" she asked excitedly walking backwards a few steps before turning around to walk at his side.

"Harrie does not like women," Willem stated his lips barely moving. "He would not fall in love with a woman – not like I fell in love with you."

"You know him better than I do," said Gloria. "But couldn't he have changed? What if Ursula was very beautiful?"

"My dear," said Willem bending his head to talk. "I am not sure a man can change in that way – liking men and then liking women. I think people are born to be homosexual or not – they do not change partway through life."

He kept his voice low so passers-by wouldn't hear him and Gloria walked close to him, with her head inclined towards him. He felt her bump against him as she almost walked into an American soldier who was exiting a bar. Willem looked up quickly and saw the sign Rathskellar above the door.

"Let's go in here," Gloria said. "It must be nearly lunchtime. Perhaps we can get something to eat."

They found a table in the nearly half-full bar. Willem noted that there were many American soldiers which might present possibilities for obtaining information. He checked with Gloria to find out what she wanted and went to the bar to see if he could order any food. Gloria handed him money. He returned in a few minutes with a sandwich to share, a beer for him and a whiskey sour for her.

When Willem returned Gloria indicated with a slight movement of her head a couple at a nearby table.

"Look at them," she said in an undertone. The man was dressed in loose-fitting pants held up with a rope. His open-necked shirt had the sleeves rolled up but the woman was wearing clothes that were too small for her. The sleeves of her top stopped just short of her wrists and her pants came to mid-calf. On her feet were high-heeled shoes.

"It looks like she borrowed clothes from someone smaller," said Gloria, "perhaps her daughter. Her shoes don't match what she's wearing."

"Those fancy shoes," said Willem "may be the only ones that are still fit to wear. Perhaps all of her clothes are worn out and have holes in them. She would not have been able to buy new shoes or new clothes during the war."

Looking around Willem noticed that he, Gloria, and the oddly-attired couple were the only civilians in the tavern. The remainder of the patrons were dressed in military garb and most of them were likely American. The man dressed in the unusual clothes approached their table and spoke in German to Willem.

"Do you and your wife want to join us at our table?" he asked. Willem answered in the affirmative and picked up his and Gloria's drinks. He explained what was happening as they walked to the next table but Gloria, guessing what the man had said, had already picked up the plate and was preparing to follow Willem.

"My name is Karl Metzer and this is my wife Rilla," the man said in German when Gloria and Willem were settled. "You're new here?"

"My name is Willem Spelt and this is my wife Gloria," Willem said offering his hand. "I'm from Holland and my wife is Canadian." He was going to say more to get the man talking but it was unnecessary.

Chapter 42:

Gloria listened without comprehending as Karl started a lengthy dialogue in German. When Karl paused to take a swig of beer Willem translated.

Karl didn't think the two countries, Germany and Holland, should have gone to war. But when the Nazis came to power all German citizens had been forced to become Nazis. No other viewpoint was tolerated. Karl and his wife became Nazis even though they did not agree with those beliefs. With the war at an end Karl and his wife were prepared to stop thinking like Nazis and to return to their former way of thinking but not everyone was. A few of Karl's neighbours declared they hated Jews and wouldn't shop in their stores even though before the war they had been happy to do so. When Willem stopped talking, Karl set his beer down with a bang and several soldiers from a neighbouring table looked their way but no one said anything.

"How long have you lived here?" Willem asked the couple in German glancing at Gloria. She nodded to indicate she was following.

"All our lives," Karl said, "both of us." His wife murmured in agreement.

"Did you know a Dirk Simmt?" asked Willem.

Gloria lost track of the conversation. She thought Willem was probably asking them if they had known Dirk Simmt but she couldn't follow the rest of the conversation. Now that she had a closer look at Karl she judged him to be in his mid-fifties maybe even into his sixties. Rilla looked to be a few years younger although both of them had the same haunted look she'd observed in people in Amsterdam. It was obvious that the war had been just as hard on German citizens as on Dutch.

After a few minutes Willem took a cigarette package out of his pocket and offered it to the couple. Karl took two smokes. He used a match to light one and handed it to his wife. Then before the flame died he lit his own. He blew out the match quickly and puffed on his cigarette.

In the silence Willem told Gloria that Rilla had known Simmt's mother and she'd been sad when both of his parents were killed. Karl didn't know if Ursula had been killed as well but Rilla thought she was dead.

"Come Rilla we have to leave," Karl said finishing his beer before dropping his cigarette butt in his glass where it sputtered before going out. There was no ashtray on their table. They said good-by to Willem and Gloria before walking away Rilla holding Karl's arm. Gloria waited until they'd moved some distance away before speaking.

"They certainly were a strange couple," she said. "Can we trust what they say? They tried to tell us Ursula may've been killed and we know for a fact that she wasn't."

"I will talk to them again," said Willem. He took the last couple of puffs on his cigarette and then stood and used the ash tray on the next table before following Gloria out of the bar.

That evening Gloria visited with Willem and Frederick.

"If it isn't too nosy to ask," said Gloria tentatively, "could you tell us what happened to Margriet's husband?" Listening to Esmee and Margriet, Gloria had heard hints of a problem and she wondered what the story was.

"We never talk of Margriet's family when she comes to visit," said Frederik lowering his voice although there was no reason to do so. "Margriet's husband Otto was killed because of Esmee's husband." Frederick expelled a breath forcefully.

"It was very tragic. Esmee's husband Luis and her son also Luis both joined the Nazi party in 1938. They firmly believed that Hitler was Germany's hope for making her a strong country again. Esmee did not join however. Everything was fine for several years. Otto did not share Luis' beliefs but since their wives were friends Luis and Otto tolerated each other's company. A few years ago now, in '43, Luis heard Otto voicing anger at what Hitler was doing to the Jews. The next night Otto went out and never returned. It was only later we learned that Luis had reported him to the Nazi officials."

Gloria gasped and reached toward Willem. He clasped her hand in his and held it on his knee.

"Luis never showed any remorse," added Frederik, "for turning Otto in. I think that is why Esmee is such a good friend to Margriet now. She feels a terrible guilt about her husband's actions."

"Where are Luis and his son now?" asked Gloria.

"They were shot at the end of the war," said Frederik standing and looking out the window. It was dark and he couldn't possibly see anything. He turned to face Gloria again. "They never caught the people who did it. But Esmee told me that she stopped loving her husband many years ago when she witnessed what he was doing as a Nazi. I think she regretted that her son was drawn into it but he was very like his father and over age seventeen. He made his own decision; there was nothing she could do to stop him."

"Thank you for telling me," said Gloria gently. "It is another tragedy of war."

After a minute Frederick opened a drawer and took out a deck of cards.

"Willem and I played bridge last night," he said to Gloria. "I understand you can play too."

They played four hands with Frederick winning two and Willem and Gloria, as a team, winning two. Frederick gathered the cards and set the deck on the table.

"I am going into my bedroom. I have some reading to do before tomorrow but you are welcome to stay here if you wish," he said to Gloria as he left. Willem thanked him and looked at Gloria.

"When do you expect Esmee and Margriet to return?" he asked. Gloria looked at the clock on the wall.

"They won't be much longer," she said. "They will call for me here when they get back." She settled back in her chair as Willem pulled his chair closer.

"We do not want to disturb Frederick," he said lowering his voice. "But we have not had much time to talk about us."

Gloria hoped the distress she felt was not visible on her face. She'd hoped to have a few more weeks before she had to deal with this. Had the talk about relationships gone bad reminded Willem that he wanted out of this relationship? She hoped not. She'd thought they were falling in love again.

"You look worried dearest," Willem said warmly. "Do you want to end our relationship? Or are you afraid I do?" He reached for Gloria's hand and tugged gently urging her to sit on his lap. When she was settled he added, "Have they not heard of sofas here?" He grinned briefly.

"I want to know how you feel about us." he said tenderly. "Do you want to stay married?"

"Yes I do Willem. I love you and even though our baby died I am glad we got married," she said letting her eyes roam over his face.

"I am glad too," he said lovingly hugging her tightly, "because I love you. I wish I could have been with you when the baby died. It is not your fault though. Do you mind talking about it? Can you tell me what happened?"

Gloria shifted her weight so she could hug him as she told him what had happened. She didn't spare any of the details and by the time she'd finished she was crying. She put her head on his shoulder and sobbed silently for several minutes. Willem handed her his handkerchief and she used it to dry her eyes. She sniffed and wiped her nose.

They stayed sitting silently with their arms around each other until a knock sounded. They broke apart and Gloria stood, wiping her eyes and handing the handkerchief back to Willem. She could feel her face getting hot as Esmee came in.

"Hi Gloria," she said her eyes traveling from Gloria's face to Willem's and back again. "We will wait for you upstairs," she said backing out of the door a small smile on her face.

"I'm ready to go," Gloria said moving toward the door. "Good night Willem."

"Good night dearest," he said.

Gloria was glad Esmee didn't talk as they ascended the stairs. Once more she had told Willem how she felt about losing the baby but he hadn't reciprocated. How could they resume their married life if he didn't let her know how he felt about the death of their baby?

Chapter 43:

"I can't see," Gloria said over her shoulder to Willem after entering the bar. "It's too dark."

Willem murmured in agreement and drew her to one side as people moved past them leaving the tavern. While waiting for her eyes to adjust Gloria searched for the couple Karl and Rilla Metzer. After a few minutes she spotted them at a table on the far side of the room. She pointed in their direction and Willem nodded. As they made their way to the table Gloria noticed the woman was dressed more reasonably today.

"Good day," said Willem in German. He added another sentence which Gloria didn't understand. Karl stood and looked at them saying something in German. He urged his wife to stand practically pulling her out of her chair.

He and Willem had a short conversation at the end of which Karl gave him what looked like a business card. Willem and Gloria sat at the table the other couple had just vacated. Willem told her that Karl had given him their address.

"He said we could visit them tomorrow," he added.

"Were they trying to avoid us?" Gloria asked. Willem looked at their retreating backs.

"I did not get that feeling," he said. "Perhaps they have something else planned for today." Gloria shrugged.

"We'll have to leave too," she added in an urgent voice as she searched her purse. "I don't think I have my money with me."

Before leaving Amsterdam, Gloria had visited Maartje to get information about Maartje's aunt and uncle who lived in Marl. Besides telling her about the family quarrel, Maartje had renewed her offer of financial assistance for the trip.

"That is very kind of you, Maartje," Gloria had replied. "I may have to take you up on it this time. My money is starting to run out and Pa doesn't have any to spare."

Maartje had handed Gloria some bills, saying that if the trip helped to repair the bad feelings among her family members, she would consider it money well spent. Gloria had tucked the money in her purse without mentioning it to Willem.

Gloria was still searching for the money in her purse when she heard Willem talking to the American soldiers at the next table. She abandoned her search and tuned into the conversation.

"I know where Detroit is," Willem said at a pause in the conversation.

"Ya know Detroit?" The soldier looked at him in surprise as he lifted his bottle to his lips.

"My wife knows better than I do," Willem admitted gesturing to Gloria. "She used to live in Amherstburg – across the river from Detroit. I have never been there myself," he confessed. "But I hear they make good cars."

"The best. The best." The soldier agreed nodding. "And you've heard of the Red Wings and the Tigers?"

"The Wings won the Stanley Cup in '43," said Willem. He knew from listening to Gloria's father, a hockey fan, when he'd been stationed in Canada. "I do not know as much about the Detroit Tigers. My father-in-law is not a baseball fan." He grinned as he shrugged.

"Bob Earle," said the soldier extending his hand and smiling. "I can't believe there are people who aren't baseball fans. It's the best game there is."

"Willem Spelt," said Willem cheerily. "My wife, Gloria." She nodded pleasantly but stayed seated. Bob glanced at Gloria then did a double-take and looked at her more closely.

"You're from Amherstburg?" he asked. At her nod he continued. "You've been to Bob-Lo Island then."

"Several times."

"I used to work one of the rides there," said Bob. "I've probably taken your money if you ever rode the Ferris wheel."

"I've only ridden it once," she said. "I almost got sick so I never went on it again."

"That happens to quite a few people," he said turning his attention back to Willem.

"You're not English, are you?" he asked.

"No," said Willem. "I am Dutch but I fought with the Canadian Army at Juno Beach."

"You fought at Normandy?" exclaimed Earle.

"Queen's Own Rifles in the first wave," stated Willem in a flat voice. "It was hell but eventually we were successful."

"I was at Omaha," Earle spoke bitterly. "It was…," he paused and looked at Gloria.

"It was another kind of hell," he said finally looking back at Willem.

After that exchange one of the soldiers pulled two empty chairs to the table and Earle invited Willem and Gloria to join them.

"We're just having a drink," he said indicating the bottles on the table. "Can I get you anything?" Willem agreed to have a beer but Gloria asked for a whiskey sour. Earle walked to the bar to place the order. The soldiers and Willem talked of general things for a few minutes until Willem was able to question them about what specifically they were doing in the area.

"We're a long way from most of the action up here," said another of the soldiers. "Not too many Nazis left to clear out. We just heard of one group and they're almost all gone."

"Ever come across anyone by the name Simmt? Either Dirk or Ursula?" Willem asked casually.

"Ursula?" asked a soldier in surprise. "A girl? In one of these groups? Not likely!"

Earle returned in time to hear Willem's question. He set the drinks on the table pushing Gloria's in her direction.

"I haven't heard of a Dirk," said Earle. "But it's possible there could be girls here. As long as you adhered to their philosophy the Nazis would accept you."

"I never saw no girls," the soldier muttered. Gloria thought he sounded disappointed.

As Gloria sipped her drink she glanced at Bob. He did look familiar now that she thought about it. But the memory didn't come from Bob-Lo. It was something else. Earle...she recognized that name. But it wasn't Bob. It was...

"Do you have a brother Brian who played for the Wings?" she asked suddenly interrupting Willem's conversation.

The soldiers stopped talking and looked at her in surprise. Bob's face broke into a grin.

"Yes. Did you ever see him?"

"My father was given tickets to a game several years ago and he took me." Gloria said blushing. "Brian scored a hat trick," she added.

"I remember that game," said Bob. "It was the first time he'd done it."

Gloria sat back in her seat as the men continued to talk about what was happening in Marl but she felt the tone had shifted. The soldiers, even Earle, were treating her and Willem almost as friends.

"What do you do?" Earle asked her while Willem talked with the other soldiers.

"I'm a nurse," she replied and filled him in on the work she'd done in Amsterdam.

"Do you speak Dutch or German?" Earle asked.

"I'm picking up some Dutch and I learned German in high school," said Gloria. "But I don't really speak either language."

Earle seemed pleased with her answer but he didn't say any more to her. His attention shifted to Willem. After a few more minutes of general conversation, Willem stood and said goodbye to the soldiers. Gloria scrambled to her feet and let her gaze sweep over the other soldiers at the table before she followed Willem out of the tavern. Once outside she asked him if he'd learned anything useful.

"Not really but the soldiers gather at this bar one or two nights a week," said Willem thoughtfully. "I may try to come back and get to know them. Perhaps I can get more information about Ursula that way. They certainly are not going to let me do any investigating on my own."

§ § §

Willem returned to the bar a couple of nights over the next week and spent time over a beer getting to know the soldiers. After talk about shared war experiences and sports Willem asked Earle how their work was going. Earle told him that not knowing the language was their biggest difficulty. When they knocked on doors and questioned the people living there most of them didn't understand what the soldiers were saying.

"Or maybe they're just pretending not to understand us," Earle admitted.

"I speak fluent German," said Willem. "Could I help?" Earle looked at Willem.

"You're fluent in German are you?" he asked. "That could be very helpful very helpful indeed. You were with the Queen's Own Rifles weren't you?" He was silent as Willem drank his beer.

"I have to talk to some people, but I'll get back to you," said Earle.

A message from Earle arrived at Frederick's apartment the next day. Willem was to meet with the Americans and accompany them as they canvassed a neighbourhood. Willem was instructed to wear dark clothing but he was not allowed to carry a gun. Willem was just as glad he wouldn't be expected to shoot anyone if it came to that. He was quite sure the Americans would have more than enough fire power to cope with whatever emergencies might arise.

When he arrived back at Frederick's several hours later he immediately went to Margriet's apartment to tell Gloria about it.

"Come in dear," said Gloria opening the door to his knock. "Margriet and Esmee are out for a bit. How did it go?"

Willem was glad he and Gloria were alone. He didn't want to have to tell the other women what had happened.

"The Germans do not like the Americans at all," Willem said when he and Gloria were seated. "I am sure many of them knew what Earle was asking but they pretended to not understand. When I spoke German they could no longer keep up that pretense but I could tell they were unhappy. They did not want to answer the questions."

"Did you come across any Nazis?"

"No but I am sure some of them might have been sympathetic to the Nazis. There was no way they would admit that to the American soldiers though." Willem shook his head. His plan to find Ursula with the Americans' help might not succeed. Earle had asked him to join them again in a few days. He would send Willem a message to let him know exactly when.

Willem and Gloria talked a bit more before he left to go back to Frederick's apartment. He met Margriet and Esmee on the stairs but only nodded at them in passing.

Gloria and Willem set out directly after breakfast the next morning and were at the Metzer's in short order. Rilla Metzer answered their knock and invited them into their first-floor apartment. It was what Gloria thought of as a bachelor apartment but the different sections of the room were separated from one another by pieces of cloth hanging from ropes. Goodness knows how Rilla had scavenged the material and the rope. Looking around Gloria decided she liked it but they weren't here to gawk at the decorating style.

"Thank you for inviting us over," Willem said using formal German that Gloria understood. When Rilla invited them to sit Willem and Gloria took seats on a couch on one side of the room while Rilla and Karl sat on another couch opposite them. They were so close their feet almost touched. Willem cleared his throat.

"We are trying to find a woman named Ursula Simmt," he said in German and repeating it in English. "You knew her I believe."

Karl and his wife looked at each other. Karl answered in German, his wife nodding in accompaniment. When he finished speaking she began to talk, bobbing her head yes and then shaking it no. She looked at her husband and he took up the tale. Gloria had no idea what they were saying but she followed the conversation between the two like she would a game of ping pong. When they settled back in their chairs Willem repeated it in English.

"They did not tell us the truth yesterday," he said. "They are saying now that Ursula was not killed when her parents were. They saw her with her friends after the building was destroyed. In fact, Karl believes Ursula went to Amsterdam in 1944 to kill Dirk."

"Why would she do that?" Gloria asked looking from Rilla's face to Karl's. She turned to her husband.

"I have to back up," said Willem, "and tell you the whole story according to what Karl and Rilla said. Dirk had left his home in Germany in the early 1930s to go to Amsterdam to work as a watchmaker. He felt the economic climate was better there. Shortly after he left home Ursula, who was only a teenager at the time, joined the Nazi Youth Movement and started going to Hitler's rallies. Up to this time she had always gotten along with her parents but after she became a Nazi they had a falling out. Ursula wanted her parents to join the Nazi party but they refused. That is when the trouble began."

"How do they know all this?" asked Gloria.

"They lived on the same street as the Simmt family," said Willem. "They've known Ursula since she was born and they think she was always a little 'cuckoo.' She used to tease younger kids and she always said strange things."

That didn't sound too bizarre to Gloria but maybe they had different standards here for what was crazy. Or maybe it lost something in the translation. Willem continued his tale.

"After the Simmt's apartment building was destroyed in 1943," he said, "Ursula told her neighbours that her father had wanted her to go to Holland to live with Dirk if anything happened to him."

"To the father, you mean?" asked Gloria.

"Yes," said Willem. "Ursula let it be known that her father figured the Allies would win the war and he was worried that if he and his wife were killed Ursula would not be treated well."

"But Karl doesn't think that's what really happened?" asked Gloria.

"Karl believes that Ursula made up her mind to go to Holland," Willem replied, "to try to change Dirk's mind and to convince him to become a Nazi too. She probably wanted him to move back to Germany with her. And once she made that decision the Nazis thought to use it to their advantage."

Willem paused and Karl spoke in German. Without waiting to translate Willem motioned Gloria to her feet and said they must leave. As soon as they were on the sidewalk Gloria spoke.

"Why did we have to leave so suddenly?" she asked walking quickly to keep up with Willem. He slowed down as they reached the corner, turned around, and watched as two men entered the Metzer's apartment.

"Karl wanted us to leave because he had another appointment." He said. "It must be those men. I wonder who they are."

"They couldn't be Nazis could they?" asked Gloria anxiously. "The soldiers said they were almost finished their work here. It does seem strange though doesn't it?" Willem shrugged his shoulders.

"They may not have anything to do with Dirk and Ursula," he said. He started walking again with Gloria at his side. "I think we need to go back to Frederick's," he said, "and write down everything we know. Perhaps that will give us a clearer understanding of what is happening."

Chapter 44:

"We know that Ursula's parents were killed in the fall of 1943," said Willem holding up his hand and ticking items off at each finger. "Harrie went to live with Simmt the fall of '43 as well. According to Salentijn Harrie was sending the Underground information about who Simmt was meeting. The Underground was gradually becoming aware of what the German army was doing to the Jews. After Ursula showed up in Amsterdam in January 1944 Simmt's activities were curtailed."

Gloria and Willem had returned to Frederick's apartment and Gloria was sitting at the table taking notes. Since she didn't know shorthand she was writing in longhand while Willem talked, having found some scraps of paper and a pencil on the desk. She raised her finger to indicate she needed more time but as she finished the sentence she indicated Willem could continue.

"Ursula disappeared and Simmt was killed in the spring of '45," Willem continued. "An unidentified body was found with Simmt's body that may or may not be Harrie's. If it isn't both Harrie and Ursula are missing."

"We also know," said Gloria setting the pencil down, "that Harrie was considered a traitor by some people as soon as he went to stay with Dirk."

"And that the Nazis didn't trust Dirk anymore," said Willem, "once they knew that Harrie was living there. They sent Ursula to eliminate him."

Gloria began writing again. Walking by the Simmt's apartment earlier they'd seen that the whole building had been destroyed by the bomb. There was no sign of a place where the Nazi Youth had met many years ago. She sat tapping the pencil against her bottom lip.

"What if Harrie pretended he was a traitor," said Gloria cautiously, "and for some reason he came to Germany with Ursula."

"You mean," Willem said slowly, "Harrie and Ursula came to Germany together at the end of the war? He let her believe he was on her side?" He stopped talking as he considered that possibility.

"No, I do not believe he would have done that," he said confidently. "He would not even have pretended to be a traitor. Not the Harrie I grew up with." He paused again. He had been hearing from all sides how different life had been during the occupation. Could he really predict how Harrie would have acted?

"But if Harrie was injured in some way," he said carefully, "unable to walk for instance perhaps Ursula forced him to go to Germany with her."

"How would she have done that?" asked Gloria.

"She would have needed help to do it," said Willem.

"Or she could've drugged him," suggested Gloria. "But she still would've needed help in getting him onto the train." She fell silent. After a minute she looked up. "Or," she said pausing for effect, "she could've used an ambulance."

She dropped the pencil in her excitement. Willem looked at her in amazement shaking his head.

"How could she have used an ambulance? I doubt they even had any here," he said. He was silent. Gloria picked up the pencil.

"Although," he added. "It might not have been an ambulance. What if she had a truck or she knew someone who had a vehicle?"

"She still would've needed help getting across the border," Gloria said. "But remember Renate said that there were men coming to the apartment to visit with Ursula – men who looked like they might have been soldiers during the war. One of them could've helped her." Willem stood and began pacing when Gloria stopped talking.

"And if she had someone to assist her," he said, doing a Sherlock Holmes imitation, "they could have brought him here and…" he turned to walk the other way. "They could have brought him here and hidden him, or they could have locked him up," he stopped talking but continued walking. He walked two lengths of the room and stopped.

"It's useless speculating," he said. "We need to find out where Ursula is and we need to talk to her." He sat in a chair beside Gloria's.

"The American soldiers are planning something," he said. "Perhaps in another few days they'll have Ursula in jail and I'll be able to talk to her then." Gloria looked at the clock.

"It's time for me to return to Margriet's," Gloria said. As if to reinforce that idea Frederick walked in.

"I'm just leaving," she said. She blew Willem a kiss and waved goodbye to Frederick.

Chapter 45:

Gloria raised her head from the pillow hearing rain against the window. She was fed up with the weather, with being in Germany, and with not being able to live with Willem. She wanted the affair resolved quickly so they could get on with their lives. She wanted to clear Harrie's name or find him if he was still alive. She wanted to know what was happening with Pieter. She wanted to go home although she wasn't sure which home - Canada or Amsterdam.

Nothing would happen if she stayed in bed however so getting up was her first task. While getting dressed, she thought about what Willem had learned from his evenings spent with the American soldiers. They seemed to be appreciative of his help but Gloria wasn't sure he was any closer to finding Ursula. Willem was planning to talk to the Lieutenant that morning and if they had the German women in jail, Willem wanted permission to talk to her. Willem had better not think he was going to confront Ursula by himself!

"Do the soldiers have Ursula in jail?" she asked when Willem showed up a short time later.

"I was not able to talk to anyone," said Willem. "Things did not go as planned apparently. The raid did not happen. We will have to wait another day. But it is raining today anyway. Not a good day to go out."

§ § §

It rained for two days – two very frustrating days for Gloria. Willem spent the days with Frederick but Gloria didn't think he gathered any more information about Ursula's whereabouts. By the third day the weather had cleared and Gloria was pleased when Willem called for her at Margriet's apartment.

"I'll be ready in two shakes," said Gloria going into the WC to put on her lipstick and comb her hair. It was long enough to pull into a pony-tail albeit a short one at the nape of her neck.

While she and Willem walked along the sidewalk he told her that the American soldiers had planned to raid Ursula's apartment the day before. He hoped that he could talk to the German woman in jail today. They were headed that way when suddenly Willem changed direction.

"Why are we going this way?" asked Gloria.

"I have just had another idea," said Willem. "We will walk by Ursula's apartment on our way to the jail."

Gloria wondered if it would be safe to go to the apartment today after the raid yesterday but she decided it couldn't be that risky. Willem didn't usually want her involved in anything dangerous although she had noticed his concern for her had lessened as his anxiety for his brother had increased.

They left the downtown business district and began walking through a residential area. Tall apartment buildings looking like one huge building came into view. At the far end of the block Gloria noticed a cluster of soldiers standing in a group. As they drew closer she recognized Lieutenant Earle standing in the midst of them. She was shocked to realize that two of the soldiers were carrying guns. She stopped and put her arm on Willem's sleeve.

"We shouldn't be here," she said in a low voice. "This looks dangerous. What's happening?"

Just then one of the soldiers broke away from the group and jogged to meet them.

"How'd you get past the guard?" He questioned angrily. "This is a restricted area. You can't be here." He turned as Lieutenant Earle came up behind him.

"Get out of here," he called waving his arm. "This is a restricted area."

"I don't know how they got past the guard," said the soldier.

"It's Willem Spelt," said Willem. "There was no guard. We just want to talk to you Bob. Have you got Ursula in custody yet?"

Earle started to answer but stopped speaking as he looked at Willem more closely. He shifted his gaze to Gloria's face. Gloria could tell he was angry.

"I'm sorry," she said. "We shouldn't be here. We'll leave."

"That would be best," said the lieutenant bitterly. "I'm sorry, Willem," he added in a softer voice after a minute. "By tonight this should be over. We can talk then. You're going to have to leave now." When Earle stopped speaking Gloria tugged Willem's arm as she backed away.

"Let's go dear. You can talk to him later." Gloria led Willem across the street but Willem refused to go any farther. He twisted his arm out of her grip and encircled her with it.

"Let's wait here to see what happens," he said into her ear. The American soldiers had moved away but at a shout from the back of the building the soldiers began running in that direction.

Less than ten minutes later a soldier approached Gloria and Willem who were still huddled on the sidewalk across the street from the action.

"You're still here," he said. "The Lieutenant wondered if you would be. She's asking for a doctor."

"Who is asking for a doctor?"

"The woman in the apartment. The lieutenant said to tell you she may have a prisoner…"

"A prisoner?" exclaimed Willem, interrupting the soldier. "How do you know?"

"The woman who lives in the apartment below the German woman's had been hearing some strange tapping for several weeks. It happened while her brother was there and he thought it might be someone trying to send an SOS, but it was very faint. He just told us about it. We can't get a doctor here any time soon." The soldier looked at Gloria.

"You're a nurse, right? The lieutenant wants you to come." He made a move to grab Gloria by the arm but Willem stepped up to block him.

"My wife is not going in there," Willem stated firmly. Gloria turned and looked at him.

"Willem, if it is Harrie …" she started to say.

"No," said Willem at the same time. "I cannot let you go in there. After talking to the Metzer's yesterday I fear Ursula is unstable and we do not know what she will do."

The soldier looked between the two of them before turning and jogging away. A few minutes later Earle appeared. He reaffirmed what the soldier had said.

"I'll send a soldier in with her," he added when Willem started shaking his head. "She'll be safe."

"Please Willem dear," Gloria pleaded. "I'll be careful. This may be the only way. If it is Harrie and he's sick he'll need our help." She looked at him pleading with her eyes. Willem hesitated.

"I do not like this," he said.

"She'll be safe," said the Lieutenant. "I'll come back to see what you decide in a few minutes." He walked away and Gloria took Willem's hands in hers turning him so she could look into his face.

"I must do this," she said forcefully. "It may be the only chance we get."

Willem looked back at her in silence. She could see the indecision on his face. Two people each of whom he loved and getting help for one meant putting the other at risk.

"I wish I could go with you and keep you safe," he said finally making a face. "But I failed Harrie before and I cannot fail him again if it is him." Willem turned to face Earle as he returned.

"What do you think?" the American said urgently. "It's now or never. If she don't go, we'll have to break in. Word has come down. We can't wait."

Gloria squeezed Willem's hands.

"I'll go," she said, glancing at her husband. He made no move to stop her as she dropped his hands and stepped back. The soldier took her arm. She tried to smile at her husband before turning away.

Chapter 46:

Willem sighed watching Gloria as she walked away. He turned to Earle.

"I hope I have done the right thing," he said.

"She'll be fine," Earle said. "We won't let anything happen to her. Who do you think the prisoner is?"

"I am afraid it may be my brother," he said quietly. When the Lieutenant looked at him in amazement Willem told him what he and Gloria had discovered. Earle listened intently and whistled softly when Willem stopped talking.

"It sounds like the woman does have a few screws loose that's for sure," Earle said, shaking his head in disbelief.

"That is why I did not want Gloria to go," Willem replied. "I do not trust Ursula one bit."

"My man will stay with her," said Earle confidently.

They stood together watching as Gloria and the soldier disappeared around the building. The sun had slipped behind a cloud. In the lull Willem started to relax. Earle was certain of his men. Perhaps it would work out with Gloria saving Harrie and them returning to Amsterdam together. Once he knew his brother was safe he and Gloria could resume a married life. He would even consider adopting Pieter since that seemed to be what she wanted. In fact —

Loud voices. A moment of silence. A gunshot. A scream. More loud voices. Soldiers began running towards the building. Willem joined them. He could hear Earle pounding behind him as he rounded the building. There was a smell of gunshot in the air. Willem stopped suddenly. Earle almost ran into him. A soldier lay on the ground his face twisted in pain. Two other soldiers were tending him — trying to stop the bleeding from a leg wound. The door to the apartment building was closed and there was no sign of Gloria or Ursula.

"Where's the woman the Canadian?" Lieutenant Earle bellowed. One of the men tending the wounded man's leg stood and saluted.

"The German woman took her," he said tersely his gaze unwavering. "She, the German, wouldn't let Mitchell here go in. She shot him, grabbed the woman, and went back in locking the door behind her."

Chapter 47:

Gloria had trouble staying on her feet as the woman pulled her into the building. Her first instinct had been to go to the man who'd been shot; she hadn't expected the woman to grab her arm. She was aware of the woman kicking the door shut and throwing the bolt.

The building was dark and smelled of boiled cabbage. The woman, Gloria assumed it was Ursula, seemed to be talking to herself in rapid German. Gloria stopped listening since she couldn't understand it anyway. When they got to the second floor Ursula opened the door to an apartment and pushed Gloria through the doorway. Gloria found herself in a small dark kitchen. Catching her balance she heard moaning coming from a room down the hall. Ursula followed her into the apartment and closed the door.

"*Neige ihn!*" Ursula commanded pointing down the hall. Gloria understood that Ursula wanted her to help whoever was moaning. She headed down the hall. The sour smell grew stronger. At the doorway to the bedroom she recoiled from the smell before forcing herself to look in. A man lay on blankets. His hair was long and matted and his eyes were closed but it was his face that drew her attention. She tried not to react. She didn't want to alert Ursula to the fact that he meant anything to her but Gloria knew immediately that she had found Harrie and he was not dead. Not yet anyway.

She had to convince Ursula that he needed medical attention. There was nothing she as a nurse could do. He needed to be in a hospital – to be hooked up to an IV and to be given penicillin for his leg wound.

"He needs to be seen by a doctor," Gloria said slowly and carefully hoping that Ursula would understand. Ursula looked at her blankly.

"*Arzt. Krankenhaus*" Gloria said, suddenly remembering the words for doctor and hospital. How could she convince the woman? Harrie would not last much longer!

Ursula handed her a cloth and made washing motions gesturing towards Harrie. Gloria took the cloth and ran it under the tap.

"It won't help," she said knowing that Ursula wouldn't understand. "Washing him isn't going to make him better. He needs to be seen by a doctor and quickly. He will die otherwise." Gloria made a half-hearted attempt to wash Harrie's torso. It pained her to look at him. Besides being unconscious he was so skinny she was afraid his skin would come off when she touched him. His eyes fluttered open as she put the wet washcloth on his arm.

"Mamma" he said. His eyes closed and Gloria blinked back tears. She couldn't fall apart now. She straightened, turned around, and faced Ursula.

"*Er muss zum Krankenhaus gehen*," Gloria said sternly. She hoped that by speaking German she had impressed upon Ursula the fact that Harrie needed to go to the hospital. She must've said what she intended because Ursula went to a window and had a conversation with someone outside.

A half hour later Gloria watched as two ambulance attendants arrived to remove Harrie. Ursula stood near to Gloria her gun in plain sight and pointed at Gloria's heart. One of the soldiers carrying the stretcher looked briefly at Ursula but for the most part they focussed their attention on

Harrie. Gloria was given no chance to signal that she needed help. It was more important that Harrie be seen by a doctor. As soon as they were through the doorway Ursula slammed the door shut and locked it.

Gloria sat on a chair waiting to see what Ursula would do. Ursula walked around muttering to herself. She stood at the window looking out at the street. After another quarter hour Gloria stood.

"*Ich werde gehen jetzt,*" she said pointing to the door. She was going to leave. It was surprising how being in a stressful situation concentrated her mind and brought the German words to mind. Ursula stepped in front of Gloria and pointed to the chair saying something as she did so. It was probably "Sit down." Gloria sat.

Ursula began talking. The only word Gloria recognized was "*Haftling*" which she knew meant prisoner. The German continued and Gloria gave up trying to decipher what the woman was saying. She seemed to be debating with herself.

"Why?" asked Gloria. "Why did you keep Harrie here so long?"

Ursula didn't even look at her. Gloria tried again.

"*Warum?*" she said. Ursula stared at her. "*Warum behalte Harrie hier?*"

Ursula let loose with a stream of German all of it unintelligible to Gloria.

Listening to the woman muttering to herself Gloria doubted that the woman herself knew why she'd done it. If Ursula wasn't insane she was close to it. Ursula returned to the kitchen and Gloria sat quietly wondering what Willem was doing. After another hour or so, Gloria needed to use the facilities.

"*Ich gehen die Toilette*" she said hoping that she'd said she had to use the toilet. Ursula ushered Gloria down the hall and stood outside the door not allowing Gloria to close it. As she sat in the living room after her bathroom break she started to think about what she would do if the opportunity to escape ever presented itself.

Suddenly Ursula appeared in front of her and motioned her towards the door. Gloria stood quickly but cringed when she noticed the gun was still in Ursula's hand. She could feel it against her back as they went down the stairs. Gloria matched her footsteps to Ursula's as they descended. She didn't want the gun to go off accidentally. When they reached the ground floor Gloria opened the back door and several things happened simultaneously.

She fell to her knees, hit the ground hard, and rolled to the right. She saw Willem running towards her and she heard firecrackers.

Chapter 48:

Willem reached Gloria and gathered her in his arms. She was covered in blood. So much blood. She must be dying.

"Gloria! Gloria! Do not die!" he cried. "I love you. I love you."

He felt her moving and he loosened his grip rocking slightly on his heels. He sat on the ground holding her on his lap. After a few minutes she stirred.

"You love me?" she questioned in a soft voice, looking at his face. "I love you too."

Willem kissed her in spite of the blood.

"I see you're all right then," said a male voice. Willem looked up to see Lieutenant Earle.

§ § §

"Ursula thought she could use Gloria as a hostage," Willem explained to Frederick.

"But I wasn't about to let that happen," said Gloria. "I dropped as soon as we were out the door giving the soldiers a chance to shoot Ursula. As I fell I saw Willem but I couldn't change my plan. He thought the soldiers had shot me."

"Why did Ursula want to use you as a hostage?" asked Frederick. The three of them were sitting in his living room discussing the events of the previous day.

"I had convinced her to let Harrie be taken to the hospital," said Gloria. "Once she realized she could no longer trade him for safe passage to America I guess she thought to use me. After Harrie left she spent a while talking to herself. My guess is that she didn't want to be tried as a war criminal in Germany."

"Earle assured me," said Willem, seeing Frederick's look of incredulity, "that they would not have let her go free but they would have agreed to her terms until Harrie and Gloria were safe."

"How is Harrie?" asked Frederick. "Have you been to the hospital yet?"

"One of the American soldiers dropped me off after we brought Gloria here last night," said Willem. "I was not able to talk to him because he is not fully conscious yet. He is receiving treatment for dehydration. The injuries on his arms and wrists indicate he fought having the cuffs on him though. He did not come here willingly."

"Harrie was in a bad way when I saw him," Gloria said. "But Ursula tried to say that they cared for each other. She insisted that the reason she kept him chained to the bed was so that her boyfriend would leave him alone. But I doubt if that's true. Given what Karl and Rilla told us about Ursula I think it more likely that she's insane."

The three of them were silent.

"I still do not know," Willem said finally, "how Harrie ended up in Germany with Ursula but I am glad he did not come to Germany of his own free will." Willem went on to tell Frederick how the Underground had sent Harrie to live with Dirk in Amsterdam.

"And Ursula was Dirk's sister?" asked Frederick. "Why did she suddenly move to Amsterdam so late in the war?"

"She likely wanted Dirk to become a Nazi and return to Germany with her," said Willem. "She did not seem to understand that the Nazis had lost the war. Harrie may be able to explain more when he recovers." Frederick sipped his coffee.

"He is expected to make a full recovery then?"

"That is the prognosis," Willem said standing and pouring another mug of coffee. He held the pot up silently asking Frederick if he wanted more and topped up his mug when Frederick nodded. Then he filled Gloria's mug with tea. Frederick put his mug on the table.

"With Ursula dead what will the Americans do now?" he asked.

"They seem to think they'll find evidence in her apartment to get the rest of the gang," said Willem with a small smile. "But that is not my problem. I just have to take Harrie to Holland."

For several days Willem stayed at his brother's bed side as Harrie slipped in and out of consciousness. One day Gloria went with her husband to be there to give support if Harrie's condition deteriorated.

"I failed my brother when he did not get out of Holland before the war," Willem said defending his actions although no one had questioned them. "I will not fail him now."

§ § §

Harrie was resting comfortably and Gloria felt she could leave for an hour or so. There was one important task to do. She sent a telegram informing Willem's parents that Harrie was alive but in the hospital. On her way back to the hospital she bought a sandwich for Willem.

Willem was sitting in his usual spot beside the bed eating his sandwich when Harrie turned his head. Gloria was on the other side of the bed but from what she could see she thought Harrie's eyes looked more focussed.

"Wil-lem" Harrie rasped without expression making the name two distinct syllables.

"Harrie! Oh Harrie! You are awake," Willem said dropping the last bit of bread as he stood.

"Harrie is awake — look he is awake!" Willem said joyfully. He leaned over the bed looking his brother directly in the eyes.

"Harrie! Oh, Harrie you are back!"

Harrie looked at his brother impassively his eyes moving back and forth over Willem's face. When his eyes closed Willem turned to Gloria.

"Is he all right?" he asked anxiously.

"He is as well as can be expected my dear," Gloria said gently leading her husband away from the bed. Two nurses approached Harrie's bed one going to each side. Gloria led William to the far side of the ward where they stood together leaning against the wall. Willem let his head fall on his chest and his eyes closed of their own accord.

"Willem," she said gently shaking his arm.

His eyes jerked open when he heard Gloria's voice and he raised his head.

"Why don't you go back to Frederick's apartment for a rest?" she said, patting his arm. They were waiting for the nurses to be finished with Harrie and even leaning against the wall, Willem had fallen sleep.

"Harrie will likely sleep for a while," said Gloria, "and you are exhausted. You'll be able to have a good rest now. I'll walk back with you," she said, "and then return to be here if Harrie wakes again."

"Perhaps I should," said Willem slowly. "I am very tired. But I am so happy so very happy that Harrie is back." He grinned at Gloria.

Willem spent as much time as he could over the next two days by Harrie's bed to be there if Harrie should awaken. Gloria accompanied him and they were both at Harrie's bedside when Harrie opened his eyes and looked at his brother.

"Where…is… Dirk?" Harrie said in a soft voice pausing between each word. He spoke in a monotone. Willem glanced at Gloria before putting his hand on his brother's shoulder.

"I am sorry to tell you this, Harrie, but Dirk is dead," he said sadly.

"Dirk…is…dead." Harrie repeated in a toneless voice. His face was impassive his lips and cheeks pale. He closed his eyes and did not speak for the remainder of the day.

§ § §

Willem wanted to spend every minute of every day with Harrie but the day after Harrie asked about Dirk Gloria convinced Willem to go for a short walk while Harrie was sleeping.

"I'll be here," she said, "if Harrie speaks again."

Willem reluctantly agreed and with one last look at his brother he left saying he'd only be gone for five or ten minutes. When Willem returned to the ward he saw Gloria waving excitedly. He hurried to Harrie's bedside where his brother was lying on his back with his eyes open. He was staring straight ahead.

"Come over here," whispered Gloria moving a few feet away from Harrie's bed. "Harrie woke up again and when he saw me he thought I was Ursula."

"What did you say?" asked Willem in an undertone.

"I had to tell him Ursula was dead," whispered Gloria.

Willem walked closer to Harrie's bed. His brother's eyes were still open but unfocussed. Willem took Harrie's hand in his. With his other hand he pulled a chair close and sat. Harrie looked at Willem and took a breath.

"Urs-la," he said with great effort.

"Harrie," said Willem. "Ursula is dead."

Without knowing what the relationship was between the two Willem didn't know how Harrie would react to the news but he couldn't lie to his brother.

"Urs-la...dead," Harrie said tonelessly.

"I'm sorry," Willem said in a soft voice.

Harrie's lips moved but he made no sound. His eyelids fluttered closed and although Willem remained for several minutes Harrie didn't open his eyes again. Willem signalled to Gloria and after one last look at his brother he and Gloria left the hospital.

As they walked home Gloria said, "His memory does seem to be returning. That's a good sign."

"How long will it take for him to remember everything?" asked Willem. "There are so many questions I want to ask him." Gloria hesitated before answering.

"We have to be prepared for the fact that he may never remember everything," she said gently. Willem looked at her sharply.

"If Harrie is not able to tell us who died," he said "we may never find out whose body it is. But at least we know it isn't Harrie."

Chapter 49:

When Willem arrived at the hospital the next day an American doctor was on the ward. Willem asked him what Harrie's prognosis was.

"We don't really know," the doctor said. "He seems to be coming along well. Keep talking to him and reassuring him that you're here. That may help. The brain is a remarkable organ but we don't understand what happens when a person is unconscious."

Willem barely managed to voice his thanks before the doctor strode off. For the next two days Willem talked to Harrie greeting him cheerily as he arrived and telling him that when he was better Willem would take him to Holland where Mamma and Pa were waiting to see him.

Willem went to the hospital alone one morning. He'd left Gloria visiting with Esmee and Margriet. Harrie had been more active – moving his arms and legs – but he had not said anything for over a day. Willem wanted Harrie to wake up completely so he could question him about what had happened. The doctors and nurses were pleased with Harrie's progress and thought he'd be well enough to travel soon but it wasn't happening fast enough for Willem.

Willem observed Harrie lying peacefully on the bed. He looked to be asleep. Willem greeted him cheerily as was his custom. Suddenly Harrie moved.

"No!" he shouted. "Klaus!"

§ § §

Willem burst into Margriet's apartment when Esmee answered the door. He was panting, his hair was wind-blown, and his face was red with exertion.

"What is it?" Gloria asked fearing the worst; Harrie must've died.

"Klaus," said Willem breathlessly. He must have run a good part of the way from the hospital. "The body," he gasped. He collapsed in a chair. Gloria moved to the sink and poured him a glass of water.

"Drink this," she said handing him the glass. He took it and drank it all pausing only to gulp air. Gloria pulled a chair close and sat beside him. When Willem finished the water, he took a couple deep breaths.

"Harrie suddenly said the name, Klaus," he said. "That's all he said, but the nurses talked about getting him up tomorrow. We can ask him then if Klaus could be who was killed with Dirk."

§ § §

Willem was just emerging from the bedroom when Gloria arrived at Frederick's apartment in the morning. Frederick had let her in as he was leaving for work.

"I was going to make tea," said Gloria after Willem was dressed. "But Frederick doesn't have any."

"We have no time for tea," said Willem. "We have to get to the hospital. We may be able to talk to Harrie today and finally get some answers."

Arriving at the hospital they went directly to the ward where Harrie was. Gloria sat on one side of the bed and Willem sat on the other. Harrie was leaning against two pillows and his eyes were open. He looked more alert. When Willem greeted him in the usual way, Harrie replied.

"Hello Willem," he said. His eyes flitted past Willem. Willem turned around and saw two nurses entering the ward. One of them was carrying a wash basin and the other was pointing at Harrie but she was smiling.

"We'll wait in the hall," Gloria said quickly as one nurse reached to pull the curtain around Harrie's bed. Gloria signalled Willem to follow her as she walked away.

A half hour later Harrie was washed and wearing a clean shirt. He sat on the bed with his back against the wall. Gloria and Willem sat together on two hard backed chairs beside the bed.

"It is great to see you looking so good," said Willem enthusiastically. He beamed at his brother.

"This is my wife Gloria," he added putting his arm across Gloria's shoulders. She smiled at Harrie.

"Do you feel like talking?" she asked kindly. When he bobbed his head she continued, "We've been trying to piece together your story to figure out how you came to be in Germany. Can you help us?"

Harrie shifted his gaze from Gloria to Willem. When his brother nodded eagerly Harrie shrugged slightly.

"What do you want to know?" he asked speaking slowly and without inflection. Willem glanced at his wife before speaking.

"We know you were living with Dirk in Amsterdam," he said tersely. "What we do not know is how you came to be in Germany and why you did not try to contact us, your family, after the war ended." Willem was trying to keep his anger in check. Gloria patted her husband on the knee as she spoke to Harrie.

"Willem has been very worried about you," she said gently. "Were you injured? Is that why you didn't leave Ursula and return to Holland?"

Harrie shifted on the bed straightening the blanket that was covering his bottom half. His feet sticking out from under the blanket were bare.

"I do not remember," he said tonelessly. No one said anything and finally Harrie gave a deep sigh.

"I remember a little," he said. He paused and looked at Willem's eager face. He started speaking again.

"Dirk's sister arrived near the end of the war, maybe in '44," he said speaking deliberately and pausing between words. "At first she was pleasant."

He stopped talking and closed his eyes taking a few deep breaths. Gloria and Willem remained silent.

After a minute, Harrie continued, "She was interested in me, I could tell." He stopped and took several more deep breaths.

When he started talking again Willem had to strain to hear. "It was very embarrassing. Dirk either did not notice or he pretended not to."

Willem leaned forward listening intently. Harrie shifted uncomfortably and Gloria looked from one brother to the other. She motioned to Willem to join her a few feet from the bed.

"Harrie is having trouble talking about this," she said in a soft voice. "Do you think he'd feel better just talking to me? I'm a nurse."

"Let me talk to him a bit more," said Willem. "If you think he would rather just talk to you, I can go to get the papers so we can leave tomorrow." They took their seats at Harrie's bedside as he began speaking again.

"She spied on us – on Dirk and me," he said, "sneaking up behind us and trying to listen to what we were saying when we were having a private conversation." He paused again taking a deep breath. "When her friends came over she never failed to mention how the Nazis did not tolerate abnormal and deviant behaviour." He stopped talking and stared off into space.

"Many times I was afraid she would just shoot us both," he said after a few minutes. "When she did not I wondered if she still had some feelings for Dirk since he was her older brother. But I also feared that sooner or later she would snap." Willem leaned forward.

"You could never predict what she was going to do," he said earnestly.

Without a noticeable movement Harrie recoiled from his brother's intense gaze. Gloria again looked from one brother to the other. She grabbed Willem's hand and suggested they go out to the hall and let Harrie rest for a minute.

"Why don't I stay with Harrie," she said when they were in the hall, "and you can chase down the papers we'll need to take him back to Holland. I think he'll be ready to go soon, perhaps as early as tomorrow." Willem closed his eyes briefly.

"That might be better," he said. "I get angry all over again listening to him. If I had made sure he was on the boat this would not have happened." He made a fist and mimed hitting the wall. Gloria reached for his hand and held it in hers.

"That may or may not be true," she said, "but I think the quicker we get him to Amsterdam the better it will be." She raised his fist to her lips and kissed it. He touched her on the shoulder before turning and walking away. She watched him for a minute before re-entering the ward.

Chapter 50:

"Willem has gone to get the papers we need to take you back to Amsterdam," said Gloria after returning to Harrie's bedside. "I think you'll be ready to travel tomorrow. If you want to continue talking to me I'm a nurse and I cared for injured men who were hospitalized in Amsterdam."

Harrie turned to look at Gloria. She thought he seemed calmer. Gloria wondered if perhaps Harrie felt that his brother didn't understand him even though they were twins. She waited for him to continue.

"One time she saw me and Dirk standing together and she was enraged," he said softly. Gloria had to strain to hear him. "We were just talking but it angered her so much she went on about it for several days. We made sure we were never alone together after that. She was getting even more volatile after end of the war and we did not want to do something that would set her off." Harrie stopped talking. After a brief pause Gloria spoke.

"How did you come to be at Dirk's in the first place?" she asked. "*Meneer* Salentijn told us the Underground had sent you there but Willem couldn't figure out why."

"The Underground knew that the Nazis wanted to recruit Dirk to give them information about Allied troop movements, but communication fell apart just as they were setting it up," Harrie said. He started coughing and Gloria passed him a glass of water. He took a few sips before continuing.

"The Allies wanted to discover exactly what his role was and they asked the Underground to help. I had known Dirk before the war and the Underground thought I could get a job in his shop."

"Surely he wasn't still doing business was he?" asked Gloria sceptically.

"Not strictly," said Harrie with a weary shake of his head. "He was not selling watches. No one had money to buy them. But he was accepting jewellery and giving money in return. Then he sold the jewels on the black market." Gloria nodded. Harrie took several deep breaths before continuing.

"Dirk was doing enough business that it sounded reasonable for me to ask for a job in return for room and board," he said. "That gave me an excuse for living there. Sometimes I thought Dirk knew I was spying on him but it did not seem to bother him."

Harrie paused and as the silence lengthened Gloria glanced at him. He had closed his eyes and was breathing deeply. Finally he opened his eyes but he didn't look at her when he started speaking.

"We both felt something towards each other, me and Dirk," he said so quietly that Gloria had to strain to catch his words. "But we fought against it. We, we, we did not want to —", he paused again, glancing at her. His eyes were full of pain. He looked away before continuing.

"Ursula thought she saw – something – I do not know what but it was nothing. I do not remember. Maybe Dirk put his hand on my arm. It was nothing - nothing." His voice was getting louder and the man in the next bed looked their way. Gloria stood and straightened Harrie's blankets as a nurse rushed over.

Harrie took a deep breath and smiled at the approaching woman. Her eyes softened as she looked at him.

"How y'all doin'?" she said pleasantly.

"Fine," said Harrie. He seemed at a loss for words.

Gloria stepped back to allow the nurse to fuss over Harrie. After straightening the blanket she left casting a reproachful glance at Gloria.

"Sorry," he mumbled after the nurse was out of hearing range. Gloria smiled and shook her head slightly. Calmer now Harrie took another deep breath and resumed his tale.

"We thought it would blow over," he said quietly. "But one day Dirk's friend, Klaus, came to visit. He was a business associate but Ursula took it in her mind that he was like Dirk too." Harrie stopped talking.

Gloria remained silent watching him. After another deep breath he continued. "She told Dirk he could not be that way anymore because she would not allow it in any house where she was living. Dirk tried to laugh it off. He was so embarrassed at having her say that in front of Klaus.

"Without warning she pulled a gun and shot them both. Bang. Bang. She pointed the gun at me and I felt a pain in my head." Harrie paused frowning in concentration. "Things get a little fuzzy after that. I am not sure exactly what happened. I may have blacked out but I think Ursula left and returned with her boyfriend. I am not sure. When she walked in I expected to die right away — I thought she would kill me when she saw I was still alive. But she held me in her arms and told her friend to help me." Harrie paused again swallowing several times. Gloria handed him a glass of water.

"The two of them got me to Germany," said Harrie. He drank the water. "I am not sure how that happened either. Parts in my memory are missing.

They moved me into a house in Marl. When I was awake I listened to what Ursula was saying and I knew the war had ended but they talked about not giving up. It seemed Ursula and her friends did not want to believe the Nazis had lost the war." Harrie yawned.

"Perhaps you should rest for a while," said Gloria. "I'll go find Willem now and we'll come back this afternoon."

Harrie nodded and closed his eyes. Gloria tiptoed away stopping at the nurses' station to say she was leaving. The nurse glanced at her briefly but didn't speak.

Gloria walked a block before she saw Willem talking to an American soldier. He ended his conversation as soon as he saw her and walked to where she waited.

"Did you get the papers? When can we leave?" she asked eagerly. "I think Harrie is well enough to travel." Willem looked calmer. He gave her a quick squeeze around her shoulders.

"The papers are here," he said patting his pocket. "We can take him home tomorrow."

"That's good news," she said. "I said we would go back to visit him this afternoon."

They turned and walked along the street until they came to a bench in an area that might one day be a park.

"What else did he say?" asked Willem when they were seated.

Gloria told him what Harrie had said although when she came to the part about him and Dirk she hesitated feeling uncomfortable. But it had to be done; she had to tell Willem.

"Harrie was adamant that nothing happened between him and Dirk," she stated. "He said that Ursula must've misinterpreted whatever she thought she saw."

"It sounds like you are not so sure," said Willem.

"Ursula was so upset it caused her to kill two men and to try to kill Harrie," she said. "She must have seen something. It could not all have been a misunderstanding could it?" She turned to look at Willem searching his face for an answer.

"Did Harrie think it was a misunderstanding?" Willem asked gently. He stood and pulled Gloria to her feet.

"Harrie doesn't remember," said Gloria as they started walking. "If Ursula really was not quite right in the head perhaps that caused her to misinterpret what she saw." Gloria paused.

"He also heard Ursula talking about the end of the war," she said, "but her group did not want to believe that the Nazis had lost." She looked at her husband frowning in bewilderment. "Could Ursula and her group really have believed that?"

"Ursula might have wanted to believe she could still be a Nazi," said Willem forcefully, "but her boyfriend would have known better. It is more likely they were out for revenge."

"Harrie was also unclear about how he got to Germany," said Gloria. She suddenly realized that Willem had taken them back to the hospital while they were talking. She hoped Harrie was rested and prepared to talk.

When Willem and Gloria arrived at the ward Harrie was being tended by the nurse but after a five minute wait they were allowed to visit with him. They were cautioned not to stay too long and to leave if Harrie seemed tired. Gloria saw the wink Harrie gave the nurse before she left. The nurse, a Black American woman at least ten years his senior, winked back.

"Gloria says you do not remember how you got to Germany," said Willem.

"I remember a dream," said Harrie. "I was in a truck with soldiers. It was night and they told me to be quiet but perhaps it was not a dream." He looked at his brother and shrugged his shoulders. Willem shared a look with Gloria and they both nodded.

"It wasn't a dream," said Gloria. "That's how Ursula did it."

"Gloria filled me in on what you told her this morning," said Willem. "Why did you not leave once you knew the war was over?"

"She, Ursula, kept me chained to the bed," said Harrie. He struggled to sit up crossing his legs under the blanket. He took a couple deep breaths before continuing. "One time I tried to escape while I was unchained for a bathroom break but her boyfriend and his friend caught me and pounded the living daylights out of me. I was in a very bad way but Ursula took pity on me and nursed me back to health. Another time her boyfriend burned my leg with his cigarette. He claimed it was an accident, but Ursula urged him to do it. Then she wanted to take care of me. Many times, it was like that.

"It was as if," Harrie paused and closed his eyes a frown on his face. After a moment he opened his eyes "It was as if as long as I was sick or in pain she would take care of me but if I started to get better she would lose interest in me. Sometimes when I was starting to get better she would forget to feed me. It was very strange."

Gloria looked at Willem remembering what the Metzer's had told them about Ursula being mentally unstable as a girl. It certainly sounded as if Ursula was a few bricks shy of a load. Harrie caught the look.

"What is it?" he asked looking at Willem. "What do you know?" Willem filled his brother in on his and Gloria's activities in Marl as they'd searched for him.

"Mamma and Pa were told that you were dead…"

"Oh no!" Harrie exclaimed, interrupting him. "They think I am dead? We have to tell them…"

"Don't worry," said Gloria, putting her hand on his arm to reassure him. "They know you're alive now. I told them when we first found you. And they'll tell Anneke," she added. "She too had been told you were dead." Harrie closed his eyes and bowed his head.

"How soon can we go home?" he asked.

"I have the papers. We will leave tomorrow afternoon," Willem said as Harrie slid down in the cot. "Gloria and I will pick you up at eleven hundred hours. That will give us enough time to get to the train by thirteen hundred hours. Gloria and I will tell the nurse on our way out."

Gloria straightened the blankets over Harrie. She and Willem waved as they walked away. They stopped at the nurses' station and Willem showed the head nurse the paper signed by Lieutenant Earle.

"I'll make sure Harrie is ready to go when you arrive," she said after seeing the orders.

Chapter 51:

Gloria was finding it hard to say goodbye to Esmee. They had developed a friendship during the time they had spent together while Gloria sorted out her thoughts about Willem having a twin brother. It was not that she was attracted to Harrie Gloria explained to Esmee. She loved Willem and never mistook one brother for the other. But she felt – something – she wasn't sure what.

"Perhaps what you think are feelings for Harrie are really a mirror of what Willem is feeling now that he has found his brother," Esmee had said. "For many years, from the time he went to Canada he did not talk about his brother because he thought Harrie was dead. Willem will find it difficult to express how happy he is now that his brother has been found alive – if he is anything like my brother that is. And I suspect he is." Gloria reflected on that.

"It's true," she said. "I do feel very happy for Willem. He suffered for many years thinking that his brother was gone and it was his fault. But now I can rejoice with him that his brother is alive."

Gloria saw Willem at the door. She hugged Margriet good-bye and picked up her suitcase. After handing her bag to Willem she hugged Esme.

"Good-bye," she said before following Willem down the stairs. In her suitcase she had two letters – one to Mevrouw Smit from Margriet and another to Theo from Hans.

§ § §

Walking behind Willem and Harrie after getting off the train in Amsterdam, Gloria observed that the two men had similar gaits; each walked with a spring in his step. Harrie seemed taller but it could've been that he was thinner and that would change as he gained back the weight he'd lost. Gloria's observations had begun as soon as she saw the two of them sitting together on the train.

Harrie had a beard and mustache while Willem was clean-shaven. Willem's eyes were darker than Harrie's brown ones. Nevertheless, the resemblances were uncanny. Standing at ease they held their arms the same way. She suspected they each had a good sense of humour although Harrie's wasn't as noticeable right now. Conversation between the two men had been strained at first but they were talking easily now as they walked.

Willem and Harrie's reunion with their parents was going to be another emotional time for all of them and Gloria wondered how Harrie would handle it. When she opened the apartment door she stepped back so Harrie could enter first.

Mamma saw him and she jumped to her feet, exclaiming, "*Oh, mijn zoon.*" Tears ran down her face as she wrapped her arms around Harrie. He hugged her back his eyes shut and his lips clamped tight. Willem stepped up and hugged them both. Skirting them Gloria went into the living room but Pa and Pieter had heard Mamma say "My son."

"*Tante* Gloria," Pieter shrieked flinging himself into Gloria's arms.

"Pieter, oh Pietje, I've missed you," Gloria crooned, standing with him in her arms. Pa rushed past them both to wrap his arms around his wife and sons and the four of them stood immobile for a full minute. Mamma released Harrie and Gloria set Pieter down simultaneously. The little boy looked at Harrie in confusion his eyes growing big.

"*Oom*," he said.

Hearing the voice Harrie extricated himself from the entwined arms and looked around to see where it was coming from. His eyes finally found Pieter's face.

He said nothing for a minute but then he mumbled, "I remember you. Pieter." Another pause. "Pieter Zweers." He pronounced it "Payter." Stumbling to a chair at the kitchen table he sat putting his head in his hands. Gloria sat on a chair beside him and beckoned to Pieter.

"Come and sit on my lap dear," she said helping Pieter to climb up. He turned his worried gaze from Harrie's face now hidden in his hands to Gloria's face.

"*Oom* Harrie has been sick," she said softly, "but he'll be better soon." The boy seemed comforted by her words and leaned back against her chest. He put his hand tentatively on Harrie's arm.

"*Oom*," he said gently.

Harrie raised his head and turned to look at the boy. A small smile brightened his face momentarily and then was gone but it was the first real smile Gloria had seen.

"Pieter," he said. "Pietje." He put his hand atop the little hand on his arm. Harrie looked at his brother and at Gloria in turn.

"What happened to the others?" he asked. "Pieter's family – where are they?"

"We'll tell you later," said Gloria quickly. Pieter spoke at the same time.

"They are dead," he said in a matter-of-fact voice. "I tried to save Tonny but I could not. He died."

"Tonny," repeated Harrie, looking at Pieter. "Tonny. I took you and Tonny to the neighbour's." he paused with a look of concentration on his face. "I do not remember his name. Soldiers came. I had to get you away before they saw us."

He opened his mouth to say more but just then a knock sounded on the door. Mamma was closest and she opened it. Anneke paused at the doorway. Her gaze swept over Gloria and Willem to land on Harrie.

"You are alive!" she said in a disbelieving voice. She stood still for a few seconds and then walked towards the kitchen table. Harrie stood as she approached and he opened his arms. As she walked into his embrace his arms tightened around her.

Chapter 52:

Gloria was feeling excited and nervous the day she, Willem, and Pieter met with the people from the Dutch Reform Church to arrange for Pieter's adoption. There was one tense moment when Pieter mentioned that he was going to live with *"Oom* Harrie." Gloria quickly assured the woman handling the adoption that Pieter did know who his new parents were going to be and it was only the excitement of seeing Harrie after so long an absence that caused the slip. Once the final papers were signed they had a small celebration and invited Anneke and her father to attend.

After dinner while they were cleaning dishes in the kitchen Anneke asked Gloria if they could talk privately. Gloria was intrigued by the request and agreed to meet with her the next day. Neither woman wanted to miss hearing Harrie's account of why he hadn't gotten on the boat to England with Willem.

"There were so many people on the dock," Harrie said, "I followed Willem as best I could but people kept getting in the way. Everyone was so anxious to be on the boat. I knew Willem couldn't see me and I tried to wave to let him know I was there. Someone bumped into me and I fell.

Then the sailors started casting off. I heard Willem calling, telling me to jump, but I could not. I just could not. There were too many people."

Gloria was watching Willem as Harrie talked wondering if hearing what happened from Harrie's own lips would finally ease the guilt Willem had felt for so many years.

"A man did try to jump but he ended up in the water and they had to fish him out," Harrie continued. "By then the boat was too far away. People were shoving and screaming, trying to get the boat to come back. I waited in the area for a few days hoping there would be another boat but no one would chance it."

He stopped talking again and Gloria was aware of a look passing between the brothers but she didn't know what it meant. Maybe it was her imagination.

"I started back up the coast heading towards Holland," Harrie said, "I got as far as Den Hague when I met a chap who said the German army was in Amsterdam. He was going to Friesland to find work with a farmer. I thought that sounded like a good idea so I changed my mind about going to Amsterdam. I did not try contacting Mamma because my new friend said the Germans were controlling everything by then. I did not want to put her or Pa in any danger.

"When we got to Friesland the chap contacted Aert Zweers and I stayed there for a year or more. When the Nazis raided his place I was able to get Pieter and Tonny to a neighbour's but I did not stick around. I contacted the Underground and they sent me to Amsterdam."

Harrie leaned back in his chair and closed his eyes. No one spoke for a minute or two. Pieter yawned and Gloria and Willem took him into the bedroom. By the time they returned to the living room Harrie and Anneke were gone. Mamma and Pa were going into their bedroom.

§ § §

"What an amazing story!" said Gloria quietly as she and Willem were getting ready for bed, "but it explains why Harrie didn't make it onto the boat and it was not your fault at all," she said. She leaned forward to kiss him.

"We can talk tomorrow about returning to Canada," she continued. "I would like to move back. I know my parents would sponsor us. What do you think?"

"I feel happier now about moving to Canada," whispered Willem. "I will begin to make enquiries tomorrow."

Shortly after breakfast the next morning Gloria said good-bye to Pieter and Willem and walked down to Anneke's apartment. They'd decided the night before the only way they could have a private conversation was by going for a walk. When they were on the sidewalk Gloria paused to look at a flower in a garden.

"It is heart-warming to see flowers struggling to grow against all odds," she said to Anneke. Anneke looked at the flower briefly but kept walking.

"I know what Harrie is like," said Anneke gently, stopping to wait for Gloria. "And it does not matter to me. I love him because he makes me laugh." Gloria looked at her sharply.

"You are a nurse," said Anneke. "You know that some men like men. Harrie says he was surprised to find that he likes women too. He asked me to marry him last night when he walked me down to my apartment after dinner," she said calmly.

"You and Harrie are getting married? That's wonderful," cried Gloria grabbing Anneke's hands. "I'm so happy for you! Have you set a date?" Anneke gently eased her hands out of Gloria's grip.

"We have not talked about a date," she said starting to walk again. "But soon I think. Harrie wants to apply to work for the Amsterdam police as soon as he is able. Being married to me will help to dispel rumours." Gloria felt like she'd been hit in the stomach.

"You don't suspect…" she started to say and stopped. Could Harrie be that mean, that calculating? Was he only marrying Anneke to dispel rumours?

"No, no," said Anneke quickly. "I did not mean it to sound like that. I think Harrie cares for me as he is able. I do love him. We will be happy." She blushed again.

The two women finished their walk and returned to the apartment building. Willem and Harrie had gone out. Gloria waited impatiently for them to return; she could hardly wait to tell Willem what Anneke had said. When Willem returned half an hour later he had news of his own. Gloria bit her tongue and listened to Willem tell his story. Willem and Harrie had gone to the police to clear up the misunderstanding about the dead body.

"We spoke to Adri who was happy to see Harrie again," said Willem. "Adri said he would contact the police in Germany and do whatever was needed to make sure the dead body was correctly identified.

"I was glad to get out of the police station," Willem continued. "Harrie seemed unaware of anything but I noticed a few policemen looking at Harrie oddly. They might have heard the story about Harrie and Dirk and it may affect how they treat him if he wants to join the police after he recovers."

Gloria was going to speak, but Willem leaned closer and spoke in a soft voice.

"You'll never guess what Harrie told me," he said. He looked around and lowered his voice even more. Gloria had a hard time hearing him.

"Harrie is attracted to women as well as men," Willem said.

"I know," said Gloria. "Anneke just told me."

They were whispering like a couple of schoolkids but Mamma and Pieter were in the kitchen not paying them any attention. Willem looked disappointed that Gloria hadn't been more surprised.

"Harrie also told me," said Willem secretly, "that is probably why he's alive today." Gloria looked at him in amazement.

"Why did he say that?" she asked.

"Harrie thinks that Ursula did not kill him because she thought he was attracted to her," said Willem. "She must have thought she could save him from being homosexual." Gloria looked at him in confusion.

"But you said that wasn't possible," she said. "You said that a man is born as one or he isn't – he doesn't change part-way through life."

"That is what I believe," said Willem. "I do not know if it is true. Ursula obviously believed something else."

"We know that many of her beliefs were foolish," said Gloria. "Perhaps that one is too. I have some news for you."

"What is your news?"

"Harrie asked Anneke to marry him last night," said Gloria. Willem looked at her in surprise.

"Well that answers that question," he said almost to himself.

"What do you mean?"

"Harrie said just as we finished talking that he wondered if he'd be attracted to other women," said Willem smirking, "so I guess he found he is!"

"Oh, Willem," said Gloria punching him playfully in the arm.

§ § §

Anneke and Harrie were married two weeks later in a civil ceremony. As the matron of honour Gloria waited at the back of the room before the ceremony started. She observed the people in attendance.

At the front were Mamma and Pa with Pieter. Mamma's face was a wreath of smiles. Behind them were Maartje with her brother and her father. Her mother was improving but she was still too weak to leave the house. Margriet and Hans were seated behind Maartje having come for a visit in advance of their move which would happen as soon as it could be arranged. On Maartje's other side was a young man who was a stranger to Gloria but she assumed this was Maartje's boyfriend's older brother Rik. He'd been out of the house when the bomb had hit killing his brother and his parents.

Maartje had met Rik once or twice when she was going with Mathias but she had never spent much time with him. Recently they had gotten together and discovered they shared a common interest in history and literature. Gloria wondered if a romance was brewing but even if it wasn't she was glad Maartje had a friend.

Dom and Jenny Molenaar had been invited because Dom had known Harrie briefly in May 1940. After Gloria had greeted Jenny, Dom spoke to Gloria.

"There's no reason not to tell you what I know of Ernst Visser now," he said. "Harrie was working as a decoy leading German soldiers away from a cache of weapons. Ernst was helping to cover for Harrie when the weapons exploded injuring Ernst. He eventually lost his leg. When he realized that Harrie had escaped uninjured he began to spread a rumour about Harrie being a traitor."

"Thank you for telling me that Dom," said Gloria. "It clears up another part of the mystery and may help to ease Willem's guilt."

Gloria looked to where Harrie was standing with Anneke at his side. Anneke was radiant as all brides should be and Harrie had gained back much of his weight. Gloria knew that Willem believed implicitly that Harrie had never betrayed his country but Gloria hadn't been able to shake her doubts. With Dom's admission she was finally able to believe that Harrie had not been a traitor.

Willem had been Harrie's best man and Gloria had been feeling the tiniest twinge of guilt that Harrie had missed out on being Willem's best man. Seeing the two brothers together supporting each other through this happy time Gloria was able to let go of that guilt.

After the ceremony, everyone gathered at the Spelt's apartment for a reception. It was crowded but everyone was in good spirits and no one minded the congestion. Harrie made a heart-felt speech thanking everyone for coming but in many ways, it was a declaration of his feelings for Anneke. Gloria hoped they would have a long and happy life together.

Chapter 53:

Gloria stood at the railing of the ship and looked out over the ocean. It felt good to stand and do nothing after the past few months of near constant activity. Her husband and her son were playing ping pong. She could hear Pieter laughing although she couldn't see him. She knew that Willem had agreed to adopt Pieter to accommodate her wishes and she'd been afraid that they would never love each other as a father and son should. The opportunity for love to grow had happened because of Harrie. She'd tried to thank him.

"Don't think I haven't noticed what you've been doing," she'd said to him before they left Amsterdam. Fortunately, they were alone in the living room and she'd been able to speak freely. He tried to feign innocence.

"I have no idea what you are talking about," he said holding his hands in the air palms up. She smiled at him.

"You knew Pieter was attached to you," she said, "and you've been helping to wean him away from you by allowing him to develop a relationship with Willem."

Harrie had always asked Willem to join in when he and Pieter had been playing a game of cards. As Pieter had gotten more involved in the game Harrie had let Willem answer his questions. If Pieter asked Harrie to go for a walk Harrie had invited Willem and put the boy in the middle so he held a hand of each man.

"Willem is his father now," Harrie said airily. "It's only right that they should spend time together."

"Yes, well," said Gloria. "I do thank you." She had leaned over to kiss him on the cheek. He had blushed and she laughed in memory of how embarrassed he'd been.

"What is so funny?" asked Willem as he and Pieter approached hand in hand.

"I'm just happy," she said. "Is your game over?"

"Yes. I won!" squealed Pieter. "I beat *Oom*…I mean, Father." Willem laughed.

"It was a good game," he said. "You beat me fair and square."

"Good for you dear," said Gloria, putting her hand on Pieter's shoulder briefly. "We're going back to our room to get ready to go for lunch."

"I'll beat you there," said Pieter walking away quickly. Soon he was out of hearing range. Gloria patted Willem's hand on her shoulder as they followed their son.

"I'm glad we adopted him," she said softly. "I will try my best to make him very happy."

"We both will," Willem agreed planting a kiss in her hair.

Pieter had been excited at the prospect of moving to Canada. He'd asked in a small voice if he could call her and Willem "Mother" and "Father" rather than using the Dutch words for aunt and uncle.

"We will be living in Canada," he said solemnly. "I will be speaking English all the time there; I do not want to call you *tante* and *oom*."

Gloria remembered how delighted she'd been at Pieter's request. These two weeks with just the three of them travelling to Canada would be a time to grow together as a family.

§ § §

After they'd eaten, Willem and Pieter took off hand in hand to do some exploring. Gloria watched them go. Willem had really taken to his role of father. He was likely aware of what Harrie had been doing but he'd been willing to accept the transfer of feelings. Pieter had an insatiable curiosity and Willem was always pleased to answer his questions. If he didn't know the answer he would look it up in the encyclopedia and tell Pieter what he'd leaned.

Later in the evening after Pieter was asleep, Gloria and Willem talked quietly. Gloria leaned her head on Willem's shoulder as they sat on their bed. Willem was propped against the wall his legs stretched out in front of him; Gloria's shorter legs were beside them.

"Thank you for coming to look for me," he said his voice husky with emotion. "I was so surprised to see you at Dom's but having you with me meant that I was able to start searching for Harrie more quickly. Although of course I had not known I was going to have to do that." Gloria shifted her body so she was more comfortable and squeezed Willem's hand.

"I came here not knowing what I was getting into," she said. "In fact I came to the Netherlands, to Holland, but I also came to the Nether-lands, the unknown!" Willem patted her knee.

"Good one, Gloria. That is a good pun." He looked at her and grinned. Gloria grinned in return. It felt good to be silly again and to think of nothing more important than word plays.

The next day it rained and Gloria was confined to the cabin although Willem and Pieter were still able to play ping pong. This time they played against another father and son who were also passengers on the ship.

Gloria knew she would miss all the people she'd met in Holland but she enjoyed writing letters and Maartje had mentioned seeing her the next time she visited her aunt in Winnipeg. Gloria didn't imagine she and Willem would be able to afford a trip to Holland any time soon. It would depend of course on what job Willem was able to get.

"I think I will make application to join the RCMP," Willem had said before they'd set sail. "I would like to be a detective eventually."

Gloria thought Willem would make a fine detective. Being with the RCMP might mean they would have to move but Willem planned to spend a year or two living in Stratford first, working for the Stratford City Police. She picked up her knitting. Mamma had helped to start her on a child-sized pair of mitts but it was slow going. She had to really concentrate on what she was doing so she wouldn't drop a stitch. How she envied Mamma who could knit while she was talking and didn't even need to look at her knitting.

§ § §

They were a week into their trip when Gloria returned to their room to discover Pieter lying on his bed crying.

"Honey what's wrong?" she asked lovingly sitting beside him and gently easing him into her arms. She held him stroking his head until he gradually stopped sobbing.

"I miss Tonny," he said gulping. "I wish he had not died."

"I know you do sweetie," said Gloria kissing him on the forehead. "I too am sorry he isn't here."

"Will there be friends in Canada?" he asked in a small voice.

"Yes," said Gloria nodding. "I'm sure you'll have many friends in Canada."

Pieter sighed and relaxed against her chest. Gloria patted his back wishing she could remove his pain. But she knew from her own experience that it would happen over time.

Willem entered the cabin just then. His eyes met Gloria's over Pieter's head.

"If the ping pong table is not being used," he said touching Pieter on the shoulder. "Do you want to play?"

Pieter sat up and dashed the tears from his face. He stood and looked at Willem.

"I would like that," he said reaching to take Willem's hand. Gloria smiled her thanks at Willem.

"Have a good game!" she called as they left the room.

Pieter and Willem headed off to the games room to see if a table was empty leaving Gloria alone. The trip was almost over. What lay ahead for them in Stratford? Her life would be very different. She and Willem would have to get used to living together as husband and wife and they had a lot to learn about being parents. Pieter was worried about making friends but perhaps she and Willem would give him a brother or sister she thought happily patting her stomach. She would have to make an appointment to see the doctor as soon as they arrived in Stratford.

Chapter 54:

Gloria was standing with Pieter near the bow of the ship a few days later. Her son's excitement was evident as he pointed to a dark shape on the horizon.

"Canada!" he called out jumping up and down.

"That's Newfoundland," said Gloria letting go of his hand and putting her arm on his shoulders. "It's an island just off the coast of Canada but we'll be able to see Canada soon. Then we'll have to travel down the St. Lawrence River to Montreal before we can land. We'll be there in a day or two."

"Is Canada a big country?" Pieter asked, "bigger than Holland?" He turned to squint at Gloria who grinned.

"Yes dear, Canada is a very big country," she said tousling her son's hair. "It's getting windy. Perhaps we should go in now."

She would be glad to be back in Canada. This had been an eventful year – full of new experiences. She had gained a new love for her husband and a greater understanding of the guilt that had been plaguing him for the past five years. She was ready for a return to ordinary life – with a new son and a baby on the way.

Willem returned an hour later saying he'd left Pieter playing with the little boy he'd met on the ship. The boy's father had said he'd watch them. Willem invited Gloria to stroll around the deck. They joined hands as they started walking.

"I confronted Harrie," Willem said, "about him not getting on the boat in 1940."

"Confronted?" asked Gloria. "You quarrelled? When was that?"

"Just before we left Holland," he said. "Remember I went out in the rain and you were annoyed with me because I had not taken an umbrella? Harrie and I didn't quarrel, really."

§ § §

Harrie had had an umbrella and he tried to hold it over both men as they walked. He didn't have much luck. Willem was glad when the rain stopped after they'd gone half a block and Harrie folded the umbrella.

"I talked to Salentijn," said Willem speaking Dutch.

"*Ja?*" said Harrie using the umbrella as a walking stick.

"He confirmed what I'd suspected for a few weeks," said Willem looking around. Even then he'd been worried about talking in the open but there'd been no one else on the street. Harrie remained silent. Willem took a deep breath.

"That story about you not getting on the boat – it didn't happen like that did it?"

The two men walked on in silence. Willem held his peace. He had to hear Harrie say it.

"Only partly," said Harrie finally. "It was too late for me to jump but you're right. I had never intended to get out of the country. I had talked to Salentijn and I knew the Underground would need men to work here but I needed to make sure you were out of Holland. I didn't want to put your safety at risk."

"You didn't trust me?" asked Willem softly.

"It wasn't a question of trust," said Harrie. "You are my brother, my twin, but you don't live a lie as I have ever since I discovered I was different." When Willem didn't say anything Harrie continued.

"I didn't know exactly what I'd be asked to do but I didn't want you caught up in it. When I went to Amsterdam and moved in with Dirk," he said, "I knew there was a possibility I would be seen as a traitor. One or perhaps two men knew the truth and if they hadn't survived the war there would be no way to prove I had not betrayed our country. I knew the risks I was taking and what might happen. But if it helped the Allies win the war it was worth that risk." Harrie paused but kept walking and Willem kept pace although he didn't speak.

"My only fear," continued Harrie "was that if I died you would never know the truth. Having other people think badly of me was normal — I've lived with that my whole life. But I did not want you to think badly of me. I almost lost my nerve when we were getting on the boat to England. I would have jumped if I could. I hated not being able to tell you."

Gloria watched her husband as he finished the story. He stopped walking and stayed at the railing near the stern of the ship. Gloria stood beside him gazing out over the ocean.

"All that time I felt guilty," said Willem wonderingly. "All that time…I felt guilty because I had not protected my brother. And he was trying to protect me!" He shook his head.

"I could almost be angry with him," he said, "if I were not so happy that he is alive."

"Ah Willem," said Gloria. "Love is never easy is it?"